A Texan's Choice

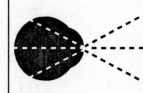

This Large Print Book carries the
Seal of Approval of N.A.V.H.

A Texan's Choice

Shelley Gray

THORNDIKE PRESS
A part of Gale, Cengage Learning

GALE
CENGAGE Learning

Detroit • New York • San Francisco • New Haven, Conn • Waterville, Maine • London

GALE
CENGAGE Learning

LIBRARY OF CONGRESS CATALOGING-IN-PUBLICATION DATA

Gray, Shelley Shepard.
  A Texan's choice / by Shelley Gray.
     pages ; cm. — (Thorndike Press large print Christian fiction) (The heart
of a hero series ; book 3)
  ISBN 978-1-4104-5587-1 (hardcover) — ISBN 1-4104-5587-4 (hardcover)
  1. Texas—Fiction. 2. Large type books. I. Title.
PS3607.R3966T45 2013
813'.6—dc23   2012044207

Published in 2013 by arrangement with Abingdon Press

Printed in Mexico
1 2 3 4 5 6 7 17 16 15 14 13

To Barbara Scott and Ramona Richards.
Thank you for making the dream of
publishing these books a reality.

ACKNOWLEDGMENTS

Thank you to my agent, Mary Sue Seymour, for championing my westerns. Thank you to the folks at Abingdon who've designed the most beautiful covers, and to the editorial team who helped me write a better book. Most of all, thank you to the readers who've given my westerns a try, told their friends about them, and made me excited to write every morning. I'm so grateful for you all.

Since no man knows the future, who can tell him what is to come?
                    — Ecclesiastes 8:7

"No man in the wrong can stand up against a fellow that's in the right and keeps on a-comin'."
                    — creed of Texas Ranger
Captain William Jesse "Bill" McDonald

1

November 1874
West Texas

They'd been waiting five days for her father to die.

Only a strong sense of duty drove Rosemarie back into the darkened room, where the scents of whiskey and sickness grabbed her the moment she crossed the threshold. When she coughed, in a half-hearted attempt to adjust to the dim, thick air, six faces turned to her in surprise. The seventh occupant was oblivious.

"Sorry," she murmured around yet another cough. "Didn't mean to startle y'all."

"Rosemarie. Hush now," her mother ordered. "You're gonna disturb your pa."

"Yes, ma'am."

Yet — as much as Rose could tell — Pa continued to lay motionless. The only sign he was still alive was the faint fluttering of the collar on his nightshirt. Though she hadn't been invited to do so, Rosemarie edged closer to the bed.

It wasn't easy to do with too many people packed into a too-small bedroom, and the place had never been much anyway.

Of course, it went without saying that their whole house had never been much. Her father had built it from a slew of cast-off boards from someone else's broken barn. Judging by the gaps in the planks, Rose had always assumed the former owners had known what they were doing when they'd left the wood for scrap before heading back east.

Her family had settled into the fifty-acre farm eight years ago, in the midst of the war. It lay just outside the borders of Broken Promise, a sorry little town if there ever was one.

But it had become home.

Her father had used every cent he had to settle them in and had promptly named the ranch "Bar C." Though the red dirt and loads of dust didn't look like much of anything, Pa had said the land was as good as any.

He was happy to settle and escape the fighting, though Rose had never understood exactly what was wrong with him.

Her mother had slapped her silly the one

time she'd asked.

Now, though, her father seemed dwarfed by his past as much as by the old iron bed frame above his head, the pair of oak rocking chairs to his left, and group of bodies surrounding him.

Rosemarie stood in the perimeter, looking in, trying to see her father's face. But all she saw was the jumble of covers covering the majority of his chest. A wide splotch of brownish liquid had soaked into the warring rings making up the quilt. The once pristine white and soothing pink rings looked like faded replicas of what they'd once been, and that was the truth.

His breathing turned labored.

"How is he doing? Any change?" she finally asked, unable to bear the silence anymore. Unable to bear the idea that the waiting would continue. And continue some more after that.

"Ah, Rose." Doc glanced her way over a pair of wire-rimmed spectacles. "I'm afraid I have no good news for you. He's about the same."

"His breathing slowed," her mother added somewhat hopefully.

With a weary nod, Pastor Colson nodded. "I believe it has. He'll be with the Lord soon, Rosemarie."

"That's good."

The comment had come from a sense that too much had happened that could never be repaired. They'd known for days now that their father wasn't going to get better, and since they'd begun the deathwatch, the atmosphere among all of them had turned into a helpless sense of inevitability.

And sickness.

Actually, the air in the room was so thick with the mingling of warm bodies, the light so dim, and the smell of sickness and despair so overpowering, Rose knew death would have to be better than the current situation.

But she probably should never have acknowledged that. To her right, her sister Annalise gasped. "Rose, how could you say such a thing?"

Though Rose knew Annalise had probably felt the same way — as did everyone else in the room — she apologized. "I'm sorry. I spoke out of turn."

"You certainly did."

"However, I dare say that heaven is a whole lot better," Rose said, not quite able to hide the irony she was feeling. After all, this place had never been good.

At least not for her.

Since Annalise only blinked, looking

determined to pretend that they were in the middle of one of those fancy homes owned by the cattle barons — and the others looked grateful to have something to think about besides her father's labored breaths — Rose continued. "Heaven is supposed to be a wonderful place, right? A whole lot better than this?" When her sister merely continued to look shocked, Rose looked to the preacher for support.

Pastor Colson, however, was praying over his clasped hands.

"You need to learn to keep your thoughts to yourself, daughter," her mother murmured. "No one wants to hear your opinions."

No one ever had . . . well, not since her brother, Pete, had died under her watch. "Yes'm."

The atmosphere relaxed a bit as all eyes turned back to Ben Cousins. With bated breath, they continued to watch Pa gasp and struggle to wheeze. No one touched him, not the doctor nor the preacher. Not Annalise. Not even her mother.

Maybe not especially May Cousins. Rose couldn't blame her mother for that, though, because her pa had never been much of a good man. In many ways, he hadn't been a bad one either.

No, more like her father was a study in what could have been. He could have been brighter, smarter, handsomer, or even nicer. Maybe even meaner. Instead, he'd often faded into the woodwork, not doing much of anything.

The thing was, no one expected him to do much, anyway. Not even to stay fighting in the war.

If Rose had been a betting woman, she'd have pretty much bet all her worth that no one had actually ever liked Ben Cousins, except, perhaps, his momma.

After all, what did you do with a man who clung to dreams like strings from kites and who made promises with the smallest amount of hope possible? Dreams only got you so far in the middle of November when the wind was howling, the fireplace was bare, and there wasn't a thing in the rickety house worth eating.

Once, when Rose was supposed to be sleeping but couldn't because her parents were going at it something fierce, May Cousins let forth a stream of dire words. "You're nothing but a waste and a wastrel, Ben. Day after day I've been waiting for you to go do something of means, but all you do is say that you don't feel well or that you've got plans in town. You're nothing but a worthless mass of bones and skin."

Rose reckoned that to be a pretty fair description.

Pa had been all of that and more. Full of shiny smiles and made-up promises. He was a shell of a man, his pride and confidence as brittle and fragile as one of the eggs the hens laid on a good day.

Now, as he lay dying, he wasn't much better.

Predictably, he was taking forever to meet his maker, holding up a mess of chores and work in the meantime.

Maybe Jesus wasn't in a real hurry to visit with him, neither.

As if reading her mind, May Cousins looked up from her perch next to her husband's side, the damp rag limp in her hand. "Rosemarie, do something to make yourself useful. Fetch more water, would you?"

"Yes, Mama."

Rose knocked into the thick door as she hastily walked back out. Her clash with the door's frame rang out a racket, drawing her older sister's scorn. "Can't you even walk right?"

Her sister's impatience was no surprise. Annalise Cousins Petula was only three years older but was comprised of a lifetime of different choices. At twenty-two, she was married, nursing a new baby, and still managed to look fresh and beautiful. Of course, Annalise had always managed to look perfect, even when she'd lived with them.

In contrast, Rosemarie, with her riot of brown curls and murky blue eyes, always seemed to be in need of a mirror.

She'd never had a patient nature, had hardly ever been able to sit still. That was surely why she'd spent the day brewing coffee, frying flatbread, and fetching for everyone else. It was why she'd gotten up early to take care of the chickens and Sam, the pig. It was why her hair was falling out of its hastily pinned bun and her bare feet were dirty.

Even in the chilly month of November.

Knowing that even if she got a pail of water and brought it back without dripping a drop, her mother would still find fault, Rose passed the pump and just kept going. She threw open the rickety back door, raced down the four steps, and welcomed freedom.

Grains of dust, cold and hard and unforgiving, spat up underfoot, mixing with the hem of her calico. A few errant pebbles scattered, flying in her path. One hit the wheel of the doctor's buggy, the sharp sound spurring his horse to lift his ears in annoyance. But no one yelled, and the air smelled clean. It felt so good to be outside.

The sun was setting, bringing with it a riot of color in the otherwise mud-brown horizon. In the distance, an owl hooted, signaling his dismay about the intrusion to the peaceful silence.

Rose didn't care. With eager feet, she passed the doc's buggy and the preacher's mare. She scurried by chicken pens. Around the gate to the garden. Finally with care, she approached the lone fence post. Pa had pounded it in the earth years ago, back when he'd intended to fence in their property. He'd never gotten any farther. It was as good a symbol as any, showing Broken Promise — maybe even the world — that the Cousins never had much and weren't likely to, neither. Just beyond their land was opportunity. Rose clasped it gratefully.

As the sun continued to set, she spoke, praying and talking. Communicating with the only one who seemed to care about her. "Why's it taking so long, Lord? I'm thinking Pa's suffered enough."

The wind howled, slapping her in the face, bringing her shame for even wishing her Pa would hurry up and do the inevitable.

After all, their neighbors, the Kowalchecks, had crops to tend to. Annalise needed to get on home to her snooty husband. And, well, everyone else just seemed plumb worn out from all the waiting.

Was wishing for death so wrong? Rosemarie wasn't sure. But there had to be hope in death if there wasn't in life, right? And, well, Doc Breane said Pa's condition wasn't going to get better. Ever. Everyone had been on deathwatch for days. Rose couldn't remember for certain the last time her pa had been awake. One week ago? Ten days? Too long, for sure.

So shouldn't they all be hoping that Pa's glorious salvation would come sooner than later?

Life, such as if was, needed to go on.

As the sun sank and darkness flooded the plains, a stillness rose. No moon, or even a star deigned to keep her company. Only the wind, that howling, never-ending factor that was always present. Cool air sank into her bones. Crept in, teasing her with its company. Spurring her to duty, no matter how unpleasant. It was time to go back inside.

But then, in the distance, a shadow appeared. As it got bigger, Rose felt the vibration of horse hooves on the ground. Who now?

Unafraid, Rose watched the rider approach. Was it Mr. Wilson, their neighbor to the north? Russ Parker, the sheriff?

Annalise's husband? No doubt he would be looking for his dinner and his wife.

But as the shadow formed, Rose sensed he was a stranger. She knew of no man who sat a horse so perfectly. And she'd certainly not seen a black stallion of that size and strength.

He came closer.

Rose noticed his boots were black. The horse's bridle had a bit of silver. His duster was long and black and worn.

Who was he? Fear rose inside her.

His horse slowed as he approached, then finally came to a stop a good four feet away. Under the brim of the hat, pale blue eyes met her own.

For the first time in her life, Rose was afraid to speak. This man looked powerful and strong. Vaguely threatening.

"Ma'am?" His voice sounded scratchy, like he wasn't used to talking. Very slowly he tipped the rim of his black hat.

After swallowing hard, she found her voice. "What do you want?"

Before he could answer, a scream tore through the night, spooking the horses, even the stranger's. After the man gained control, he glanced at the window, then looked at

21

her in concern. "What just happened?"

Rose knew. She knew as sure as if she'd been asked to stand by the bed, been allowed to hold her pa's hand. Loosening her right hand's death grip on the post, she pointed behind her. "I do believe my pa just died."

The sound of crying curled through the loose planks of their home, then dissipated into night air. To her surprise, Rose found she was not immune. Tears trekked down her cheeks — though maybe her eyes were watering from the cold that had suddenly engulfed her.

In front of her, still mounted on his very fine, very tall horse, the man in the black Stetson cursed under his breath. Finally, he spoke again, his voice low and husky. "Now, don't that beat all? My timing never was worth beans."

"Mister, who are you?"

After a lengthy pause, he spit out the words. "My name is Scout Proffitt."

Even someone as isolated as Rose knew the name. "You're an outlaw." Dime store novels told his tales. He'd killed before. Whispers hinted that he'd done worse.

All the novels also claimed that he wore only black. And this man, well, he certainly fit the bill.

"An outlaw? That's putting things a little harsh, don't you think?"

She thought it suited him just fine. "Why are you here?" Rose gripped the post as if her very livelihood depended on it.

"To claim my property . . . if this is indeed the Bar C."

She heard the hint of sarcasm. The mess of boards and barbed wire in the middle of nowhere certainly didn't look in need of a name. "This is the Bar C. But it isn't your property. It's ours."

"It is now." A drop of humor and something else entered his eyes. As he leaned back in his saddle, he almost smiled. Almost. "Your pa bet this place and lost."

Rose struggled to grasp what he was saying. "My pa bet our home? Our land?"

"He did. Last time he came through Shawnee." His voice drifted off as he scanned the area. With one pass, he seemed to take in everything. The scraggly mesquite trees in the distance. The weed-filled garden. The planks in the house with the strangely beautiful door. The sorry state of the barn. The red dust that covered it all. "Though, by the looks of things, I reckon I might have come up as the loser after all."

As the crying continued in the distance, and the hens squawked their discomfort, as

23

Rose heard her mother call for help and felt the burst of wind blow yet another curl loose from its pins, Rose had a feeling that he might be right.

"Rose? Rose! Where are you, girl?"

The gunslinger's mouth twitched. "Is that you? Rose?"

Wearily, she nodded.

"Rosemarie! Now!"

With a look of sympathy, the outlaw pushed back his hat. "I guess you're needed. Go on now. Don't worry, I'll still be here when you come back."

She figured he would. After all, he'd come to claim her home.

As Rose turned and ran, she wasn't sure if she was afraid of that or very, very glad.

One more time, her sister yelled her name. "Rose, get in here!"

"I'm a-comin'!" she yelled, back to the house where she'd always wished she'd never been. Back to the home she'd always wished she'd never known.

2

After Rose had gone into the house — such that it was — Scout threw his leg over the horn and slid to the ground. Figuring the lone post was as good as anywhere, he tethered Rio to it. And then took a good look around.

The house was made of planks, sprinkled liberally with mud. The windows were glass, but dirtier than the depths of a murky pond stained with silt, making his view of the inhabitants hazy at best.

The house was a sad and ugly thing. Not near as pretty or large as the house he'd grown up in with his brother and sister.

It was even smaller than the house he'd lived in with Corrine during the war, back when it had been basically just the two of them since Clayton was off fighting Yankees as soon as he'd been able.

But one thing that the house did have going for it was a curiously attractive door. It looked to be solid oak. A master carpenter had carved an arch on the top, making the panel curved and pretty. But the nicest thing about the door was that it was painted a bright shiny red.

The door reminded him of some of the city houses he'd seen out in St. Louis. The door looked stately and high class and so completely out of place that it seemed like a bandit must have stolen the thing and attached it to this grandiose shack.

Just for kicks.

Beyond it was a ramshackle barn, made of faded golden wood. And though it looked to be in dire need of someone sticking a match to it, it did look to be in better repair than the house. Perhaps it was the scattering of hardy wildflowers that were growing around the perimeter.

Scout wondered who would have taken the time to plant flowers along such a sorry spot and how they'd managed to thrive in the midst of such cold weather and lack of care.

Uncomfortable with the way his mind was going — it kept veering toward sentimental nonsense all the sudden — he ruthlessly moved his gaze toward the next portion of the place.

Just beyond the barn were a few pens.

Dead grass and dirt covered most everything else. The pair of oaks in the midst of it all climbed tall and straight, though. Almost like they could hardly believe they were still standing in the midst of the place.

He understood the feeling.

He'd been just about to look for water for Rio when a woman exited the home.

She was everything like the girl he'd first met, and nothing, too. She had the same blue eyes and high cheekbones of Rose. But in place of a lithe figure and pale pink cheeks, the woman's waist was thick and her skin tone sallow.

Everything in the woman's body looked labored and worn out, though from exhaustion, not grief.

A better man might have met her halfway. Scout stayed by Rio.

He was selfishly content to watch her march toward him, her footsteps sure and solid, the skirts of her faded calico grazing the dirt like a broom. All of it curiously reminded him of a marching soldier.

Slowly, he tipped his hat. "Ma'am."

She stopped three feet away. "And who might you be?"

Beside him, Rio shifted, obviously feeling the waves of distrust emanating from her. It was on the tip of Scout's tongue to say

27

something vilifying and mean.

He was used to "decent women" not thinking he was good enough to share the same air they breathed. He was used to people looking the other way when he approached, desperate to put as much space as possible between themselves and the notorious gunslinger.

Usually, he paid them no mind, granting them their due. No one wanted another man's blood on their hands — even if that blood was merely just a reputation.

But instead of sassing the woman, he kept his peace. From the depths of his childhood, he recalled a faded photograph of his mother. It was washed out but crystal clear in his memory. She'd had full cheeks and creamy shoulders and kind eyes. She'd been the type of person to make a son pull his shoulders back and respect others.

Well, so he'd been told.

So, even though she'd died giving birth to him, Scout couldn't quite gather the gumption to be cruel — at least not to a woman who'd just lost a husband.

He settled on honesty. "Name's Scout Proffitt, ma'am. I'm sorry for your loss." And he was sorry. That was true. If that Ben Cousins had stayed alive, he wouldn't be reduced to standing next to a worn-out

28

post, claiming the property like the worst sort of scavenger.

Her back stiffened. Obviously she, too, had heard of his name. Fear entered her eyes. Just as if she expected him to start raping and pillaging any moment. "Mr. Proffitt, what is your business? We have no food to spare for you."

For him. She had no food for him.

The words found their mark like a sharp arrow to his heart. Though he made sure he remained motionless, Scout felt his temper start to flare. "I didn't come here for food, ma'am."

The door to the house opened again. Raising his head slightly, he looked to see Rosemarie walking toward them with a purposeful stride. For a moment, he stood in awe, unable to tear his eyes away from her. Her auburn hair was now completely unpinned. It hung in curls around her shoulders, flowing down to almost her waist. It was beautiful. And Scout knew he wasn't immune to its appeal.

Mrs. Cousins cleared her throat. "We are also in no position to entertain today. And I'm sure we have nothing here that you'd like. So, therefore, it would be best for everyone concerned if you'd best be moving on."

"I'm afraid that won't be happening." From the corner of his eye, Scout continued to watch the young lady's approach. Noticed that a hint of a delicate figure was hidden in the ugly brown sack of a dress.

It was truly the ugliest dress he'd ever laid eyes on.

Next to him, the woman was getting more agitated by the second. "Mr. Proffitt, if you didn't come here for food, and you don't want to leave . . . may I ask what you have come here for?"

"Mr. Proffitt says Pa bet our home and lost," the lady — Rosemarie — blurted just as plain as day.

"Bet?"

"Pa gambled our house and farm away, Momma."

Her lack of emotion and obvious lack of surprise made Scout a bit uncomfortable, and he hadn't thought he could ever get that way.

He kept his silence as Rosemarie made her way to stand in between him and her mother, her petite frame and glorious hair drawing his eye in spite of his best intentions.

Little by little, Rose's words seemed to register with her mother. Some of the visible fear seeped out of her expression as she obviously attempted to wrap her head around the news.

"This is yours?"

Scout looked at the pitiful house and the beat up barn. Yes, this was all his. Such that it was. He nodded.

When she continued to eye him, he cleared his throat. "It was back in Shawnee, ma'am. In Oklahoma."

Rosemarie now stood close enough for him to smell the hint of lavender on her hair. He wondered why she was so close. Was it to protect her mother from him . . . or the other way around?

Mrs. Cousins frowned. "He was there two months ago. I recall he was mighty quiet when he returned. You'd a thought he could have told me about that. Of course, he was feeling rather poorly by then. He was ill, Mr. Proffitt."

"So it would seem." Given that the man had just died and all.

Beside him, Rose closed her eyes.

Scout searched for something to say. "It took me some time to get here. I had to wrap up a couple of pieces of business first."

Actually, he'd had to find a way to deal with a young girl's death. Somehow, in the midst of Kansas, a girl named Kitty had asked for his protection. Feeling sorry for

31

her, he'd reluctantly given her aid. When she'd died, he'd mourned deeply for her. Both for her loss and the fact that the only person he'd taken it upon himself to care for instead of kill had committed suicide.

But that mourning time had also done some good. For the first time ever, he'd begun to see himself as something other than a hired gun. That maybe there was more to him of worth than a steady hand and a lack of conscience.

And so he'd made a choice to become a different person. If it was at all possible.

A look of distaste crossed the older lady's features. "I imagine you had all kinds of business to finish up, Mr. Proffitt," Mrs. Cousins said. "Even I have heard of your taste for blood."

"I don't have a taste for blood, ma'am. Just trying to make a living."

"With the Walton Gang?" Her voice was thick with derision.

"We all make our choices, ma'am. I'm not about to start defending mine."

There was nothing he could add or explain, anyway. Nothing that was worth explaining to a pair of women who had no idea what he'd been through, at least.

Instead, he concentrated on the women in front of him. The lithe woman with the attractive auburn hair and smooth pale skin. Her mother's barely concealed anger.

And both women's complete lack of tears for Ben Cousin's death . . . and only sadness, not true surprise by the man's penchant for giving away the only thing in their lives of value.

Was she surprised at all? Perhaps . . . or perhaps not. Maybe his first impressions hadn't been far off the mark. Ben Cousins hadn't been worth much to his kin.

Not even the knowledge that he'd left a family without property in death didn't look like it came as a surprise. He was just about to try to explain away the poker game — which, by the by, really didn't need explaining — when the girl started speaking again.

"We need to let Mr. Proffitt get settled, Mother. Need to let him water his horse."

Finally after a good long minute, Mrs. Cousins looked worn down. "Do you have any proof of this acquisition, Mr. Proffitt?"

"I do." Carefully, he unfolded the paper Ben Cousins had given him. Well, had tossed into the pile of chips and assorted worldly goods. As he handed the paper to the widow, he wondered if maybe he should have just walked away. He didn't need the land, and these folks looked to already be fallen on hard times.

It was downright sinful to be taking their home, too.

Behind the women, men were already carting the body into a wagon. The dead man's weight seemed to weigh them down — there was a fair bit of grunting and such as they shuffled him across the parched ground.

Seconds later, the wagon groaned under the new weight. Bridles jangled as two horses were hitched up.

Neither woman in front of him turned to watch.

Strange, but, in a way, somewhat impressive. Most folks liked to take their time before depositing loved ones into the earth.

Mrs. Cousins made quick work of examining the paper, then nodded. "That is my husband's handwriting," she said. "Such as it was." Handing it back to him, she met his gaze. "I reckon this place is yours, all right."

Rosemarie looked horrified. "Momma? You're not thinking of just letting this man have our home . . . are you?"

"What am I going to do with this place without your Pa, Rosemarie?" The woman's voice was as hard and brittle as the circumstances. "Till the soil every morning?"

"No, ma'am. But what should we —"

"Hush now."

Behind them, an almost fine-looking quarter horse whinnied as its bridle was adjusted. Wind swirled around them as fine red dust flew into pores and settled in.

"May?" one of the men called out. "We're ready for ya."

Scout noticed not a one acknowledged the girl.

The air stilled with expectation. Finally Mrs. Cousins swallowed. "Mr. Proffitt, I hope you'll excuse us for a moment. Why don't you find a stall for your horse in the barn and water him? Then we'll discuss when I can leave."

"Yes, ma'am."

She turned and started walking. When Rose still stared at Scout, lost, and almost defiant, her mother's voice turned hard again. "Rosemarie, come with me. We best go bury your father. No more dawdling. People are waiting."

"And they've sure waited long enough," the girl muttered. Turning a wide blue gaze to him, she said, "Will you still be here when we get back?"

"I will." He kept his voice hard. Clipped. Did his best to hide any misgivings he had, and the truth — that he had nowhere else to go.

Something resonated in the girl's eyes.

"Then I suppose I'll see you then."

Slowly, he nodded. Just as another woman exited the ramshackle home. "Rose!" she called out, raising her chin enough that tightly curled blond ringlets bounced around her shoulders. "Rose, come on. You're making us wait."

The woman's voice was shrill and strident. He'd never gotten used to a woman's need for order in a disorderly world. Perhaps that was why he'd made certain to only keep company with women who didn't care for order. Or perhaps they'd just given up on the idea of it long ago.

Kind of like the slip of a woman standing not five feet away from him. Everything in her posture spoke of better days and a sadness that couldn't be erased.

And since he was well acquainted with that sort of feeling, he gentled his voice. Even though there was little in his body that was gentle. "You'd best get on now."

Rosemarie Cousins shot a look his way. Before his eyes, her lips parted and her wide eyes turned languid. For a moment, he thought she was about to speak, then abruptly, she shook her head and scampered to meet her family.

Around them, the sun sank another few inches as twilight approached. The wind picked up.

And a funeral procession began.

Scout kept his place by Rio and looked on. He tipped his hat as the motley crew walked past him — Mrs. Cousins riding on the wagon beside the pastor, and Rosemarie, the blond lady, and two others walking slowly behind — each of them hardly seeming to notice the ruts in the dirt or the pebbles kicking up from the wagon wheels and hitting their shins.

The prayers were short and to the point. "The Lord is my shepherd, I shall not want . . . ," Pastor Colson intoned as her pa was lowered into the ground, his body already fitted into the plain pine casket that had been waiting in the barn's loft for weeks.

"Even though I walk through —"

Rosemarie seemed to be the only one to have been bothered by the idea that a casket had been waiting for her pa. The hole had already been dug, too.

The preacher's beautiful, even voice continued on. "You prepare a table for me in the presence of my enemies —"

Quietly, without skipping a beat, her mother tossed a handful of dirt on the pine box. Her sister followed suit. Obligingly, Rose tossed some on, too.

Ten minutes later, it was done.

As the doctor and preacher nodded to each other and then went on their way, Annalise turned to their mother. "Of course you can stay with us, Mother. I'll help you get your things together. We should be on our way in no time."

Rosemarie raised a brow. Waited. But no invitation came. After too much time passed, she looked at her sister. "What about me?"

Her sister's cheeks flushed, but she didn't look away. "I don't know what to tell you. Carson and I can't feed two more mouths, Rose. We have a baby."

As the words sank in, true dismay overtook her. "But what am I going to do?"

Annalise shrugged. "Maybe Mr. Proffitt will give you a day or two to figure out where you can go."

"That's it?" Panic brought the tears that grief hadn't allowed. She grabbed at her mother's hand. "Ma —"

"There's nothing I can do, Rose," she said as she pulled her hand away. "You turned down two marriage proposals last year. I told you then that I was washing my hands of you."

The men had been friends of her father's. Old. Almost as worthless. Of course, unsaid was the tragedy that always separated her from the rest of the family.

Her part in Pete's death.

But even living alone was worse than being ignored. What would she do? Where would she go? Desperate, she pushed down what little pride she still possessed and reached for her mother's hand again. "But, Mother. You know I —"

"That's enough, Rose," Annalise interrupted harshly. "It's time you grew up. It's time you realized that life isn't full of dreams and wishes. A woman has to look out for herself. Once more, she needs to do what needs to be done, no matter what. You should've accepted one of those offers. Or you should have made other plans. But you didn't."

Dismay held Rose motionless as she watched her sister curve an arm around her mother's shoulders and guide her home.

Pride held her captive as she wiped the last of her tears from her cheeks.

Only the sense that she wasn't alone gave her the strength to breathe deeply. To turn. And to walk toward the man who still stood alone in their field. Watching.

3

Russell Andrew Champion stabbed his father on a Saturday afternoon in the middle of July. The day had been warm, his father's temper far hotter.

But it didn't matter. Russell had had enough.

When Russell raised his bowie knife and his father saw the blade coming his way, they'd both known there was no going back. Russell intended to do justice, and that intention had nothing to do with the sun beating down on them.

Instead, it had everything to do with his father forcing himself on Russell's girl in the front parlor. Nora had cried out, which had made him come running. And when he'd seen what his father had intended, Russell knew it was time to take matters into his own hands.

After a lifetime of beatings and skipped suppers, some things just couldn't be forgiven.

Pushing the knife into the soft skin of his father's chest had been surprisingly easy. The blood that had stained his hand and clothes hadn't bothered him a bit.

His only surprise had been his lack of regret or shame.

Or guilt. He hadn't felt guilty at all.

That event — such that it was — had surely been the tipping point in Russell's life. With little compunction, he'd pushed his father's bleeding body to the ground, told Nora his pa wouldn't be bothering her no more . . . and then faced his future like a man.

He'd been fifteen.

After Nora had left in a haze of tears, Russell turned to face his mother. His father — her husband — had been a cheater and a philanderer and had taken great pride in bullying anyone weaker than himself.

Russell had been more than ready to accept his mother's thanks, then profess to take care of her forever. He'd been prepared to treat her with the dignity that she deserved. To promise that no one would ever lay a hand on any of them again. He'd been prepared to shoulder the responsibilities of his actions, knowing that whatever punishment he received or pain he suffered would be worth it.

Because he'd saved his girl and helped his mother.

But instead of embracing him and offering her sympathy and undying gratitude, his mother had backed away in fear. "Russell Andrew! You're a murderer."

He knew that was true. "He was forcing himself on Nora, Ma. He was going to harm her. He was going to take her innocence."

When that didn't get much of a response, he added, "Ma, he beat me something awful almost every day of my life. He beat you, too." What he didn't add was that there hadn't been a doubt in his mind that his pa would do it all again, if given the opportunity. And again.

He'd had to take matters into his own hands because sometimes pure evil had to be fought with evil.

But his mother had glared at him like he was a stranger . . . or maybe even something worse. "You need to leave this house, Russell."

Her cold tone stung. It had scared him, too. "Ma, we'll think of something to tell people . . . and I promise, I'll go tell the sheriff." Almost desperately, he added, "Ma, I'll even go turn myself in."

"You'll do no such thing. Just go. I don't

want you here."

He'd been so taken aback, he'd been practically struck dumb. "But, Ma . . ."

Her eyes turned flinty. "Don't call me your mother. Look at you! You're standing before me, covered in blood. Talking about what you did without a lick of shame. *You killed your father,* Russell!"

"He . . . he was hurting Nora."

"You are a true sinner. I'm sure God will punish you the rest of your days."

He flinched. Feeling hurt and betrayed, he'd been tempted to tell her that from his point of view, God had already been punishing him well and good his whole life. And though Russell figured he'd done plenty lately to deserve it, he knew he'd hadn't deserved a slew of terrible whippings when he'd been four.

His mother pointed to the door. "Get what you need, get your horse, and leave. And don't ever come back."

He hadn't hesitated. After washing the blood off as best he could in the spigot out by the barn, he packed up a saddlebag, took his father's best horse, and went.

Forty minutes later, he was in Nora's front yard. His heart skipped a beat when she threw open her home's front door and ran out to see him. An ache had rushed through him at the sight of her, at the sight of her hurrying to him. Welcoming him with open arms.

At least he'd done one thing right in his life. He'd saved her. She was unharmed. Just seeing her smile made him sure that everything was going to be fine.

He was filled with so much emotion, it almost hurt to talk. "Nora, it's so good to see you, honey," he said, his husky voice hardly sounding like his own.

She halted a good five feet from him. "What's going on?"

"My ma kicked me out." There was no other way to talk about it.

Her pretty brown eyes widened as her step faltered. "What happened with your pa? Did he really die, Russell?"

Something in her expression made him temper his words. Made him try to sugarcoat things. "Everything is fine. I promise you, honey, he won't bother you ever again."

But instead of dissolving into tears of relief or running to hug him, she took one step back. "Did he die?"

"He did."

"You murdered him. Russell, you took another life."

Her eyes were wide with fear. He'd been tempted to comfort her. To ease her mind.

To promise her that everything was going to be just fine.

Then he realized she wasn't concerned about his father. No, this time, he was the one who frightened her. Russell swallowed hard and tried to think of soft words to ease her worries.

But all that came up was the awful truth. "I killed him for you, Nora. And I don't regret it, neither. Fact is, I'd do it again." His words weren't the complete truth. He'd killed his pa for a whole lot of reasons.

Him roughly pawing Nora had simply been the final straw.

She looked devastated. "Russell, you shouldn't have done that."

"He shouldn't have touched you. He shouldn't have come near you. But it's okay now, right? Justice was served."

"What are you going to do? Are you leaving town?"

He hadn't thought that far. He hadn't thought about what he was going to do — beyond seeing Nora and reveling in her goodness and love. "I don't know."

Actually, he'd kind of thought she'd offer him shelter. He'd imagined she would have been so grateful for his interference and so eager to show her love for him, too, that she'd want to reach out to him in any way she could.

But instead of welcoming him, she turned and slowly walked back inside. Never saying another word.

He'd stood, watching her retreating back in shock.

He'd killed his father, left his home, and ruined his life . . . all for the love of a girl who didn't love him back.

Shoot, maybe she never had loved him. Maybe he'd been so desperate for love, so desperate to be loved, that he'd been willing to imagine another person cared for him more than any other.

While that all spun around in his head, he turned his horse and rode west.

That day, he'd become a little bit harder. A little bit tougher and a whole lot smarter, too.

Seven months later, Mr. James Walton offered him a place in the Walton Gang. Russell accepted gratefully.

It had been hard, living on his own. Harder than he'd ever imagined. He'd been forced to do things he'd never done, forced to steal and lie and hurt in order to survive.

That first night, when he'd sat in the back of a saloon, next to the great Mr. Walton and staring at Addison Kent, Will McMillan, and the notoriously infamous Scout Proffitt,

46

Russell had known he'd finally made something of himself.

And that he'd finally been accepted. Finally, after a whole lot of hardship, someone else cared whether he lived or died.

He'd realized then that it hadn't been all that hard to do, either. Matter of fact, it had been real simple.

All he'd had to do was become the type of man he'd never wanted to be.

The chilly evening air was starting to take a toll on Rosemarie's bare feet, but that pain was insignificant to what was happening to her heart. Little by little, layers were getting peeled away as she watched her mother and sister prepare to leave her.

Their movements were methodical and even. Not rushed. Actually, it kind of looked like they were spring cleaning — and it took everything she had to pretend that their final betrayal wasn't killing her inside.

When she'd entered the house a few minutes earlier, she'd been dismayed to find her mother and sister packing up belongings like locusts were on their heels. "I can't believe you're packing so fast."

"It's time we got on our way," her mother stated as she folded a quilt. "That Mr. Proffitt might have swindled your father out

47

of our home, but he's not entitled to everything inside, too. And furthermore, I have no desire to remain in his company for longer than I have to."

The dresser was now practically empty. What was she going to do if she had nothing but the threadbare clothes on her back? "You two can't take everything."

Annalise paused long enough to stare at her curiously. "We've left plenty for you. There's a nightgown and another calico, too. What more could you possibly need?"

Besides a loving family, Rosemarie thought her needs were pretty obvious. "I need something to sleep on."

"The bed is still made up."

The bed was made up with the sheets and quilts her father had slept in. Had died in.

Feeling like she was two steps away from falling off the edge of a cliff, Rosemarie said, "I deserve some of the items in this house as much as anyone. I didn't gamble away the house, and I didn't kill Pa. I'm not even stopping you from leaving me. But I deserve more than just the clothes on my back."

Annalise sniffed. "Rosemarie, as far as I'm concerned, you deserve nothing. You killed Pete. You're lucky we didn't send the law after you."

It always came to that, didn't it? When

she'd been eleven, Pete had drowned under her care. Though his death had surely been an accident, no one in the family had ever forgiven her for it.

Far from it.

Now, she was too tired and too desperate to once again try to tell her side of things. "I know you think so," she said quietly. "But I've lived with you for ten years since Pete passed away. I don't deserve to be left without even a means to cover myself when it gets cold. Mama, even if you don't like me, I still am your daughter."

For the first time in her life, her mother seemed too ashamed to look at her. "I'll leave you some bedding, Rose. All the kitchen things and dishes, too."

"Thank you for that." She didn't even try to hide her sarcasm.

When neither spoke another word, Rose left and took up her current spot on the porch, watching the shadows of their bodies, hearing the low murmurs of their voices. Keeping her company was her firm resolve.

There was no going back. All she could do was stand to one side and pretend their abandonment wasn't the final straw to an already bad day. To an already bad life. She needed a new plan, a new direction, or she was going to drive herself crazy.

That is, crazier than she already was.

But, of course, for a woman like herself, there weren't a whole lot of options, no matter how many twists and turns she tried to give her situation.

Actually, there was only one thing to do, and it didn't matter if it made her quake in her boots.

She needed to throw out the last bits of pride she still possessed and go ask Mr. Proffitt for a job. The sharp, bitter taste of regret stung her mouth. Humiliation threatened to curve her spine. But she forced herself to walk forward, shoulders back, chin up.

She forced herself to do what had to be done. Because the only thing worse than working for a scary outlaw was going out into the world by herself. Chances were very good that she wouldn't last more than a day or two on her own, especially in the company of strange men. She'd rather take her chances with just one man. She wasn't blessed with a whole lot of smarts, but she certainly wasn't a fool.

The steps toward the man didn't get any easier, but she found if she didn't look backward, it was easier to pick up the pace.

As if he had all the time in the world, Scout Proffitt stood by his horse and watched her approach. As they'd been when they'd buried her father and when he'd told them the news about the farm, his arms were crossed over his chest, his dark eyes staring at everything, taking in everything.

Giving nothing away.

His stance was loose and easy.

As she got closer, she became aware of two things: her feet had turned bitter cold and that Mr. Proffitt had most likely had a whole lot of practice of standing and watching, his gaze barely free of the low brim of his Stetson. He seemed to be a real champion of patience and silence.

She was not.

Finally, she stopped in front of him. Waited for him to say something.

He didn't. Instead he just stared, his gaze slowly skimming down the path of buttons of her dress, following the ragged hem in need of a press and a needle and thread. Stopping on her cold, curled bare toes.

Only then did his gaze travel upward again.

She licked her lips and forced herself to do what had to be done. "Mr. Proffitt, I believe it's going to take some time for you to get settled. The house is dirty." Realizing what an understatement that was, she amended her words. "That is, it's in terrible shape. Real bad."

"And?"

"And, well, sir . . . I'd like to stay on and clean it for you, if I could."

Slowly his left hand repositioned his hat, bringing her face to face with the notorious killer's lethal stare. "Say again?"

His voice had somehow become even more gravelly. She cleared her throat and fought her fear. "Mr. Proffitt, what I'm saying is that I'd like to offer my services to you."

Even in the dim light of early evening she could see disbelief shine in his expression. "I'm obliged. However, I have no need for *your services,* ma'am."

She flinched, realizing now that he thought she was offering a much different type of service than cooking and cleaning.

With some dismay, she realized that if the man had wanted her for other nefarious reasons, she probably wouldn't have the strength or willpower to refuse him. The sad truth was that she had no money, no family, and no prospects. All she really had was an inherent need to survive. If it came down to honor or survival, she knew which she'd choose.

She'd learned the hard way that pride and honor didn't keep a woman warm or fed.

All it did was provide the barest amount of comfort in a hard, brittle existence.

And because of that, she knew she couldn't give up or give in. She had no other options.

"Mr. Proffitt, I'll be happy to live in the barn," she continued, talking quickly. "We don't have to converse. We don't have to have much to do with each other. I'll cook your meals and help you clean the house. Believe me, you're going to want someone to help you with that."

"What about your mother? Your family?"

"I'm afraid they're moving on."

"Without you?" His voice was incredulous. And a little bit horror-struck.

As if on cue, the door opened, and her mother and sister came out. The gunslinger paused to watch, and Rosemarie turned as well.

Her sister's and mother's arms were heavy with their burdens. Likely they were surrounding most of her mother's worldly goods. Well, such as they were.

The man standing so straight and tall seemed mesmerized. "Looks to me like they're taking everything they can get their hands on."

"I stopped them from taking it all, but most likely they took everything of worth,"

Rosemarie agreed. "To be honest, I had no idea there was all that much worth taking."

Unspoken, of course, was that she was getting left behind with the other belongings that weren't valued or that didn't amount to much.

As they watched the women load up the buggy, Mr. Proffitt spoke. "I'm not in the habit of living in the company of women. Not even cooking and cleaning ones."

Rose supposed that was true. Frozen with worry, she turned to watch her mother and sister finish moving their belongings.

Eventually, they approached Rose and the gunslinger. "I believe we have everything," her mother said.

"Except your daughter," Scout pointed out.

"Rosemarie stopped being my daughter the day she killed my son, Mr. Proffitt."

He glanced away, obviously startled.

Annalise noticed. "You see, Mr. Proffitt? You aren't the only killer standing on the property. You and Rose have something in common."

The outlaw's jaw tightened, though he said nothing.

Rosemarie didn't say a word. There was no reason to, anyhow. She could never rewrite the past. No matter how many times she'd wished for things to be different, or how many times she'd wished to erase the memories, doing so was a thankless and difficult task.

She knew because she'd tried.

As Annalise turned away, her mother spoke. "This isn't the future I would have wished for you, Rosemarie. But you are strong and you are willful. I feel certain you will do whatever it takes to survive. That should get you somewhere."

Then she turned around and joined Annalise at the buggy. Moments later, they were gone, leaving only the faint trail of dust in their path.

The air around them quieted as she stood next to Scout Proffitt. Beside him still stood his horse, sixteen hands tall. Pawing the hard ground with a hoof.

Everything else in her life was gone. And all she had left was a gunslinger, her memories, and two dollars that she'd managed to somehow scrimp and save during the last five years.

"Is that true about your brother?" he murmured, still staring straight ahead.

Though she burned with the need to tell him the full story, experience had taught her that excuses didn't matter all that much. "Yes."

A moment passed. Then two.

"What happened?"

She swallowed, then knew she had no choice but to share the story. It didn't matter anyway. The story would either stay with her or linger between them. "He was four and I was eight. It was my duty to watch him, but he fell into a pond. Neither of us knew how to swim. I tried, but I couldn't reach him in time."

The air around them seemed to still — so much that even her toes stopped hurting. Maybe they, like the rest of her, had finally become numb.

"Stay," he murmured, then pivoted on a heel and walked toward the barn, leading his horse.

She wondered what was going to happen next. Would Mr. Proffitt shoot her in the back? Kill her in her sleep?

Bring the whole Walton Gang over to roost?

All she seemed to be able to do was close her eyes and pray that it didn't hurt too much to die.

4

As Scout strode into the barn, he cursed both himself and his fate. Only he would win the world's worst farm in a poker game. And only he would discover that a woman nobody wanted came with it.

And, it seemed, only he would keep both.

He could hardly believe the turn of events. When the heck had he gotten so soft? For his whole life, he'd prided himself on putting his survival first. Always. A man had to do that or else reap the consequences.

And those consequences were all about pain and suffering.

Pacing back and forth, he stomped, letting out his anger and frustration with his feet instead of his fists or his mouth. Or his gun.

This new way of dealing with things almost felt good. Kind of peaceful.

Almost.

He stewed some more. He should have

pointed a finger to the horizon and told that girl to scoot. Instead, he now had her living with him. If James Walton could see him now, he'd probably have put a bullet in his head.

The turn of events was almost dizzying, for sure.

The three horses whinnied and snorted in their stalls. Obviously, they were sensing his displeasure. Realizing his pacing probably sounded like a stampede, the way his hard steps were echoing off the rafters, he stopped in front of Rio's stall and breathed deep.

"Sorry, boy," he murmured, scratching the gelding around his ears the way he liked. "I'll settle down. Eventually."

He would settle down, he was sure of it. As soon as he figured out when he'd started caring about what happened to abandoned women.

The answer didn't hit him like a lightning bolt or even as a surprise. Because it all boiled down to one person who had changed his life: Kitty.

When he'd made the choice to try to rescue that poor girl, he'd changed his heart, too. Something had happened in her company. Her questions and temperament had given him an excuse to think about somebody else.

Her death had made him think about himself.

And her burial had made him think about what he wanted out of his miserable life.

And realize that he didn't have much of one. He'd already lived too long. If he'd gambled much longer with his odds, there was no question that he'd surely lose everything.

It was inevitable.

As the horses whinnied again, he paused and took a look around and noticed for the first time the stream of light that peeked in through the slats in the wood, making curious sunbeams shine on the ground.

One stopped right at his feet.

The beams of light were bright and beautiful. And made him think about God and His ways.

And calmed him.

He stood there and just watched the beams, enjoying the sight. Enjoying the site, too. These were his beams, his barn.

After all this time, he finally had a home of his own.

A lot had happened to Miles Grant over the last two years. He'd listened to his sister get beaten, and had stood to one side while another man escorted her to safety. He'd gone on a long journey with his stepfather, discovering while they rode that the journey had become as much about finding God as tracking down his sister.

He'd been given a Bible by a man who'd made it his business to teach others about the Lord. And he'd read it by firelight to pass the time while his stepfather tasted the charms of any number of cathouses.

And just as he'd accepted the Lord as his savior, he'd cast himself a sinner by committing murder. He'd shot his stepfather when he'd dared to touch his sister.

He felt bad about what he'd done, but he also had few regrets. Some things couldn't continue. And when he'd pulled the trigger, he'd realized he couldn't continue to let other men do as they pleased.

Not when it hurt others. Innocents.

He'd been prepared to go to jail for what he did. Maybe even die, getting strung up on a nearby oak. He'd been prepared to do it because he'd known taking Price Venture's life was the right thing.

If committing murder could ever be seen in that way.

However, the sheriff, influenced no doubt by Miles's brother-in-law's reputation and the unyielding character of John Merritt, the man whose land they were on, had acquitted Miles. After listening to a whole lot of tales, one more sordid than the next, he'd put an end to the matter by deeming Price Venture's death justifiable. After all, Price had been eager to shoot them all. Only Miles got to him first.

Yep, the sheriff had called the whole thing self-defense. Which was almost the truth.

But he still woke up in the middle of the night remembering what it had felt like to pull a trigger. He remembered the blood pooling on the ground and the startled, shocked look of awareness in his stepfather's eyes.

Taking another's person's life did that to a person.

Now he was sole owner of the Circle Z ranch, and doing his best to right a lifetime of wrongs. He'd invested in more cattle, gotten lucky at market, and used the profits to improve the ranch.

He'd also spent much of the last year working hard to earn the hands' trust. These men had seen him do next to nothing for most of his life. Miles realized it would take time for them to see that his dedication wasn't a passing fancy.

But finally, after watching him sweat by their side for a spell, the hands slowly began to joke with him.

Just last week, Frank "Slim" Cayman, Miles's dedicated, fairly quiet foreman, had introduced Miles as his boss in town. Miles hadn't taken that title lightly. Thing was, Slim would never have referred to him that way if he didn't mean it.

Receiving that respect had surely been one of the highlights of Miles's life. Right then and there, he'd again felt like he'd made a huge stride in becoming the type of man he wanted to be.

He would have given just about anything to feel that way again. Because at the moment, he was standing next to Laurel White, and she was making him a nervous wreck.

They'd gone into Camp Hope for supplies and a much-needed break from the constant braying and bawling of cattle. The last thing he'd intended happening was getting propositioned by the most beautiful woman in the whole state.

She'd spied him outside the post office and hadn't wasted a minute to float across the dirt and mud to stand by his side.

"Mr. Grant, are you ever going to ask anyone to Friday's dance?" she asked prettily.

Miles gulped. Laurel's eyes were the kind of brown he'd seen in the outskirts of New

Mexico Territory, that surprising mix of sand and stone that seemed to shift every other minute.

Every time she turned that gaze of hers on him, he felt a lump form in his throat, followed by a need to lose his lunch.

It wasn't pretty but it couldn't be helped. Fact was, from the time they'd first got to talkin', Laurel White had had that kind of effect on him.

"I . . . well. I don't know," he mumbled.

"Whyever not?" Her lips puffed and pouted. And he couldn't help himself . . . he gazed at them a little too long.

Struggling to remind himself to talk, he said, "Well, Laurel, the thing is . . . I don't rightly know if I'll be going to the dance."

"You should." She leaned back against one of the wooden poles that lined the front of the mercantile. Months ago, someone had decided to paint them red. The brightness flanking her on either side accentuated the rose in her cheeks and the lovely brunette locks that curled down her shoulders and back. "Everyone's going."

He glanced at her pretty hair again, imagined how soft and silky it would feel against his fingers, and felt his cheeks heat. "A lot of folks are, that's true."

"Miles, you wouldn't believe it . . . but I

don't have an escort." She blinked prettily.

He could believe it. Laurel half-frightened him. She had too much femininity and wiles for the likes of most of the poor cowboys in their vicinity. "You don't need one, Laurel. Everyone just goes. You know that."

Her eyes widened, then after an awkward pause, narrowed. "I see. So you don't intend to take me?"

"No, I don't."

Pure surprise lit her eyes. He felt ashamed. Years ago, back when his real father had been alive, Miles had been taught how to treat the fairer sex.

It wasn't by speaking bluntly.

But before he could try to soften his words and try to figure out a way to tell her that he meant no disrespect, what he said wrong, she presented her shoulder to him and flounced away.

Behind him, Slim chuckled. "Oh, ho! Looks like Miss White ain't happy at all with you, Mr. Grant," he said over a fifty-pound bag of flour on his shoulder.

"Come on, it's Miles, Slim. You know you don't need to be calling me Mr. Grant."

The usual fun-loving gleam dimmed a bit in the foreman's eyes. "It's better for everyone if I call you by your rightful name in town," he said seriously. "You deserve it, too, sir. Don't let anyone think you don't."

Since he trusted Slim more than himself, Miles let the comment slide. "Do we have everything we need?"

"Yep. All we gotta do is wait for Big Jim to finish his business at the livery."

Miles glanced at the Golden Star Saloon. Even two years ago, the scruffy town of Camp Hope was known as a hotbed of saloons and loose women. But over the last year, as more and more men down on their luck headed out to Colorado Territory in search of gold or into the ranks of soldiers fighting in the Indian wars, the place had become far more settled. A few more ranchers had moved into the vicinity, and someone had even started talking about maybe building a school.

Camp Hope still wasn't all that special of a place, but it wasn't as bad as it once was.

The Golden Star was just about the only saloon left. "You're welcome to go get a sarsaparilla or something. I don't mind waiting."

Slim looked mildly interested. "You gonna partake, Mr. Grant?"

"Nah. I don't have a taste for liquor. But I'm in no big hurry, neither. All we got back at the ranch is more of the same that was there this morning. A break from cow punching might do us all good. I don't mind waiting."

"Obliged." Slim nodded. "I'll go see what's keeping Jim then meet you back here in an hour or so. There's been talk of some rustlers circling around here, too. I'm going to see if I hear some news about that."

No one had ever dare to mess with the Circle Z's cattle, so Miles wasn't worried about rustlers. However, he figured Slim was right to stay informed. "That's a real good idea," he said. "Take your time. Like I said, we only got more of the same waiting for us."

Miles felt good about letting his foreman have some time off and would have felt better if it hadn't been so warm.

Even though it was November, the sun didn't seem to have gotten that message. Currently, the sun was beating down on them all something awful. Just when he'd wiped his kerchief over his forehead and had decided to move to the shade of the church's covered porch, he saw Tracy Wood walking down the road. Her arms were so full of laundry that it was a wonder that she knew where she was going.

The next thing he knew, he was striding toward her, helping her carry a too-heavy load of sheets.

"Let me help you, Trace," he said, grabbing a pile off of the top. Well, of course, his action caused more than a few to topple down onto the dirt beneath their feet. "Sorry 'bout that," he said as he bent down and picked them up.

Eyeing the now mud-stained sheets, she glared. "Mr. Grant, I've told you before, I don't need any help."

"I know you're strong. But there's no shame in accepting a helping hand, Miss Wood."

A faint sheen of rose flooded her cheeks. "You're the only man in fifty miles who calls me that."

"I shouldn't be. It's the proper way to address a lady."

"We both know I ain't no lady."

"If you aren't, it's because you never sit still long enough to act like one. You're the busiest gal I know." Inwardly, he winced. Though he didn't mean to embarrass her, he knew his voice had a touch of disapproval in it.

He couldn't help it, though. The work she was doing was really too difficult for a slip of a thing like her.

To his surprise, she chuckled. "I suppose you're right. I don't know how to sit still."

"Or accept help."

She shrugged, his advice rolling easily off her shoulders. "It's always easier to do it myself."

"I promise, we all need help every now and then."

Tracy had cinnamon-colored freckles dotting her nose. Those freckles never failed to make him smile. Now with a better grip on his load of sheets, he stepped to her side and walked in time with her. "How are you, Miss Wood? I haven't seen you lately."

Still looking straight in front of her, she mumbled. "I've been busy."

Both her parents had passed away about a year before. They'd been good people, but never rich. Mrs. Evans at the hotel had taken Tracy in, and now Tracy seemed to work too much all the time.

But she never complained, and Miles had always had a soft spot for her. He treated her like a little sister, like the way he should have treated his own sister, Vanessa, years ago. Eager to see her smile, he said, "What have you been so busy with? Washing sheets?"

By this time they were at the Chinese laundry. "No. I've been carrying around sheets, not washing them. No one in Camp Hope can do laundry like Jon."

She had a point. One day last year, the

Chinaman had appeared in Camp Hope, let the word out that he did laundry, and waited for business. By Miles's estimation, it only took the man about twenty-four hours to make everyone in town a believer of his services. The man had a real way with a washboard.

In front of the weathered boards of Jon's business, Tracy called out, "Jon?"

The little man appeared in an instant, his long black braid swinging down his back as he moved. "Tracy, what you got?"

Right before his eyes, Tracy Wood gave the querulous Chinaman the brightest smile in all of Texas. "I've got five sets of sheets for you. Do you think you can manage to get them back by tomorrow?"

Out went a palm, all five fingers spread out in a good imitation of a spider. "Five?"

"Uh-huh." She smiled again. "Five sets. One has mud on it, though. It might take little bit of extra work."

"I can do tomorrow. Come at noon."

"I will do that. Thank you." When Jon nodded abruptly, followed by a little bow, to Miles's astonishment, she did the same. "You have a good day now," she said sweetly.

After the man grunted his good-bye and turned away with his arms full of sheets, Miles held the door open for her and followed her out. "You seem to have a smile for almost everyone, Miss Wood," he said.

"It's nice to be nice," she said over her shoulder as she walked back the way she came.

Just to tease her, he said, "How come you never have a smile for me like you do for the Chinaman?"

"You don't wash my sheets."

"Oh, come now. Why are you so prickly near me?"

"'Cause you don't give me much to smile about, Mr. Grant. And you never call me by my first name."

"Calling you Tracy is all it takes it get in your good graces?"

She froze for a moment. Stared at him like he'd just done the strangest thing imaginable — then turned and walked on.

Leaving him standing there in the dust, more confused than ever.

When he got to the wagon, his ranch hands chortled. "It takes a real man to run off two women in one hour," Slim said, revealing Miles's misadventures with the women had been duly noted. "Remind me to keep far away from you at the dance. If I'm by your side, I'm sure to be a wallflower for sure!"

Big Jim chuckled, as did Luke, their newest hire.

"Slim, if no girl wants to dance with you, I promise it has nothing to do with my way with women."

"Maybe," Slim said with a drawl. "Or . . . maybe not," he said with a grin.

That dance. It was all anyone could seem to talk about. And it was definitely the last thing he wanted to think about. "Don't worry. Y'all won't be having to dodge a thing. I won't be going to the dance. I've already made up my mind about that."

The four of them hopped in the wagon, Slim taking over the driving as he usually did.

After Slim had snapped the reins and the horses moved forward, Big Jim — sitting in the middle but taking the space of two men — looked at him curiously. "How come you ain't going?"

"Why do you think?" Miles asked. "I'm no good with women. Being around them makes my palms sweat." Plus, he didn't know how to dance. And the thought of embarrassing himself like that with a slew of onlookers watching him made his mouth go dry.

"Laurel wanted you to ask her . . ."

"Laurel frightens me," Miles admitted. "She wants something and is always staring at me like I should read her mind." Shaking his head, he said. "The problem is, for the life of me, I can't figure out what it is."

"That's easy. She wants a ring and a ranch," Slim said. "*Your* ring and *your* ranch."

"You really think so?" Just imagining Laurel White living by his side — greeting him in the morning and walking to his bed in the evening — made his pulse race.

Unfortunately, he didn't know if it raced because he was taken with her or because she scared him half to death.

"I'd watch her, Mr. Grant," Big Jim said. "That Miss White is about the prettiest thing in two states, but she's a real live wire, too."

"She'd be a constant source of heartbreak, for sure," Slim added.

"I'm going to continue to give her a wide berth," Miles decided.

"But Tracy, on the other hand, she's a peach," Slim said with a smile.

Tracy? A peach? "Do you like her, Slim?"

"Oh, no more than most men, I guess."

Miles looked at his foreman and noticed the way his eyes were diverted and his body was stiff. "Maybe you should ask Tracy to the dance."

"I couldn't. Besides, I ain't got no call for

courting. I'm just a foreman. She's most likely looking for a home with her husband."

"You should ask her to the dance, Boss," Luke said.

"Tracy doesn't even like me! Shoot, she runs from me every time I'm near her."

When Slim and Luke looked at each other, they grinned.

Miles was offended. "What are y'all smiling about now?"

"She runs because you're so clueless, Boss," Luke said. "That Tracy's got a crush on you, and she's had one for a while, too."

"Since when?" He couldn't have been more shocked if they'd said he'd contracted the clap.

"Since forever," Luke said.

"Or at least since her parents passed on," Big Jim said. "I reckon she's upset that you never give her the time of day. That's why she's always skittish around you."

"Hmm." He'd just assumed she didn't care for him or maybe even treated him like a brother.

"I know that's the reason," Jim said slyly. "I mean, I know that's the reason, sir."

"Shoot." Miles didn't know if he was more shocked by the men's words or the fact that he'd been oblivious to all the undercurrents with the women.

Or that Slim was sitting right there in the middle of it all, quiet and easy. Like he thought that Miles would be a better match for the girl he fancied.

And right then and there, Miles realized he still had more to learn. But this lesson might be even harder than figuring out how to run the Circle Z. This time, he was going to have to figure out a woman's brain.

A terribly confusing notion if there ever was one.

5

"What, exactly, am I supposed to do with you?" Scout Proffitt asked Rose when he strode into the kitchen around supper time. "I can't hardly believe you're here."

"Believe it."

His arms curved over his chest. Frowning. "Living with a woman was never part of my plans."

Rose wasn't surprised. In all of her twenty years, she hadn't been a big part of anyone's plans. But that didn't make her expendable. All it did do was make her dig in her heels. "Like I told you, Mr. Proffitt, I can cook and clean for you. Besides, I don't want you to 'do' anything with me. I may be in a bad situation, but I'm not in any hurry to start answering to your beck and call."

When his eyes narrowed, she lifted her chin. Because, well, she had to do something in order to not appear weak and foolish.

However, he didn't seem to be struck by

the power of her gaze at all. In fact, he looked pretty darn incredulous. Like she suddenly had more gumption than he'd counted on or planned for and he wasn't happy about it. "Not at my beck and call? For some reason you expect us to get along well?" he asked, his voice rising like the harsh, high-pitched squeal of a lit firecracker.

As she continued to gaze at him silently, the sarcasm in his voice thickened. "What did you expect? That I would get used to you? That we'd find a way to suddenly start making a life together?"

Her throat went dry.

"Are you ever going to speak, girl?"

"My name is Rosemarie. Rose. Not girl. Uh, Mr. Proffitt," she tagged on unnecessarily. After all, he wasn't known for putting up with folks who irritated him. "And I have to tell you that I'm fairly surprised by your attitude. When I talked to you earlier, you didn't sound all that put out about me being here."

"I felt sorry for you."

"Well, I'm grateful for your concern, but I promise you, I don't want to be a burden. You'll soon be very glad you let me stay."

A muscle in his cheek twitched. "I am beginning to understand why you were left behind, ma'am."

Shame filled her soul, but it was now habit to cover up disappointment with words. "Considering my father just passed away hours ago, I think you are being terribly unkind."

For the first time, he looked at a loss for words.

And she was right.

Almost as if he was actually embarrassed.

Which was why she decided to take pity on him, though she didn't really think he deserved it. But perhaps that was the point. He didn't deserve it.

But his words weren't completely without merit either. For most of her life, she had tended to talk too much. Usually at the wrong time.

"I do apologize, ma'am."

"Mr. Proffit, I've been thinking about things, and it's occurred to me that you go about your business . . . whatever that is. And I could make sure you did it clean and well fed."

Warming up to the conversation, she added, "I'd stay out of the way and take care not to be seen when you entertain."

An incredulous look hit his eyes hard. "What in the world?"

Though she felt her face — and her neck

— heat up with embarrassment, she soldiered on. "The dime novels say you always had a ladybird around."

One black eyebrow rose. "Did you see a woman by my side when I arrived?"

"Well, no . . ."

"So you think I'm going to conjure one up out . . ." He interjected, looking around like he'd come to the ends of the earth and then arrived at her doorstep. "Here?"

"I don't know." Truly, she hadn't thought that far ahead.

He stared hard at her again, then seemed to visibly collect himself. "I appreciate your offer, but I won't be taking you up on it."

Stung, she nodded. "I'm only trying to help."

"I gathered that."

She looked him over, noticing that his eyes were the darkest shade of gray imaginable, a true mix of dark pewter and blue. Beautiful. And that his jaw was strong and perfect. That he was more than six feet of man and muscle.

But coated over that was a cloak of black and maybe grime, too.

"I hope so."

A muscle twitched in his jaw. "How old are you, anyway?"

"I just turned twenty."

"Seriously? You look like you're about twelve."

"Being petite ain't my fault. I wanted to be taller. It just never happened."

"Petite?"

"Petite means short. Small," she clarified. "But not childlike."

"I see."

Before he could figure out something else to get on her case about, she marched back to the stove, where she was frying up dough with some potatoes, carrots, and what was left of the rabbit Annalise's husband had brought by the other day. "When was the last time you ate?"

"I have no idea."

"If you don't know, then it's past time you sat down and ate something, don't you think?"

He looked like he started to sit down, then stopped himself. "Rosemarie, do you even know how to cook?"

That man was so ornery, he could drive the top off a turnip. "I'm standing here at the stove, aren't I? I lit it and cut up vegetables without your help. And now I'm offering you food. To me, those seem like pretty good clues that I can cook."

"They're clues, but just because you can start a stove doesn't mean you can put it to

79

good use."

Without thinking, she waved her wooden spoon in his direction. "I better write that saying down. It's right up there with you can take a horse to water but you can't make him drink."

"Are you now acting offended? After I've given you shelter?"

She wasn't acting, she was offended. Even though she had no right to be, because the fact of the matter was that they hardly knew each other at all. And what they did know wasn't any good and should probably be forgotten, anyway.

"I'm telling you what, Mr. Proffitt, if you give me any more compliments, why you're going to make me blush. Sit down, now. Food's done." She placed a generous portion on one of the few plates her mother left then walked it over to him. "Eat while it's hot."

To her surprise, without another word, he sat. He stared at the plate for a long moment, then glanced her way. Almost like he wasn't used to anyone doing favors for him. "You might as well join me."

She sat down across from him. "Wanna pray?"

In a flash, he looked her way. "For what?"

"We could give thanks for the food. That's

the usual thing to do."

"Such that it is."

"Don't knock a free meal, Mr. Proffitt. This might be the last one you ever receive."

His dark gray eyes widened in surprise. And if she didn't know better, it kinda seemed like he was trying not to smile. Making a decision, he said, "Let's do it, then. You say the prayer."

Folding her hands, she spoke to the Lord, deciding to keep things easy and simple. "Dear Lord, thank you for providing us with food for this meal. I appreciate it."

"We," Mr. Proffitt corrected. "We appreciate it."

"Oh, we sure appreciate it, God. Thanks again." She paused. Waiting for a moment, certain he was going to add another word or two. But when he didn't, she finished things up right. "Amen."

"Yes. Amen."

Embarrassed about her clumsy prayer, she dug in. And though it wasn't much, Rose figured it tasted pretty good.

Across from her, Scout Proffitt ate his food in a meticulous way, carefully taking measured spoonfuls. He sat up straight and chewed with his mouth closed.

Almost elegantly.

She ate at a slower pace. With each bite,

81

the mixed-up day and the loss of her father threatened to get the best of her. It didn't seem fair that she'd already lost her father and her mother in one day. And though she couldn't claim she'd had much of a relationship with either one, a living relative was more desirable than a dead one, she figured.

She was so tired, too. So tired of worrying and waiting.

All too soon, the meal was over. And because they had nothing in common, and certainly nothing to talk about, the only thing left to do was more work.

She chose the option with pleasure. "I'll wash up now."

He let her take his plate but looked uncomfortable. "Obliged. For the meal, too. It was just fine."

As compliments went, his wasn't good.

But, considering how she hadn't been all full of sweet words and compliments either, it sounded like music to her ears. "Thank you." Conscious of him still standing there, watching her, she turned and started cleaning off the plates. She heated up water so she could clean things up right.

After a while, he cleared his throat. "I just wanted you to know that I'll be sleeping in the barn tonight."

Relief poured through her as she realized

that meant that for one more night, at least, she had a place to call home.

But her pa had lost the building in a wager, and the man lurking behind her had earned the right to take his rightful place. "No sir, you will not. I'll be just fine in the barn."

"I can't take you from your home. I can't let a woman sleep in a barn while I sleep in here."

"This is your home now, Mr. Proffitt. And, well, you and I know that as homes go, this one ain't much. It's gloomy and needs to be aired out. And that's just to start with. But even so, it's yours, and you should be able to sleep in the bed."

"The bed that your father just died in?"

She supposed he couldn't help but be a little incredulous. "I'll change the sheets, of course."

He gaped at her, then shook his head as he tried to find the correct response. Looking like he was mad enough to spit nails, he stood up. "You never fail to shock me."

"I'd be flattered, if I thought I wanted to be shocking."

"This arrangement, us living together, I'm afraid it isn't going to work out."

She paused. "Perhaps we only need it to work for tonight."

"Is that enough?"

"I hope so. I'd really love to know where I was sleeping tonight."

Once again, Scout stared at her, then simply waved a hand at her and walked outside.

After she cleaned off the dishes and set things right, she attacked the bed. It smelled like sickness and her father and death. The scents brought back a wealth of memories, some sweet, most bittersweet.

Her eyes filled with tears, but she pushed them back and concentrated on what needed to be done. Fixing up the bed.

Fixing up a place so Scout Proffitt could sleep. And maybe if he slept, he'd let her stay a little longer.

Once she was satisfied that the bed was as good as she could make it, she went to her dresser drawer and pulled out her brush and nightgown. Grabbing a blanket, she left the house and walked to the barn.

She found Mr. Proffitt sitting outside his horse's stall. His black boots were spread out in front of him, his black Stetson tilted halfway down his forehead. When she got closer, he lifted his chin and stared.

"I, uh, made your bed, Mr. Proffitt. It's ready for you now."

"And where do you intend to sleep, Rose?"

"The last stall's pretty clean. I was thinking that would be a good spot for me."

He straightened. "You sure you're okay with being out here?"

"I am."

With a long, last look at his horse, he got to his feet and walked away.

Seconds later, the door to her house opened and shut. She took that as her signal to put on her nightgown and brush out her hair. Then, she took Mr. Proffitt's spot and began the long road to a hundred strokes.

Right around number fifty, her eyes started watering. By seventy-five her bottom lip trembled. And by eighty-five, she'd given up on having healthy hair and gave into her sadness. She cried for her father. And for her place in the world.

And for her mother leaving her in the company of a man like Scout Proffitt.

And then, even though she wasn't real proud about it, she cried for herself.

And when she caught her breath, she cried some more.

6

Just like an unwanted illness, the dreams had come again, hitting him hard in the middle of the night. The visions were vibrant and disturbing. With a sputter and a start, he'd come awake with a jerk, gasping for air like a dying man.

As reality returned, Russell inhaled, then exhaled again. Breathing like an old man while he did his best to convince himself that he was now living at a far different place. Living in a far different time. He wasn't getting beaten, and he wasn't covered in blood. He wasn't standing guard for Mr. Walton either.

Instead, he was okay.

'Course, that didn't make Russell Champion feel any better. With all his heart, he wished he was back in Texas. Living a different life than the one he was neck-deep in.

Conscious of the other men near him,

Russell blinked away the last vestiges of his dream in the dim glow of the campfire and tried to calm his breathing. The last thing in the world he wanted was to draw the attention of any of the other men he was with. They would only use his weakness to their benefit. And oh, but they'd use it, of that he had no doubt.

"Russell? You okay over there?" Joe Bob asked, not unkindly.

"I'm fine."

"Sure 'bout that? Because you sound like you just got done chasing a heifer. You sound plumb wore out."

He felt that way, too. "I'm fine," he repeated, his voice turning a little harder. The last thing in the world he wanted was for the other men in his company to start thinking he was a weakling.

"Oh, well, all right," Joe Bob said. "Just askin'."

When Joe lay back down, Russell did the same and closed his eyes. And when he did, he searched his brain for something better to think about than his past or his current situation. Being a member of a ragtag group was a difficult thing. Mr. Walton had been hanged with much anticipation, and Scout had run off.

So he and a couple of others had joined

with two other men, Joe Bob, a.k.a. Joseph Robert Sloan, being their unofficial leader.

All of them were currently trying their hand leading almost-lawful lives. So far, they'd been on a number of roundups, helped on the railroad, and even worked in a lumber mill for a couple of months.

But the work was hard to get, and with no one leading with an iron hand, well, there was a whole lot of complaining.

Almost every day. Which made him, of course, wish for something better. Or at least something not quite as bad.

Because of that, he'd taken to dreaming about a future not laced with uncertainty and the surety of death. He'd start imagining somehow becoming a rich man — or at least a man with money in his pockets — then going back to Texas and visiting Nora.

And this time, in his dreams, she would beam with pleasure when she saw him. And of course, she'd ask him to never let her go.

The home he'd won was barely one step above a cesspool. It smelled like death, and, Scout reflected, he ought to know. He'd killed a lot of men in his time.

Though, to be fair, for the most part he'd just left them lying on the ground. Or in their chairs.

Searching back in his memory, he grimaced. Or in the bed they were sleeping in.

No, there had only been one time, in his recollection, when he'd put the dead in front of the living.

And that had been in the middle of Kansas, with a pretty, terrible girl who went by the name of Kitty.

She'd adopted him — there really was no other term for it — when he'd been on the hunt for a man on the run from the Walton Gang. She'd shown up in the middle of a saloon, looking scared and brave and desperate.

And had offered herself up to him if he killed her stepfather.

Even now, the idea of it all made his stomach turn.

He hadn't meant to take her up on her offer. She'd been little more than a child. And though others might have thought differently, even he had limits on how bad he could be.

Shoot. Some might even call what he had values. And those values prohibited him doing something so evil as taking advantage of a girl like her, someone who had been so lost for most of her short life that she couldn't imagine ever expecting more from a man than the very worst. He'd meant to leave her be. Even a life with a man like her stepfather was better than being on the trail with a man like him.

But then her stepfather looked down at his feet, and Scout knew it was best to take Kitty and walk on.

He'd meant to find a foundling home or a convent or someplace good for the girl. Someplace where women lived who might not judge a girl like her too harshly.

But Kitty had had other plans. She wanted to stay with him.

Oh, not because she lusted after him. Or because they had any sort of relationship. Nothing like that.

No, she'd yearned to stay by his side because he'd kept her safe. And feeling safe could never be underestimated.

Days passed. He'd almost become used to her. But not quite. When he'd gotten lucky and found his target, he'd made the mistake of telling Kitty that he planned to drop her off at a convent or something soon after.

None of that meshed with her plans, so she'd taken her own life rather than be passed on again.

He'd found her in a tangle of blood and sheets, and against his better judgment, he'd sought out the aid of the man who he'd once planned on killing. Because, next to his brother, Will had been the most upstanding man Scout had ever met.

He'd been prepared to do whatever it took to get Kitty a decent burial, whether it meant paying with gold, threatening with violence, or using the full strength of Will McMillan's authority as a U.S. Marshal to get his way.

It turned out that neither the pastor nor the undertaker had needed that much encouragement. The four of them had braved the cold weather and buried Kitty in the dead of winter. Using brawn and pick-axes to make a burial site.

And he'd cried.

The memories of his pain still shocked him.

As the cold feeling of disappointment and regret sank deep into his skin again, mixing with the cool night air and pressing him deep, he couldn't help but think about Rose.

Rosemarie Cousins.

He felt bad about leaving the girl in the barn, but not bad enough to change places with her. Besides, if they were both honest, the barn had a certain charm that the house lacked. At least there were living animals there, with their comforting smell and noises. Their body heat would keep her from being too cold.

Here in this dusty ramshackle shack, there seemed to be only miserable memories and the remnants of a lifetime of pain and disappointment.

He washed up in the kitchen and stoked the fire in the stove a bit, generating a thin thread of heat that circled his body and provided a sense of relief.

Thinking of how nice it would be to sleep in comfort, he walked to the bedroom and half-circled the bed. Though Rose's mother and sister had stripped the bed of a pair of quilts, a feather bed remained. On top of it, Rose had made it up neatly, even adding another quilt — where she'd located it he'd never know.

The sheets smelled clean, but the rest of the room smelled like old clothes and old men, mixed in with a good portion of desperate pain.

That, he couldn't take.

He ended up pulling out his bedroll and lying down on the floor of the kitchen. Without a doubt, he trusted his blanket more than the feather mattress. Besides, now he was near the fire and the heat it allowed.

His muscles creaked and popped when he relaxed enough to lay flat on his back. The movement of his muscles and bones adjusting felt welcome. Too many days in the saddle had made him ache for some days off.

The night before, he'd been about to take a bed in a hotel when someone had informed the sheriff that Scout Proffitt had come to town. The law had gingerly stood in front of him and directed him out of their town.

Scout had been tempted to remind the man that he hadn't done a thing to warrant the eviction. But if he had done that, he would have been setting himself up for a night of watching his door.

Because if there was one thing he'd learned, it was that even though he was bad, there were a whole lot of other men on the earth who were bad, too.

Just nobody knew it.

He'd ended up riding out onto the plains on Rio. Early in the morning, he'd grown too tired to keep his eyes open and had set up camp near a piddly creek and a patch of grass.

Rio had been obliged for the break, and Scout had slept like the dead.

However, now, he had to admit that having a roof over his head was a welcome thing. Feeling like no one was getting ready to shoot him in the back had a certain appeal as well. It had been so very long since he had felt like he was safe.

Little by little, he began to relax. And then, it was a simple thing to finally close his eyes. And if he took a moment to give thanks for his life and his blessings, well, that wasn't anyone's business but his own.

The next morning, as the pale yellow sun struggled to rise over the chilly horizon, Rosemarie quietly opened the door to her almost home, then just about tripped over Mr. Proffitt when she entered the kitchen. The man was sprawled out on his back, one of his arms under his head, his other spread out along with one of his legs. To her eye, it looked like he was attempting to take up as much space as possible. He looked like a flattened spider, caught in the act. Well, one of those with a good portion of his legs chopped off.

The position was really different from the way she'd observed him being the afternoon before. Then, he was completely composed, every word measured. And his gaze had seemed to light on a hundred things all at once.

Rose doubted a lizard could slither in Scout Proffitt's path without receiving permission first.

She was still standing there, staring, when she became aware that she was getting stared at, too. In the space of the last second or two he'd come awake and had pinned those pale blue-silvery eyes on her.

"What are you doing?" he asked. Still lying flat on the floor.

"Sorry. I didn't mean to stare. You being here caught me off guard. You were supposed to be sleeping in bed."

A pained expression crossed his face. "I couldn't do that."

"I changed the sheets."

"I know."

"Did they smell? I'll wash them today."

"It wasn't that, though I'd be obliged." He propped himself on his elbows. "I've been doing some thinking about you, and I've decided that you can stay for two weeks and help me clean this place up. What do you think?"

His words had neither a hint of optimism or promise in them. Instead, they were said matter-of-factly. Like it was a business proposition he was offering, not charity.

Not that she could have refused either. Fact was, two weeks was good. Not wonderful, but two weeks meant she was going to have fourteen days of knowing where she belonged. She'd take that. Even if it did mean she was going to be at the mercy of a hired killer.

"Two weeks sounds good."

"Sorry I can't offer you more."

"I didn't ask for more."

That seemed to take him aback. "Are you afraid of me or just used to nothing?"

His words created a pain that even her father's passing and her mother's abandonment hadn't. This stranger had summed up her whole life in one question.

It made her pull out some pride, though she hadn't known she possessed much. "Shouldn't I be afraid of you? I mean, all the stories can't be lies, can they?"

He moved to a sitting position, his wrists lightly resting on his knees while his scowl deepened. "Do you want them to be, sugar?"

There was anger in his voice. And a new slick anger. "Of course not. I'm at your mercy."

"I'm surprised you think I possess mercy."

"Well, I guess we'll see if you do, won't we?" While he chewed on that, a new feeling of worth flickered through her. Seeming to wake up spunk she had forgotten she had.

Stepping over his foot, she bent and got the stove going again. It took little time to bring the embers back to life. For a heartbeat, she let her fingers hover over the heat. Then she straightened and faced him. "Mr. Proffitt, how 'bout some coffee and breakfast?"

"Both would be welcome."

"After you eat, if you help me take the feather bed and quilts outside, I'll wash them and air everything out." She smiled slightly. "That means by nightfall, you'll be sleeping on a bed, not on the floor."

"That's not going to bother you none? Me sleeping in your family's bed?"

She wondered why he even cared. Surely a man like him would never think about such tender feelings?

However, the fact was that she had no desire to sleep in that bed anytime soon. She hadn't been allowed near it when her father was alive, and she sure didn't want any part of it, now that he was dead and buried. "No sir, it won't bother me none at all."

With an easy, smooth motion, he got to his feet. "I'll go check on my horse."

"I've already fed and watered him."

He paused. "You didn't need to do that."

"Since he and I are roommates and all, I didn't see how I could overlook him, you know? He seemed real appreciative."

"From now on, I'll see to my horse."

97

"Well, all right, but it seems a waste of my time and kind of cruel to your horse."

"Cruel?"

"Walking by him without feeding him."

Scout paused, looked for a moment like he was going to comment on that, then shook his head without a word and walked out.

Rose breathed a sigh of relief. Being around him scared her, and that was the truth. Oh, not because of his reputation. No, it had more to do with how she reacted to him. She didn't fear him, even though she knew she should. Instead of fear, she found herself thinking that he brought safety to her life.

Safety in the form of a hired killer? Now, how about that? She was surely a woman who wasn't good for much.

Shaking off her thoughts, she heated water, then pulled out flour and the last two eggs the hens had given out. In no time at all, she was making flapjacks and piling a plate high.

"I hope flapjacks are okay with you."

"Anything, as long as it comes with coffee."

She placed a cup next to his plate and then handed him a fork. "Here you go, Mr. Proffitt. Coffee and breakfast."

He looked at her. "If I told you no one's taken such good care of me since I was living with my older sister, would you be offended?"

"I wouldn't be offended at all. Matter of fact," she said with a bit of sass, "I'd say you were probably due for some coddling."

"Coddling?"

"Of the breakfast sort."

When she turned her back, she could have sworn he'd chuckled under his breath.

7

Holding a large china coffeepot in one capable hand, Annabeth Wayne, Miles's formidable housekeeper, sauntered in the dining room at exactly six thirty in the morning. Just like she always did.

Sometimes, he was tempted to tell her that she was more reliable than the Union Pacific, but he knew she wouldn't have taken kindly to being compared to a locomotive.

But she had a forceful way about her that was as difficult to ignore as a runaway train.

As he smelled the rich scent of darkly brewed coffee, mixed in with a liberal smattering of starch — her dresses could probably stand up by themselves — he smiled her way as he held his cup out toward her. "Thank you, Miss Annabeth." She'd informed him that "Miss Annabeth" was her preferred form of address. Even though when she'd hired on, she'd said she was a widow.

He'd been so cowed by her personality, he'd simply nodded.

"I tell you what, sometimes I am positive that you and your coffee are the best part of my day."

"Hmmph," she said.

But instead of pouring him a cup of the badly needed brew, she tossed him a look that would have had jaded gunslingers shaking in their boots. And she set down the coffeepot.

"Is something wrong?" he asked.

To his dismay, she slid the coffeepot even farther from his grasp. "Mr. Grant, it's like this. I heard Laurel was looking your way in town."

"And?" Getting into his personal business was not something she usually did. Warily, he glanced at Miss Annabeth and wondered how he'd managed to have the bossiest housekeeper in the great state of Texas. And the one who also had her pulse on every bit of gossip and goings-on in a fifty-mile radius.

"And I have opinions about that."

"How thoughtful of you to gossip about me, ma'am," he said sarcastically. Holding up his coffee cup, he cleared his throat.

"Now, may I have some coffee?"

"In a minute." Her bright blue eyes narrowed, fastening on him like a half-starved tick stuck in a nether region. "But I ain't gossiping, Mr. Grant."

"Hmmph," he said.

"All right. I might be gossiping," she grumbled, looking away. "Some. But not all that much." She picked up the pot again.

Hopeful, he, too, lifted his cup. Looked meaningfully at it. "Coffee?"

"Um-hum." She worked her bottom lip. "It's just, well, Tracy is a real fine gal, too."

Still the china coffeepot hovered over his cup, teasing him with the brew. The spout was tilted slightly, just needing the merest fraction of an incline to proceed.

But amazingly, not even a drop poured out.

To his dismay, she set the pot down once again and drew a breath. It was obvious that she was fixing to begin a whole sermon on the subject.

Well, that settled that. If she was going prattle on nonstop, he was going to make sure he had coffee inside him while he pretended to listen. "Hand me the pot, Miss Annabeth. If you're going to start talking about women, I'm going to need some sustenance."

"Hold, now —"

"I want some coffee now, ma'am. Truth is, I've got to have some coffee before I expire right here in this chair."

"Mr. Grant, I'm getting to it." She paused, looking him up and down. "And you won't expire."

"I just might," he murmured. Then did a reach and grab. But just as he was reaching for the pot, she stole it out of his reach.

"Oh, no, Mr. Grant. You can't pour it yourself. That's my job."

Sometimes he wished she'd known him before he was "Mr. Grant," back when he'd been just Miles — too weak to be much good to anyone.

Back then, he'd done all kinds of things. And on the trail with his stepfather? Well, back then, no job or service had been too small.

But, of course, she didn't know any of that. Maybe it was best that way. But at times like these, when she was bound and determined to "do right" by a man of his status, he wished she saw them as equals. "Then pour it. Please."

"Oh, yes, sir. And I will, just as soon as I tell you —"

His patience was gone. "Miss Annabeth, pour me some coffee now," he ordered, in a

103

tone that brooked no argument.

She stared at him like he'd sprouted horns and was fixin' to charge.

"If you please," he murmured. "Or, just hand the pot to me and I'll do it."

"Well, my goodness."

"I'm sorry for my tone. But you know how I need my coffee."

"I do now." Her lips pursed as she poured him a full cup. After he took two sips, she sat down to his right.

Just like she had that right.

And perhaps she did. About four months ago she'd shown up at the Circle Z's doorstep announcing that she was in need of a job and that she'd heard that he was in need of a housekeeper.

"A man like you shouldn't be doing housework yourself, Mr. Grant."

He'd been so stunned about the way she'd said, "a man like him," he'd invited her into hear what she'd had to say.

Before he'd knew what he was doing, he'd been giving her a tour. All the while, she'd taken pains to tell him how just plain awful everything had looked.

And he'd taken pains to not tell her that he'd thought her saffron yellow dress with its flounce of lace was the ugliest garment he'd ever seen in his whole life.

Somehow they'd bonded, and an hour later, she was wearing a starched gray dress and white apron and bustling about like she owned the place. The ranch had never been the same since.

Nowadays, it seemed she was getting even more comfortable.

"Maybe you should go grab yourself a cup as well, ma'am?" he murmured sarcastically.

She waved his comment away. "Oh, you. You know that wouldn't be proper."

He waggled his eyebrows. "If you were improper, it could be our little secret, though."

"Oh, you." Her cheeks bloomed with color. And for a moment, she almost looked young enough to be his sister.

"Suit yourself," he murmured. He sipped his coffee until the cup went dry, then glanced her way pointedly. Without missing a beat, she filled it again.

And then she sat down. "Mr. Grant, I really think we should think about you getting a wife."

Curving his hands around the warm china, he murmured, "We think I should, huh?"

"Yes. This is a big house. A real big house. And it's just you here."

"You're here."

"You know what I mean. This place was meant for a family. Not a bachelor."

"I'm well aware of that." His father had built the home with great things in mind. Everyone who knew him agreed it was a crying shame that he'd died so suddenly.

"Rooms are made to be filled, Mr. Grant."

The idea of marrying in order to fill an empty home didn't appeal to him. "My sister and her husband were here four months ago. With their babies."

"And that was real fine. Mr. and Mrs. Proffitt are real fine folks. But now it's just you again." She got to her feet and stood over him like some kind of soldier. "We need to fix that."

"I'm doing my best."

"I'm sure you are doing your best. But truth be told, sometimes men can get sidetracked from the best and get taken in by a pretty head of hair."

Ah, that's where she was headed. "And you're worried about me doing that with Laurel?"

"I am." Placing both palms flat on the oak table, she said, "Miss White would be a real difficult woman to work for, Mr. Grant." She sighed. "Some might even find her challenging."

With effort, he kept his expression solemn.

106

"Yes, I can see how she might be." Never mind that he should be looking for a wife he could love . . .

She smiled brightly. "I'm so glad you understand. Now, what about Tracy? Are you going to ask her to the dance?"

"I don't know." Actually, that would be a very big no.

"Are you not going to ask her because she only works as a housekeeper?"

Miles looked at Annabeth in surprise. "No. I happen to think being a housekeeper is a fine profession. You've done wonders here."

For that, his coffee got topped off without as much as a cajoling look from him. Then, her expression turned serious. "Mr. Grant, you're not getting any younger, you know. I hope you'll get to thinking about marriage and children."

"I will," he promised. Not that he really would, but he didn't want to make her feel bad. "Miss Annabeth, are you going to the dance?"

"Me?" she reddened. "No."

"Why not? The dance is for everyone."

"It's not for me." She bit her lip, looked like she was about to say something, then headed back toward the kitchen. "You sit

107

tight and I'll bring you your breakfast in a jiffy."

Something was off here. "Is something bothering you?"

"No, sir. Well, nothing that time won't take care of." She looked at him carefully, then planted both of her palms on the table. "I have a bit of a confession, Mr. Grant. See, um, I'm not really a widow. I've never actually been married."

Miles was completely taken aback. "Why would you say that you had been?"

"I thought being a widow made me sound more respectable. And, the fact is, I have, um, given my heart to a man."

"Is that right?"

She nodded. "Years ago, I had a beau. He was in the war."

"What happened to him? Did he die?"

"No. But I heard he was wounded something awful." She lowered her voice, slipping each word out like it was a painful thing. "He got some burns on his face. Bad ones."

Miles frowned. He'd seen more than a handful of men still suffering from the ravages of war. "Poor man. Where is he now?"

"I don't rightly know. But when he got injured and was in the hospital, he wrote me a letter, sayin' he didn't want me no more. Fair broke my heart, it did."

"A lot of men say things when they're in the depths of despair. He might feel differently now."

Hope shone in her eyes for a good long minute, then faded again. "Maybe."

"Maybe you should write him again. His feelings might have changed but his pride's holding him back."

"Do you think that really ever happens?"

Miles recalled the uncountable foolish things he'd done over the years that he wished he could take back. Too many to name, really. "It happens all the time. You really should write to him, Miss Annabeth."

She laughed, though the sound was hollow and broken. "Mr. Grant, the day I start tracking down that man is the day you get engaged."

His interest was piqued. "You mean that? Because that almost sounds like a bet."

"If it was a bet, it would mean I had a chance of winning it. You, sir, have just told me you've no interest in changing your situation," she said over her shoulder as she headed back into the kitchen.

Miles figured she had a point. After all, he had no intention of finding a bride. Even he knew he wasn't husband material — shoot he only recently had the respect of his field hands!

But as Miss Annabeth clanged the dishes with enough gumption to make him fear for the china's safety, he began to think about the possibility of the house being filled again. This time with feminine laughter and children's voices.

Wouldn't it be something, to walk into a room and see a pretty smile directed his way? To end each day with a hug from children? To walk the land next to his son, knowing that he was passing on a legacy.

All of that was terribly appealing.

And it left Miles to wonder if maybe he should go ahead and ask Tracy to the dance after all. Just in case they did suit and she really did have her eye on him.

After all, he had his housekeeper's future happiness to think about.

Just as he was about to pour himself another cup of coffee, Slim wandered in, Big Jim behind him, their expressions serious.

He sat back down, gesturing for them to sit also. "What's going on?"

"Trouble," Slim said. "Mr. Grant, those rustlers hit over at the Millers."

"How many head did they take?"

"We're still trying to figure that out," Big

Jim said.

Miles was surprised at the answer. "And why is that?"

"Because the rustlers not only stole the cattle, they killed Mr. Miller."

Miles closed his eyes and quickly said a prayer for Madison Miller. "Know anything else?"

Big Jim looked at Slim, then nodded. "Sheriff Brower thinks even the Circle Z ain't safe."

Feeling the cloak of responsibility heavy on his shoulders, Miles nodded. "Then I think we'd best come up with some plans to make things safer. I don't want a single cow stolen . . . and I sure don't want a single man on my land hurt."

Slim smiled in obvious relief. "I was sure hoping you were going to say that, Mr. Grant."

"Grab some cups from the sideboard, pour yourselves some coffee, and let's get to work."

They talked for a while, ate some eggs and biscuits and sausage, then talked some more.

Finally, they had a workable plan.

It was time to meet with the sheriff, hire a couple more hands, then begin nightly patrols.

"Just tell me which group you need me to go on patrol with," Miles said.

The hands looked at each other, their eyes reaching an agreement under the brims of their hats. "Appreciate it, Mr. Grant, but I think it might be best if we handle this first."

"You sure? I can ride as well as any man."

"It's not that, sir." Slim shifted uncomfortably. "You're right, you ride as well as any of us."

"Then what's the problem?"

"You're our boss, Mr. Grant. It ain't seemly."

Everything inside Miles wanted to argue and fight. But he'd learned that God provided men with opportunities. Nothing was ever left to chance.

So perhaps he should accept the men's judgment. "All right, then," he said quietly. "Big Jim, you ready to go to Camp Hope? I'd like you to accompany me when I speak with Brower."

"Of course, sir. I'd be happy to."

Miles said nothing, but inside, he had to smile. He wouldn't have expected anything less.

Sheriff Brower seemed to get more apprehensive and perturbed by the minute as they were talking.

112

"Jim, did anyone at the Millers get a good look at 'em?"

"I don't think so."

"You sure? 'Cause I could sure use a witness."

Miles leaned forward. "What's bothering you, Sheriff?"

Sheriff Brower pursed his lips. "A couple of things. Mainly that this is the latest in a string of thefts in the area." He lifted a paper with a sketchy, hand-drawn map of the land surrounding Camp Hope. On the paper were several circles, showing where the rustlers had hit.

"How come I didn't know things were this serious?" Miles asked.

"It didn't seem that way at first," Brower said. "These men have been getting more daring and wicked with each attack. No one had even been harmed before last night."

"We need to stop them and fast," Jim muttered.

Brower nodded. "I agree, but things don't look good."

Miles brushed a hand along his jaw. The sheriff looked worried — and like he was still holding something back. "And why is that?"

"I'm afraid your rustlers are Harlan Jones and his crew."

Even Miles had heard of him. "I thought Jones only pulled cattle from Oklahoma?"

"For a time, that was true. But then the law there got close on his tail. Jones and his band holed up for a while — so long the law there moved on. But now it seems that he's resurfaced and come to Texas."

Big Jim cracked two knuckles. "Well, he picked the wrong state," he said, his voice full of bravado. "I'll get out my Winchester and make sure they realize their mistake. The other men in our outfit will do the same."

Miles nodded. He didn't like the direction their talk was going. But sometimes violence was the only answer. He knew that for a fact. "I've already told Slim to hire on as many men as we need to patrol the Circle Z. One of them will capture Jones, I'm sure."

Sheriff Brower raised a hand. "It ain't that easy, Mr. Grant. Jones is an experienced outlaw. No offense, but a couple of men who've only shot at rabbits or deer ain't no match for him. What we have is a real problem."

"What's your solution then?"

He looked away, as if he was weighing his words that were at war with his personal morals. "I've been in contact with a couple

114

of other sheriffs during the last twenty-four hours. One of them has a pretty outlandish idea."

"And what is that?"

"We hire some men who are cut from the same cloth as Jones."

Miles was shocked. "What are you saying? We hire outlaws to fight Jones?"

Brower cleared his throat. Obviously, even the idea of it didn't set well with him. "Not outlaws . . . but men who've known men like Jones. I think we should hire some men who are used to being desperate and have been hired to shoot and ask questions later."

Miles was dumbfounded. "You're willing to go against the law? You're willing to kill Jones instead of capturing him and taking him to a judge?"

"I'm willing to do whatever it takes to put a stop to this," Sheriff Brower said harshly. "You may never have had to be involved in something like this, but I have. If we hesitate, things could get real bad in a hurry. A lot more landowners could get killed. Maybe even women. I don't want that."

He swallowed hard and continued. "Sometimes the only choice is between a rock and a hard place."

The words hit a chord with Miles. He'd been in situations like that. Reluctantly, he knew the sheriff was right. "Got anyone in mind?"

"Maybe." The sheriff looked away. "I'll ride out to your place when I get some names and a plan."

Big Jim scowled. "And in the meantime?"

"In the meantime, get out that gun and protect your livestock, son. Just don't expect to win."

Minutes later, as they were leaving in the buggy, Big Jim shook his head. "You know, I've always respected Brower. But today? He was sure spouting off crazy things."

Miles nodded. But inside, he wasn't too sure. He'd done things he'd never thought he'd do when he'd been pushed harder than he'd ever thought he'd be pushed.

He needed help, and he needed advice. If he could temper his pride enough to tell his hands that he'd follow their advice, then he needed to do something else, too.

He was going to send a telegram to Clayton Proffitt. Clayton had been the foreman of the Circle Z for years. He knew every bush and rock and creek bed.

He'd also commanded dozens of men.

If anyone could help, it would be Clayton.

And that help was worth its weight in gold. Even if it meant everyone on the ranch would end up comparing Miles to Clayton.

And in every way possible, Miles was sure to come up second.

"Let's stop at the bank for a sec, Jim. I need to send a telegram."

Without a word, Jim turned the corner and headed to the bank. Miles knew when they stopped, he was going to be inviting his past back again.

All of the sudden, he wished he only had dances and women to worry about.

8

Scout was uncomfortable with the idea of working side by side with Rosemarie. It had been a long time since he'd been in the company of a woman for very long. Especially a reputable, decent sort of woman. He didn't really know how to act. And though Rosemarie didn't seem to need or expect much from him, he expected much from himself.

And tried not to think too much about how he'd once had a very brief relationship of a sort with a gal named Kitty.

Kitty had barely been more than a girl, and if she had grown up, she would have been farther than a stone's throw from being a lady. Some women were in the category, he figured. It couldn't be helped, it just was.

Now, Rosemarie, however, was a curious mix of ladylike manners and childish naiveté. Scout wondered if it was her nature or if it was because her mother and sister had treated her like a servant.

Because of those issues — such as they were — Scout decided to keep his distance. Until Rose was out of his life, the less he was around her, the better for the both of them.

So he'd had gone out straightaway to the barn to clean out stalls and repair a couple of damaged posts and doors. They were the type of chores he'd done as a boy. And though his hammering skills were a little rusty, he knew what to do.

It was just too bad that his body was telling him that all the hammering and carrying on wasn't just something he used to be able to do. After an hour or two, he'd begun to realize that killing for a living and being a part of the Walton Gang didn't use a whole lot of muscles. Mainly all that was involved was gumption and a steady hand. He was sure to be stiff and sore by nightfall.

There was another reason he was happy to be away from Rosemarie and her messed-up, ramshackle shell of a home. Fact was, he wasn't comfortable with anything to do with homes or houses. Even houses as small and poorly built as the one he'd recently won.

He knew the reason for his reluctance,

though. It had come from doing without a home for much of his life.

Though he knew his brother and sister had done the best with him that they could, he still only felt sadness when he thought about the house he'd grown up in. Before their pa had gone to war and gotten himself killed, their home had always felt dark. His father had been a silent man.

A good one, for sure. Never in Scout's life had his father ever laid the blame on him for his mother passing.

But for the most part, Scout found he didn't need his father's guilt in order to be certain that his being born had ruined everyone else's life.

Later, after Clayton had joined their father and become destined for great things, Scout had moved on with Corrine to their aunt's home.

That, too, had been a forlorn and haunted place.

All he remembered about life in the quaint four-room house was an elderly aunt content to stay in the past, little to no food on account of the Union blockades, and the dark and steady knowledge that most everyone they knew was going to die sooner or later.

Death had become a certainty.

When Corrine and her husband, Merritt, had told him that no way, no how, was he going to be allowed to fight and serve the Confederacy, he'd decided to take the future into his own hands. He'd taken off in the middle of the night.

He'd been so full of himself and what he thought he should be doing. But, in truth, all that had happened was that he'd left his family with valiant intentions and misplaced honor.

Things hadn't gotten a whole lot better after that. In the next few months, he somehow started to associate heroism with the ability to take another life.

Within a year, he'd forgotten he'd ever known any other way to live. Soon after that, killing other people had a special way of reminding him that he was still alive.

And now, here he was, reminding himself that there was so much more to life than death.

When he'd told Rose what he was fixin' to do, she'd mentioned that she was going to tackle the bedroom.

A good three hours had passed before he walked outside. Like a coward, he stayed in the shadows, spying on the girl.

And that's when he realized she was intent on emptying out the whole entire blasted contents of the bedroom on to the home's front lawn.

Well, patch of grass, such as it was. It was fairly evident that even when he'd been in better health, Ben Cousins hadn't been one for sweat. Or cleanliness.

When he'd first seen her trudging with the pitiful amount of quilts that had been left behind, followed by a rag rug that had seen better days before the War of Northern Aggression had broken out, he'd been tempted to offer to help.

The rug was big and no doubt heavy with dirt and dust.

In the end, however, he'd decided to keep his distance. She still eyed him with a healthy kind of wariness, and he couldn't say he blamed her. Being alone in the company of a hired killer wasn't the stuff of any girl's dream, he supposed.

And actually, he was circling her in much the same way. When he'd first decided to let her stay, he'd imagined he'd feel toward her much the same way he'd felt around Kitty. Brotherly. Protective.

Instead, he'd noticed her trim figure and fine form. He'd noticed the way her hair glinted in the sun and the way her blue eyes were just two shades short of being brown.

After sweeping away cobwebs and getting

rid of the dirtiest hay he'd seen this side of a couple of seedy mining camps gone to pot, he'd ventured out to check on her.

The contents of the ground looked to be freezing up nicely. They'd be lucky if it all hadn't turned into stiff boards by the time Rose was ready to take it on in.

Curious as to what she was doing, he peeked inside. And got an eyeful of the little slip of a woman washing the floor on her hands and knees. Sweat made a damp line along the center of her back, making the already thin fabric resemble sheer muslin.

And from the angle he was observing . . . well, suffice to say she was definitely not a girl but a full-grown woman. Hastily, he looked away. Reminded himself that the way he'd caught himself looking at her was just asking for trouble.

If he didn't get his mind out of the gutter, he was going to make things worse for the both of them by beginning to think of her as a woman instead of as a scrawny victim.

But some things just couldn't seem to be helped.

"You almost done?" he asked. His words came out a little sharp, a little husky.

But instead of being full of sass like she'd been at breakfast, Rosemarie jumped about a foot. "Oh!"

Now he felt like the worst sort of blackguard. Spying and frightening, all at the same time. "I'm sorry. Didn't mean to scare you." He took a chance and ventured in closer.

"Don't you take another step."

He backed up like there was a bed of scorpions underfoot. "Why?" He looked around, his body tensing, looking for any hint of trouble.

"You're going to get everything dirty, Mr. Proffitt."

He was so relieved to hear her reason, he almost grinned. After all, it was unlikely that anything surrounding them was actually clean. Except for, perhaps a bar of soap. But then he noticed that she wasn't sharing his smile. No, she was completely serious. The woman was delusional and a hard worker.

Keeping his safe distance, he called out, "You need some help? Some of what you're doing takes some umph." Feeling prideful, he flexed a bicep that was already aching from his fence mending. "You need some muscle behind that carpet beating."

She raised her chin, looked him over, then shook her head. "I am just fine."

"Sure? 'Cause all the bedding is about to freeze solid outside. That makes it heavier, you know."

"I'll get it in before too long." She made a shooing motion with her hands. "Git on now. I've gotta finish this then get supper going."

The problem was, he knew she intended to do just that. She intended to work herself ragged in order to earn her keep on this worthless piece of property.

And that wasn't even taking into account the fact that she was waiting on a man like him. A man whom she was afraid of. "It's not necessary to wait on me like this."

She sat back on her heels and looked at him directly in the eye. Showing yet another side and fold of her mercurial personality. "I'm afraid it's very necessary. I'm going to make this place right for you."

"You offered to help me out," he corrected. "Since I'm the one who accepted, I think I should be the one who decides how much you do."

"Mr. Proffitt, it's better this way." Just then, a line of worry formed on her brow, in direct opposition to what he was coming to see as her usual obstinate self. Letting him see that she, too, was trying her best to negotiate this strange and foreign relationship they were having.

He was inclined to argue, but then he

began to see her side. Perhaps it was better this way, after all? In two weeks, they weren't going to ever see each other again.

He turned around and strode back outside, wondering as he did what he'd done to deserve a woman like her. She was everything contrary and prickly that he'd hated in the feminine form.

Everything wiry and tough and nothing soft and supple. Kind of like eating stewed rabbit when he'd been promised roast chicken.

Rio neighed a greeting to him when he entered the barn again.

"Hey, girl. Quite a sight we are to see, huh? Never thought either of us would be itching to go for a ride, but right now that seems like a good idea, don't it?"

Rio's ears perked up in interest.

And that was really all it took to persuade him to push aside the hammer and nails and saddle up his roan. In mere minutes, he was mounting her and gazing at the house.

For a second, he thought about letting Rose know that he was going to go for a ride. Just to get a lay of the land. But that would mean coming in contact with her thin dress and sharp tongue.

And so with a gentle nudge of his heel, he

and Rio trotted off. Ready to see the land that was now his, and his alone.

He did his best to pretend that was what he really wanted.

A lifetime of existing in squalor hadn't done the bedroom any favors, Scout decided several hours later. When he'd returned, he'd half-expected to see her still out on the front lawn. But when there was no sign of her, he decided to discover what Rosemarie was up to next.

He'd found her sitting on the floor of the bedroom, folding sheets that looked like they'd been old before the war.

"I've been looking for you," he said.

She popped her head up, then wearily got to her feet. "Well, you found me."

Scout looked at the pile of items that now littered the floor. From under the bed, it looked liked she'd pulled enough old clothes to outfit an orphanage.

If they didn't mind a decade's worth of grime and neglect.

In a yellow dish were a collection of ugly pins and buttons. And in the corner was a pile of debris. "How about I sweep that up for you?" he offered. It looked like it had already taken her forever to sweep away all the debris that had accumulated over the years.

"I've got it. Don't pay it no mind."

"Rosemarie, you're going to work yourself into a tizzy — if you don't collapse first. Let me help you."

"There's no need."

"There's every need." Scout knew this because he'd taken to checking on her a couple of times during the day. Just to make sure she wasn't wearing herself out.

Each time, she'd looked at him like he'd sprouted horns. "I'm fine. Mr. Proffitt. I'm used to working hard."

"When I said you could stay and help me clean, I didn't expect you to work like a slave. You're flitting around this place like your pants are on fire."

"They certainly are not." Her cheeks bloomed red.

He'd embarrassed her. "I'm sorry. I meant no disrespect."

"Listen, Mr. Proffitt, if you don't mind, why don't you give me a couple of minutes in here alone? I've got to wash up and then cook supper. It would be a whole lot easier if you weren't standing around, watching me."

"All right," he said, but he went reluctantly.

After standing outside with Rio for a few minutes and looking at Sam, Rosemarie's pig, he opened the beautiful red door and went on inside.

But instead of hearing her at the stove, he spied her sitting on the floor of the bedroom, crying her eyes out.

And because he wasn't a gentleman and had never claimed to be . . . because he'd only been around other people as greedy and hard as himself . . . he did the first thing he thought of.

He cursed.

She looked up in shock. Her eyes widening, her expression pained.

A better man would have walked to her side and tried to comfort her. After all, her father had just died, her mother had left her, and she was now cooking and cleaning for a known outlaw.

But he wasn't all that good. And he didn't have all that much to offer her.

So he did what was surely best for the both of them: he turned around and spent the rest of the night in the barn.

His transformation from the boy with big dreams to coldhearted gunslinger was now complete.

9

Yet again, the four of them were sitting around a campfire and wondering what to do next. Russell had been feeling especially restless — his birthday had been yesterday. He was now eighteen years old and had no more of an idea about what to do with the rest of his life than he had two years ago.

Only one thing hadn't change — he desperately wanted to stay alive.

He'd been sitting and stewing on that and wondering if Nora ever still thought about him, when Joe Bob spoke up.

"What do any of y'all know about Camp Hope? It's near Lubbock."

"Not much," Russell muttered.

"I can tell you that *we're* near Lubbock," Andrew pronounced with a grin.

Russell barely resisted rolling his eyes. Andrew loved to joke around.

"Camp Hope's on the other side of Lubbock," Joe Bob retorted, not even realizing that Andrew was just playing with him. "We're west, it's east."

"You sure?" Andrew scratched his head.

Tuff chuckled at Andrew's ribbing, then faced Joe. "I don't care where it is. I've never heard of Camp Hope. Have you ever been there, Russell?"

Russell could've sworn he had heard of the name, but he couldn't place it. "I don't think so." He didn't think so, but he wasn't a hundred percent sure he hadn't. All small towns looked the same.

With a beleaguered sigh, Joe Bob sat up straight and began talking, slow and easy. "It's about fifty miles from us, give or take." He paused, then added, "Folks say that there's a cathouse there. It's fancy, the whole place is painted red. Guess it did a good business during the war."

Tuff rolled his eyes. "Shoot, Joe, that's not news. Where ain't there a brothel?"

"And while I'm intrigued by all that red . . . it's not enough of a draw for me to go out there," Andrew said. Tapping his heart with a hand, he said, "Besides, you know I'm saving myself for Betsy."

Russell smirked but remained silent while Joe Bob started looking mad enough to spit nails. "You guys need to shut up for a moment! I'm trying to tell you about this place."

"Then start talking," Russell snapped. "So far, all you've told us is there's a place called Camp Hope that had loose women. Who cares?"

"Well . . . I was in Jackson, talking to some of the ladies . . ."

Russell scowled. Joe Bob had never met a skirt he didn't want to get close to. He'd never been able to understand it.

But of course, most men didn't have a woman in their past like Nora. He secretly doubted that even Andrew's Betsy could measure up to her.

Tuff spit on the ground then grinned. "So . . . you're anxious to check out the ladies in Camp Hope, Joe Bob?"

He shook his head with a hard jerk as he finally lost his patience. "I'm trying to tell y'all that the women said the law's all riled up there."

Russell tensed as the other men around him grew serious. "Because?"

"They've got rustlers. And not only have the rustlers been pulling cattle, they've killed two men for going after them."

Russell stilled. "Did they mention our names? Are they thinking we had something to do with it?" That was the very last thing any of them needed. They'd been walking on the legal side of the law for months now, but each of them had done their share of thieving.

Thinking about his time with the Walton Gang, he closed his eyes. He'd done far worse.

Joe Bob considered Russell's question for a moment, then shook his head. "Nah. Don't think so. I guess this has been going on awhile." He cleared his throat. "But get this. They're looking for men willing to go up against the rustlers."

Tuff scowled. "That's what the law is for."

"The women said the law don't stand a chance against these men," Joe Bob said almost patiently. "They're outnumbered and have too much else to do. So . . . they're hoping to hire some men who are willing to take a chance to take out the rustlers."

Sounded to Russell like the law didn't want to kill themselves trying. Smart men.

"I don't cotton with stealing cattle, but that don't mean I want to start sidling up to the law," Tuff said.

Russell and the others nodded.

But then Russell noticed that there was a new gleam in Joe Bob's eyes. He still had some news up his sleeve. "Joe Bob, what's in it for us?"

The brightness in Joe Bob's eyes spread over his whole expression. "Freedom," he said succinctly. "If we can put down the rustlers, our records get cleaned. We won't be running no more. We'll be heroes instead of wanted men."

Andrew stilled. "You mean we could do anything we want? We won't have to hide out no longer?"

"That's exactly what I mean. Shoot, you could even get married to your Betsy, Andrew," Joe Bob said with a wink. "That is, if she'll still have you."

"She'd want me," he said quickly. "I mean, she said she would, if I ever started making a decent living."

Tuff stretched out on the rock he was sitting on. "I've long given up walking free and easy down a Main Street. Do you think this story of the women is even true?"

"I think it is." Joe Bob continued. "The women said that the sheriff is so desperate he'd be willing to give a man amnesty for past crimes. As long as he ain't a current killer or nothing."

Russell could hardly imagine such a thing. Just thinking about living his life as a free man, without the constant feeling of doom looming over him? Before he thought of how childish he sounded, he cleared his throat. "Do y'all think we should give this a try?"

"I've been ruminating about the idea of chasing murdering rustlers for a few hours now," Joe Bob said. "Ever since I saddled up and left Camp Hope."

Tuff grunted. "And?"

"And, I don't think we should go it alone. We're good, but we're not that good. Here's what I was thinking. . . . We need to go get Scout Proffitt and bring him onboard."

"Scout Proffitt's a real good idea," Andrew said.

Russell looked at Andrew — his best friend in their ragtag group — and frowned. "Scout? Why do you say that?"

Andrew scoffed. "What do you mean, why? He's *Scout Proffitt,* that's why. He's the toughest son of a gun in Texas."

"Heck, the man could probably shoot the head off a rattler at a hundred paces," Joe Bob said.

"While riding hell-bent for leather on horseback," Andrew added with a grin.

Scout was certainly all that. He was a hired gun with a reputation that surpassed just about everyone on the outskirts of the law. He'd killed men for money, and he'd killed men in duels.

But what the other men didn't know was

that Scout wasn't necessarily a man interested in good deeds.

And he'd never been known for working well with others. Even when both he and Russell had been working for the Walton Gang, Scout had kept to himself. "I know he's a great shot, but that don't mean much," Russell said slowly. "And it don't have anything to do with us."

"Sure it does," Joe Bob said. "If we could tell that sheriff in Camp Hope that Scout was a part of our gang, we'd get the job for sure. He's the scariest man I've ever met, and he's the best shooter in the world."

"Yeah," Andrew said.

Russell wondered what Scout would think about this reputation of his. "Drew, I didn't think you knew him. When was that?"

Andrew looked down at his scuffed boots — boots that he was constantly griping about, saying that they weren't good enough for a man like him. "Well . . . I haven't actually met him. But you have. Shoot, you know him, Russell."

"But —"

"He'd do it," Andrew said quickly. "I bet he would. I've heard things. He ain't all bad."

Russell just bet he had heard things. A whole lot of things. Scout was scary, and he was near amazing with a gun.

But more than that, Russell privately thought Andrew had it wrong. Scout Proffitt wasn't the best with a gun in the region, he was likely the best in the whole country. He'd seen him in action enough times to never doubt his aim or his intellect.

But that was beside the point.

No way did he want to go ask Scout to join them. No way did he want to go up to Scout Proffitt and start talking like he thought they were equals. Because they sure as heck weren't. The last time Scout had seen Russell, Russell had been trying not to pee in his pants when the U.S. Marshals had surrounded their train and Kent had been shooting hostages.

"It don't matter whether or not Scout Proffitt can help us. Fact is, he's long gone. Y'all know the story as well as I do. Scout took off after Will McMillan and never came back."

"McMillan ended up being a Marshal," Tuff said, his voice full of bluster and swagger as usual. "Scout was most likely afraid he was going to get taken in. Heck, I'd feel that way."

Just as if Tuff's reputation was right up there with the famous man in black.

"Maybe he did do that."

"If he did take off running, we can't be holding it against him," Joe Bob said, his cheeks flushing. "I mean, sometimes running is the only way to stay alive."

Andrew nodded. "That is true."

The other men's words, spoken with such surety, got Russell feeling a little more apt to speak. "What McMillan did wasn't right," he said with a little more force than usual.

"He's a liar, that's what he is."

"He betrayed all of us on that train," Russell said.

And though Scout Proffitt himself would have cuffed him good for getting way too involved with a bunch of men who got hired out to kill people, Russell couldn't help but feel a bit of betrayal every time he thought about Will's lies. Out of everyone in the gang, he'd trusted Will the most and had tried his best to stay by his side.

Now he knew it was because Will hadn't been an outlaw at all. He'd been working for the Marshals surreptitiously, trying to discover who in the railroad was tipping off James Walton as to when the trains were carrying the loads.

Russell had trusted the only really good man in their midst. And privately — well, when he couldn't sleep in the middle of the

night and no one was around to notice —
Russell thought Will's honor had risen. It
turned out that the man really was better
than the rest of them.

But Scout hadn't been all bad, neither.
Especially if you looked beyond the fact that
he'd killed more people than most men
could probably count.

For one, he hadn't enjoyed torturing
people like Kent had. And Russell had never
seen him abuse women, neither. Actually,
Scout would have seemed almost like a
soldier if he hadn't killed for money.

He would have seemed like a godly sort of
person if he hadn't killed with a blink of his
eye, then walked on. Never looking back.

Upstanding, yep, that was the word. Scout
Proffitt was upstanding in his own
twisted-up turned-about way. "Even if we
could find him, he'd never join us without a
good reason."

"Money ain't good enough?"

"He told me once he'd banked a lot of
the gold he'd been paid. I don't think we
could ever pay him enough. Not enough to
come out of hiding and start shooting
again."

"Well, I have a reason," Joe Bob said. "The
same reason we'd all take this job. If it
works out, we'll never have to worry about

hiding out in caves and shacks ever again."

Russell realized right then and there that he wasn't the only one who wanted clemency. With some surprise, he realized he wasn't the only man to start thinking longingly about having a home and a wife and children.

Against his will, he thought of Nora, and her pretty blue eyes, and the way they'd used to soften his way. The way she'd smile when he'd play with the curled ends of her long blond hair.

The way her lips had parted into a sigh when he'd almost kissed her.

And even if she never gave him the time of day for the rest of her life, he knew he'd like to sleep at night knowing that he was worthy of her . . . if he'd ever gotten the nerve to go see her again.

And so, he asked the question. "Joe Bob, what's your plan?"

"I say we go find Scout and tell him about those cattle rustlers near Camp Hope." He paused, letting all of them get good and irritated by that.

Russell knew Joe Bob was smart to do that. If there was anything that all men, no matter what walk of life they took, could agree on, it was that rustlers were the lowest of the low on the Plains.

"Scout Proffitt is enough of a hero in some parts that they're not real anxious to start killing him. But the thing of it is, if we do this one job, we'll be home free." Looking at all of them, Joe Bob added, "We could settle in somewhere. Get married, have families. And Scout could, too. He could be known as something besides a cold-hearted killer."

In short they could do all the things most men took for granted. Because only to them did the responsibility of land and cattle and a woman to hold them close at night sound like heaven.

"So that's our choice, huh? We either get it all or nothing. If we can convince Scout to go along with us."

"It's a hell of a choice," Tuff murmured.

The other men's silence told all the story. Men who had nothing were at the mercy of everyone else in the world.

Joe Bob looked at them all, his gray eyes piercing and quiet. "Who's in?"

Russell wanted to be in, but he was afraid. "Do we even know where Scout is?"

"I do," Tuff said, surprising them all. "He won himself a farm in North Texas."

"You sure about that?" Russell couldn't imagine Scout even knowing which end of a cow to milk.

"Positive. Last time we were in Oklahoma, I sat in the very bar where Scout won the farm in a poker game." Like a carnival hawker, he added, "The ranch's name is called the Bar C."

Impressed, Russell said, "Tuff, you happen to know the town's name, too?"

"Broken Promise."

Joe Bob's eyes narrowed. "You in, Russell?"

He almost pretended to consider it, if only just for show. He wanted to be thought of as a leader, not a follower. But fact was, he wanted to be in. He wanted to be a part of this. The temptation to have a future different from the one he'd thought he'd had to claim was beyond tempting. "I'm in."

After all, it wasn't hard to be in when there wasn't a whole lot to be out of. He was either going to die convincing Scout to join them or die at the hands of rustlers. Or at the end of a Ranger's or sheriff's rifle.

But any way it all happened, at least he'd have a little bit of hope before he died.

Which would be quite a bit more than he'd had for quite some time.

10

Like an apparition, hazy shadows appeared on the cusp of the horizon of the Bar C Ranch. Though she was caught off guard by the approaching riders, Rosemarie didn't dare look away. Pretending they weren't coming didn't do any good.

She'd learned from a young age that surprise visitors never meant anything worth smiling about. Men had come to remind her father that he owed money. They'd come to inform her mother that the influenza had hit Broken Promise. They'd arrived on Sundays to ask about why they'd never attended church.

Each time, visitors had been met with resentment and confusion.

Now didn't seem like it was going to be much different.

Little by little, the figures took shape, becoming faint outlines of men and horses. And since there was nothing in between the ranch and the ends of the earth, it stood to reason that the men were headed their way.

Standing in the cold morning air, Rosemarie looked around, ready to pull sheets off the line or set a pair of muddy boots off to one side. To do anything to make the place more presentable. But the front lawn was now as clean as it had ever been.

No trash or broken farm implements or old washrags littered the area. For once, the patchy grass had been raked clean of twigs and rocks.

It looked neat. Almost well-cared for.

A burst of wind brushed her cheeks, pulling stray strands of hair away from her face and then leaving it all loose and curled. With a sudden sweaty hand, she attempted to calm it down.

Considered going inside and rebraiding it. But another gust of harsh wind brushed her skirts, kicking up dirt and embedding it in her skin.

It reminded her she shouldn't think too much of herself. She was, after all, only human. And really nothing more than a too-skinny woman used to being left behind.

Rose considered running to get Scout but quickly disregarded the notion. By now the men had seen her, so it was too late to run. She'd also learned that running did little good, anyway.

The sound of hooves pounding against the ground joined the picture her eyes were seeing. She wiped her hands against her skirts.

As the figures became clearer, Rosemarie realized it was four men, not three who approached. Their pace was steady and intent — they weren't in a hurry. No, they were merely determined. Within seconds their forms became clearer.

Which was when she recognized two of them.

Actually, Mr. King and the banker were hard to miss, being the most important men of Broken Promise, such as it was. Mr. Anthony King — known to his friends as "Ace" — was an upright man. Married and successful, he was a pillar of the community and cut a resplendent figure. He owned the majority of the land in the area, at least five thousand acres. Rumor had it that he owned a lot of other things, too.

He probably did. She'd seen his daughters' beautiful gowns that they gotten clear from Fort Worth. Both Elizabeth and Katherine King's complexions were lovely and creamlike, their hands slim and elegant, encased in perfectly white, perfectly fitted kid gloves. Rosemarie had seen the gloves up close when they'd traipsed by her seat on the aisle at church.

She doubted they'd paid her even the slightest bit of attention. No one in Broken Promise had ever wanted to have a lot to do with the Cousinses. Their last name had never garnered a lot of respect. She, being the murderer in the family, was even lower on the food chain.

Her sister, Annalise, had fought against the prejudice by using her beauty and cunning to claim a husband clear from Texarkana. Her mother had just kept her head down and her disappointments private. At home, though, they'd spent many an hour in sheer disappointment. Though the other women in the family had spent hours berating the good citizens for the prejudice against them, Rose had never held the Kings's opinions against them, and especially not Mr. King's disdain. She knew what her father was . . . and who Mr. King was. They were worse than complete opposite. In some ways, it was a miracle they breathed the same air.

But perhaps her viewpoint had come from a lifetime of being held in worse regard than her lack of money — owing to her perpetually down-on-his-luck pa — after all, she had her brother's death on her hands.

As the dust rose around the incoming

horses' hooves, she rested a hand over her eyes to shield the sun's fading glare. Squinted a bit to see if she could recognize another of the men. And started wondering how she was going to explain her presence. By now she was sure Annalise had told everyone with ears that Rose had decided to live for a time with the outlaw. That news alone would paint Rose in the worst sort of light.

And it was so shocking, the community would easily find it in their hearts to forget that not a one of them had offered her a different place to stay.

Underfoot, she felt the vibration of the horses' hooves and could now see the men's narrowed eyes as they took in her form and the stark emptiness surrounding her.

Her mouth went as dry as a riverbed in August. How in the world was she ever going to face those men right here in the yard? How was she ever going to attempt to hold onto her pride while she did it? The little bit of it that was left, anyway.

"Rosemarie?"

The deep, raspy voice felt like a soothing waterfall against her body. "I didn't know you were here," she murmured, still looking in front of her.

"It's hard to ignore riders coming. Any

idea who they are?"

She pointed to the beauty of a horse — cream with speckled on its hindquarters. "The man on the Appaloosa is Mr. King."

Beside her, Scout shifted. "Who might he be?"

"Biggest landowner in the area. He's . . . he's a very fine man."

"Do you know him?"

"No. I only know of him." Eyes still trained on the riders, she exhaled. "The man just to his right is Sheriff Parker."

"So now we know two of our guests."

She like the way he phrased it. Almost as if she didn't have to be afraid all over again. "Yes."

"Mr. King and the sheriff. The company sounds exalted. I suppose we should feel honored."

His comment held a thick trace of sarcasm. She wondered why . . . and was afraid to guess. "They aren't bad men," she blurted. Then wondered why she'd been in such a hurry to defend them. Had either ever gone out of their way for her? She couldn't recall.

"You don't know that. Just 'cause someone's got money doesn't mean they're of worth. You should know that by now."

"I'm not a child, Mr. Proffitt. I know how

the world works."

He laughed, the sound once again sounding like a cross between anger and mirth. "Sugar, I promise, you know nothing about how the world works. You, here in this sad little town so aptly named for its lost hope."

Again, she sensed there was more to his words than mere bitterness. "Do you fear you're in danger?"

She felt his body stiffen behind her. "You worried about me, sugar? Are you trying to find a way to protect me?"

Because she still hadn't turned around, she didn't know how to judge his words.

It felt like a betrayal of his honor to say that she worried he might come to harm, that he couldn't take of himself. "I . . . I just don't want to be left alone. Or have you walk into a trap." She definitely didn't want to get him hurt.

She definitely didn't want to lose him.

He chuckled low. The sound made goosebumps rise on her flesh, though it made no sense for her to react like that. They were strangers, and he didn't even like her.

"Rosemarie, if they had intended to catch me unawares, they wouldn't be showing up like they are. They'd come alone. Sneaking in the dark. That's the way to kill me. Believe me, I know — I've usually been on the other side."

Slowly, she turned around to face him. But as she predicted, his expression yielded no hints of what he was really thinking. "That's happened, hasn't it? Men have tried to kill you when you're sleeping."

He shifted his gaze to settle on the horizon instead of her face. "It's to be expected. And once more, I deserve their vengeance."

Perhaps he was right. Perhaps if a person took another life then he deserved no less than a sure death, too. "Perhaps," she whispered, thinking of herself.

He took a step backward. Making her feel ashamed. "I've been thinking of myself, not you, Scout." The moment she felt his name slip off her tongue, she felt herself blush. She'd begun to think of him as a man, as almost a friend.

Her breath caught as she waited for him to comment on her slip. But all he did was talk some more. Just like he hadn't even noticed the change.

"I don't deserve much."

"We all deserve God's grace, though. Don't you think? I mean, that's what Pastor Colson says in church."

But no matter how many regrets they each might have had, she knew there was only one step forward. And that was to concentrate on the men coming closer.

"Do these men often come around?"

She almost laughed. "They never do. In all honesty, I've been wracking my brain, trying to figure out why the men would be here, but I have no idea."

"You positive?" His voice was hard. "I don't like being taken off guard. I want to know what you know."

Daring to take her eyes off the approaching riders, she turned to him. "M . . . Mr. Proffitt, I couldn't begin to guess what they want."

By this time, the four men were clear enough that Rose saw their gazes were skittering around the area. Taking note of the lack of refuse on the ground. And examining how close she and Scout were standing.

She imagined they thought her to be Scout's ladybird. She wasn't sure if that reflected worse on herself or on Scout. She was so thin and flat, she was sure a man like him was used to fancier company, or at least women blessed with a few more curves.

Beside her, Scout adjusted the brim of his hat. As if he, too, had taken note of the other men's gazes. His voice turned frosty. "Go on inside."

With a sense of panic, Rose knew she'd managed to hurt his feelings. He still hadn't looked at her. Not really. Instead, he didn't take his eyes off the approaching horses even for a moment.

Perhaps he thought she really had found a way to call the men over. Perhaps he even thought she was turning him into the law? "I don't want to leave you," she said. "There's as good a chance they're coming to see me as you. I think I have just as much of a right to hear what they want."

"Because they think so highly of you?" He quirked an eyebrow up. Embarrassing her.

Just as she was about to turn around, preferring to imagine him behind her than to come face to face with his dark expression, she noticed that his right hand hung loose. He didn't have on his holster. Or his guns.

"Where are you weapons?"

"In the barn."

Though she'd been afraid of him, and afraid of all the killing he'd done . . . now she wished he was loaded down for bear. "I didn't know you went anywhere without them."

"I'm not anywhere. I'm home."

Home. He said the word like it meant something to him. Perhaps *home* had a different connotation to him than to her. For her, *home* meant everything that wasn't.

Not wanting to see the shame she knew she wasn't capable of hiding, Rose turned back to face the riders. And focused once again on the company they were about to have.

"Do . . . do you think you should go get your pistols? Just in case there's trouble?"

11

The tension between them grew so thick and dark, Rosemarie became frightened. Had she questioned him one too many times? Would he now turn on her?

After a good, long minute, he spoke. "I'm not going anywhere."

"All right," she said. But it wasn't all right. She felt torn. She wanted to trust Scout more than the approaching riders, but common sense told her that she'd be a fool to put her faith into a man like him.

"It's like this, Rosemarie," he drawled. Still not looking at her. "I'm in no hurry to start killing again."

Killing *again.* The phrase told it all. Taking a life wasn't a question with him. Or an imagined thing.

No, he'd done it many, many times. "You wouldn't have to shoot them. Maybe if they saw you were serious . . ."

"I don't wear guns for show, sugar. If I'm

armed, I'm going to point my gun and shoot. It's what I know."

"I should have remembered that. Remembered who you are."

He inhaled sharply behind her. As if her words had stung. "Frankly, I'm surprised you forgot."

Rose sensed his feelings were hurt. But instead of saying another word that didn't mean much, she just stood and watched the riders slow down.

"The third man is the preacher."

"How do you know?"

"By his seat. Pastor Colson hails from a city up north somewhere." She'd heard he came to Texas in disgrace after the war, but she didn't trust Scout enough to share that detail.

"He's a good man, but his riding has kind of been a source of amusement for most folks."

"How so?"

"The pastor, he rides like a city woman. Too stiff," she explained. As he came more into focus, she could tell that the two-week break from him hadn't changed a thing. He still had the worst seat she'd ever seen on a man in the state.

"Where up north?"

"Philadelphia."

"He's a Yankee?" Though he was a notorious outlaw, his voice held the same shock and contempt most southerners felt for interlopers. "Why's he here?"

It seemed there was no choice about giving up what she knew. "I . . . I heard he married a woman with a lot of property who promptly up and died in childbirth," she said, hating to gossip. "There's also word that he did something to cause shame during the war."

"Cause shame? What could he have done?"

"I don't know that answer."

"So now we know who three of them are. Wonder who's the fourth?"

She raised her hand again to shield her eyes, but there was little need for it. Now that the men were closer, she recognized them all. "The fourth is Mr. Kendrick. He's the banker."

Scout walked forward, stopping so he was slightly in front of her, dwarfing her with his height. "We've got the richest landowner in town, a preacher, the law, and the money. That's quite a posse, wouldn't you say?"

His sarcasm made her feel at a disadvantage. She didn't know how to react to it. "I wouldn't know."

He chuckled low again. Opened his

mouth, no doubt to say something sharp and cutting. But the neighing of one of the horses halted his quip.

She looked forward. All four men were stopped in a row, ankle to ankle. Hoof to hoof. About two hundred yards away. The horses stomped and fussed restlessly in the cool air, but otherwise held steady.

As steady as Scout's gaze on the men. "Don't you move or say a word, Rosemarie," he whispered through his teeth. "I'll see what they want."

She didn't argue with the directive. Her feet felt as frozen as a wet sheet on a line in February. Her body? Too tense and taut.

She'd hoped to get to pretend that nothing was wrong in her life for at least a little while. That she and Scout were going to be able to get along for a while.

That for once, she would be safe.

These men obviously weren't of the same mind.

It was truly amazing how she felt more comfortable next to Scout than with people she'd known all her life.

To her surprise, it was the banker, Carroll Kendrick, who raised his hand in greeting. "Evening."

Scout raised his hand as well, then without a word stepped forward a good five paces more. Shielding her from view. A classic protective stance.

The men on horseback looked at one another. She kept silent. As she watched the sun begin to set beyond the men on the horizon, she felt her stomach do a summer-sault.

"Rosemarie, it's good to see you." Pastor Colson asked with a nod. "Are you all right?"

Was she?

Time seemed to stand still as they all awaited her reply — as if it mattered whether she was well or not.

She was too afraid of breaking her promise to Scout to utter a word. Or to even raise a hand. Finally, she made do with nodding.

After a scant minute, the group turned their attention on Scout.

"Mr. Proffitt, how do you do?" the banker asked. "I'm Carroll Kendrick." Scout nod-ded.

The men traded uneasy glances. "We were hoping to speak with you for moment," Mr. Kendrick said. He cleared his throat. "Please meet my companions, Ace King, Pastor Colson, and Sheriff Russ Parker." When Scout still made no reply, he raised his voice and made it slicker. "I'm sure you've heard all about us from Rosemarie."

"Why on earth would Miss Cousins be speaking about you?" Scout had put emphasis on the "Miss," just as if he were giving them a lesson in manners.

The question seemed to catch all four men off guard. Almost as much as a lesson in etiquette from a known killer. They looked at one another, presumably waiting for someone to break the silence.

"We represent Broken Promise," Pastor Colson finally said.

"Is that right?" Still standing alone and true, Scout gazed at them all with hard eyes. "To what do I owe the pleasure of your company?"

The pastor dismounted. Holding his mare's reins, he led his pretty mare forward. "We've come to check on Miss Cousins."

"Have you, now?" Scout murmured.

Rosemarie held her tongue. But in truth, she couldn't have been more surprised. Never in her life had these men come to check on her for any reason.

Pastor Colson continued. "Mr. Proffitt, it's come to our attention that you've got yourself a situation here."

Scout crossed his arms over his chest. "And what kind of situation would that be?"

Obviously taken aback, the pastor looked at the others. Mr. King dismounted. With a wave of his hand, he stilled the horse, then joined them. "I don't want to offend, but I think you know."

Scout's stance stiffened. "I won this farm fair and square. You won't be taking it from me."

"Oh, we know all about that," the banker said, with a grimace the sheriff's way. "Left to his own, I doubt Ben Cousins could've held on to his boots. Shoot, they'd surely would have walked off by themselves if they could." He paused for a moment, looking slightly guilty. "No offense, Rose."

She shrugged off the remark. Mr. Kendrick wasn't telling her anything she didn't know to be true.

Mr. Kendrick continued. "Fact is, most of us are real grateful that you've taken over ownership of this place. It's harkened for a steady hand for some time now."

In unison, the sheriff and the banker dismounted and joined the others.

Rosemarie felt rather than saw Scout glance her way with a warning. But she knew better than to do a thing. She wasn't going to move or speak if she didn't have to. Pure fear held her in place.

After he glancing her way, Scout rocked back on his heels. "I'm afraid I'm going to have to repeat myself. What may I help you men with? If it's not a concern about the land, I'm afraid I'm at a loss for the reason of your visit."

The men exchanged glances. Finally, Sheriff Parker cleared his throat. "Care if we step closer? I'd like us to talk without fear of you taking advantage of the situation."

Rosemarie ached to point out that if he'd been armed and had a mind to it, Scout could have shot them all when they were barely on the Bar C property.

But all Scout did was lift his hands, showing the waistband of his denims, free of his holster. "You can do whatever you want. I'm unarmed."

With Scout's permission, the men walked their horses to the solitary post near the barn. Scout took Rosemarie's arm and guided her to the side. Out of everyone's way.

Then, still holding her arm, he waited on the quartet, staring at them with a blank expression. But she felt the tension rise inside him. No matter how calm and cool he looked, he wasn't pleased with the unannounced visit.

With barely controlled temper, he stood stiffly by her side. Imposing. "Gentlemen? If you could state your business?"

Pastor Colson cleared his throat. "Well, see . . . it's like this, Mr. Proffitt. It's come to our attention that the two of you have been living here together. Alone. In sin." His voice seemed to get steadier with each word. Just as if he was at the pulpit and delivering the Word.

Rose had never thought she'd feel so low. So full of misery. She fought against the urge to pull away from the group. Worse, she'd always thought Pastor Colson had been sympathetic to her situation. Now he was making her sound like the worst sort of woman.

But moving out of sight wasn't possible because Scout still gripped her arm. Lightly, his fingers curved around her forearm, his skin warming her own through layers of cotton and wool.

Seconds passed. Every once in a while Scout would glance her way, just as if the two of them were out for a Sunday stroll and he wanted to stay close to her side. And wanted to make sure she was all right.

"Mr. Proffitt, what do you have to say for yourself?" the pastor asked.

To her shock, Scout yawned. "I haven't felt the need to defend my actions since I was beaten good by an old soldier with one arm" Looking bored, he stared hard at the preacher. "Got anything else you feel the need to add?"

The preacher flushed. "To add? Well, yes. I, for one, think it's time we did something about this situation you two are in."

"This situation?" Scout released her arm and stepped away. Obviously, he was ready to face the four men on his own.

It made Rose yearn to reach for him, just so he would know that he wasn't alone. Though he probably had never cared about that. As the tension increased, Scout's face turned blank. "I've sinned more than most, Pastor. There's no disputing that. But Miss Cousins hasn't done a thing to be ashamed about."

The four visitors looked skeptical.

"Depends what you consider shameful, I suppose," Mr. Kendrick drawled.

Rose gasped.

But Scout didn't so much as flinch. His face turned as still as marble, and his voice had turned twice as cool. "If y'all have got something to say to me, I'd advise you to start talking. Patience has never been a virtue of mine."

12

Scout Proffitt had killed in the heat of an argument and in the heat of an armed robbery. He'd killed rapists, and he'd killed in cold blood.

He'd even shot a man from forty paces for money. It hadn't been his finest moment. When the unfortunate man had tried to gasp — producing only a steady stream of blood instead of words — Scout hadn't thought much beyond being glad nothing had soiled his new boots.

But even Will McMillan telling him he'd been working undercover for the U.S. Marshals hadn't struck him dumb like the preacher's sanctimonious speech.

He was used to people looking down on him, fearing him. As far as he was concerned, he deserved every bit of grief and disdain that could be shoveled his way.

However, the lady by his side definitely did not.

"Are you thinking to marry us for appearances' sake?" he asked, his voice slow and cool. Just to make he wasn't misunderstanding a thing.

"Don't play dumb, Proffitt — if that's even your real name," the mustache-wearing Mr. King snapped. "You know what's right and what ain't. What you and Rosemarie are doing ain't right."

No, Scout didn't believe he did know what was right. Most likely had no inkling of what was good and acceptable in this world. Because at the moment, if he'd been carrying his guns, he'd be tempted to shoot all four of them. Then Rosemarie would never be subjected to their sneaky, holier-than-thou knowing glances.

Warily, he glanced Rosemarie's way. As he'd suspected, her posture had wilted and her head hung in shame. All hints of the spunk and fire he'd gotten a taste of when they were alone had vanished the minute that foolish preacher had delivered his sermon of shame.

The other men in attendance watched her with expressions of acceptance. As if what was happening wasn't a surprise, just an unfortunate circumstance.

Scout widened his stance. "Mr. King, I'm afraid you're giving me more credit than most. Most folks have long since given up on me recognizing the difference between right and wrong."

"We're here on a service mission, Proffitt. Don't make this into something it isn't," Mr. Kendrick stated. "We're just trying to keep things right and proper in Broken Promise."

"That so?" The truth of it was that he was feeling irritated. "My understanding of right and wrong might be skewed, but I do believe you men have delivered a whole new definition to such words."

The sheriff stepped forward, light of foot like a popinjay. "Proffitt, what the heck is that supposed to mean?"

Scout didn't even try to keep the contempt from his voice. "It means that when I arrived, I discovered Ben Cousins had sold his farm out from under his family's feet for a card game."

Beside him, he felt rather than saw Rosemarie flinch. Though he was disappointed to be causing her discomfort, Scout was more intent on protecting her reputation. And the last remaining bits of her self-confidence. Heck, even a woman living alone in the remains of the most threadbare shack he'd ever seen deserved someone to stand up for her.

It might as well be him.

Continuing on, he kept his voice hard and unyielding. "I may be just a hired killer, but the fact that her father sold her house right from under her doesn't sound very upstanding to me."

As he'd expected, the four men exchanged wary glances.

It was Sheriff Parker who broke the silence. "Mr. Proffitt, what Ben did was no business of ours."

"Then whose business was it?" He turned to the preacher. "Yours, Pastor Colson? You were here burying the man when I rode up."

"I'm well aware of that."

"But you left without seeing to Rosemarie's needs."

The preacher cleared his throat. "I had greater things to concentrate on than Rosemarie at that moment. Ben Cousins was going to the Lord."

Though he knew he would be the last person in the world to discuss a soul's passing, the preacher's excuse didn't sound plausible to Scout. "But what about after?"

The preacher's eyebrows snapped together. "After?"

"I watched Rosemarie's relatives cast her aside." Remembering the way Rose had lifted her chin and had tried to smile in spite of the pain, Scout shook his head. "Her own mother left her. I've seen a lot of cold-hearted mothers in my lifetime, but May Cousins's abandonment of her daughter might be the coldest."

"Hard to imagine you being shocked, sir," the banker snapped. "I must also add that while what Mrs. Cousins did was unfortunate, it was none of our concern. None of us is ready to go out policing the way other parents treat their children."

"Exactly!" Mr. Kendrick, the banker, said with a laugh. "Why, if we started poking our noses into other families' concerns, not a lick of business would get done, we'd be so busy."

The three other men smiled sheepishly.

Scout did not. Instead, he eyed each of the men one by one. "I was shocked because no one didn't do a blasted thing," he said slowly. "At least, not to my knowledge."

The pastor raised his chin. "We most certainly did. We're here now, aren't we?"

"Two weeks later?" Scout shook his head in disgust. "Y'all come out here, like some sorry kind of musical quartet. Speaking of morality when you obviously have none to speak of."

"I resent that," Sheriff Parker said.

"I would, too, if I was the kind of man to

168

look the other way when my citizens were being mistreated and didn't have the gumption to come by myself. Not a one of you offered to take her in. And as far as I can tell, none of you asked for assistance for Rose from any of the families in the vicinity, either."

"Mr. Proffitt —" Rose interrupted, her voice tearful.

Scout felt sorry for what was being said, but he couldn't stop just to spare her feelings. "How could y'all have left her that way? How could y'all have forsaken her?"

Each man suddenly looked a whole lot shorter and as if the bluster had just been tossed out of them.

Finally, Mr. King cleared his throat. Still only looking at Scout — all of the men seemed to be too abashed to look Rose's way — he stepped forward with his hands up. "I hear what you are saying, Mr. Proffitt. And, I suspect, much of what you say makes sense." He lowered his voice, turned it more congenial.

As if they were playing poker in a noisy saloon.

"Fact is, I reckon that maybe we all should have been looking out for this woman's welfare a little better." Sparing Rosemarie a look, he attempted to look shamefaced.

"However, no matter what our past transgressions, it's all beside the point."

Scout glanced Rose's way. During the conversation, she'd seemed to have lost her spunk and had retreated back to herself once more.

Though he didn't think he had a heart, he did feel an ache in his chest as he watched her become less of a woman before them all.

It was now more than obvious that something had to be done. "And what is your point?"

"Rose here has been living alone with a man. Her reputation is now ruined. You need to do right by her and marry her."

Rose inhaled sharply.

Afraid to look her way, afraid if he did he'd see her face pale and her expression falter somewhere between pain and hopelessness — and then he'd become some kind of sorry savior.

Better to keep his voice hard and his words cutting. "Marry her? You came here to force a wedding between me and Rosemarie?" Scout asked, then laughed softly in an effort to keep the focus on him and not on the poor woman barely hanging onto her emotions. "You actually think being shackled to a gunslinger is going to improve her reputation?"

Ace King shrugged. "Couldn't hurt. She won't be accepted anywhere as she is now."

"You didn't accept her before."

When Rose's breath hitched, he turned to her. He held out a hand for her to grasp. After a second she took it. He looked over her, and what he saw nearly broke his heart. Her eyes were watery with unshed tears.

To keep her steady and offer what little support he could, he squeezed her hand gently. Then he spoke, keeping his gaze on her, steady and solid. Ignoring all the others. "We need to talk, honey. Now."

After a pause, she nodded.

She was trembling under his touch, obviously just two heartbeats from falling apart right there in front of them. And they'd all be responsible for her unraveling.

"Gentlemen, please give us a moment. But feel free to make yourself at home . . . in the yard," he said over his shoulder as he took her elbow in one hand, carefully wrapped his palm around her opposite shoulder, then escorted her into the house.

Rosemarie accepted his touch easily and followed his lead just as compliantly as if she was a mare on a tether. She didn't say a word as they walked down the short dirt path snaking through the now neatly trimmed grass.

Her sudden silence wasn't a gift. Instead, it made his chest ache again, imagining what life must have been like for a woman virtually alone in the world. Her needs disregarded until they made others feel ill at ease.

Once the pretty red door was shut behind them, Scout breathed deep, then dropped his hands and faced her. The first thing he noticed was that her cheeks were pink from the cool air and her eyes were still shiny with a mess of unshed tears.

Her breath came in short pants. Only by sheer will was she not breaking apart.

For a split second, he panicked. He was no good with a woman's tears and had even less experience with how to salvage a decent woman's reputation. But then he remembered his time with Kitty and the way that poor beaten girl had trusted him.

For the moment, he considered the best way to handle things. After some deliberation, he recalled living with the Walton Gang and the shining look of hero worship he'd sometimes spy in Russell Champion's young face.

He decided a tearful woman without a lot of options needed a little guidance in order to keep things nice and easy. Matter-of-fact.

"Miss Cousins, what do you want to do?"

The question seemed to startle her out of her sadness. After sniffing noisily, she swiped a cheek with the side of a palm. "Mr. Proffitt, you know there is no decision to be made. I cannot marry you. It would only complicate your life."

He wasn't surprised at her words. Everything she said was true. He hadn't planned on marrying, and if he were to, he hadn't imagined it would be to a too-skinny girl with unruly reddish-brown curls and a feisty attitude when it came to cleaning.

However, it had been a long time since anyone had put his needs before their own, and that made him want to do something for her, too.

But he did find himself a little taken aback by the sudden feeling of disappointment and regret stirring inside him. "I agree, sugar. Tying the knot with me is pretty much a guarantee to wearing widow's weeds. Chances are good that I won't be on this earth long." What he didn't add was that he had a sneaking suspicion that any woman he claimed as his wife would be a target for a would-be killer as well. Anything he cared about would be seen as a weakness and therefore an opportunity to do harm. And imagining Rosemarie bearing those burdens — or adopting those kinds of fears — was difficult to accept.

Her eyes widened. "That wasn't what I meant at all!"

"Maybe you should tell me what you did mean."

"Scout, I mean Mr. Profitt . . . you can't saddle yourself with the likes of me."

He knew he shouldn't press her on this, but he couldn't seem to help himself. "And why is that?"

A flash of mutinous irritation filled her gaze. Lifting his heart a bit. He was so glad she wasn't completely beaten down.

"I can't believe you're going to make me say it." She popped her chin up. "All right, here it is. I'm a woman with not a lot going for her, Mr. Proffitt. I am too skinny. I have red hair. I'm worse than dirt poor. And now, well, my reputation — which had been terrible before — has even managed to sink lower." She blinked, just like she was trying to come to terms with that one.

He flat-out hated hearing everything she had to say. Clasping one of her hands, he pulled her to a kitchen chair. Then he knelt at her feet, just so he could look into her eyes straight on. "Listen to me, Rosemarie, and you listen to me good. You do indeed have value. You are a worthy woman.

And . . . and your red hair is more of an auburn. It's real fine." Truth was, he'd spied it last time she'd washed it. Spread down her back, lit by candlelight, it had been just about the prettiest thing he'd ever seen.

Her long hair, that mass of curls, the color playing on each other in shades of fire and sunrise, had transformed her. Suddenly, her petite form looked endearing. Her thin frame looked delicate and fragile. And her blue eyes turned dark, almost the color of bluebonnets.

She'd been more than attractive — she'd been desirable enough to make him look a little too long.

Not that her beauty was any concern. His hands clenched, aching to give her family and the town folk a piece of his mind. "I promise, Rosemarie, you will make any man a fine mate."

Her eyes widened at the term. Then, just as quickly — just as was right — she looked away. "Marrying me would be a mistake," she whispered. "We both know that."

Getting to his feet, Scout stepped back and leaned against the door frame. He'd taken her into the house against his better judgment, feeling only pity toward her. He'd intended to let her get over her father's death and her mother's abandonment, then give her some money and let her get on her way. He'd been going to encourage her to leave this ramshackle place, leave Broken Promise, and go somewhere and start anew.

But now he was thinking that being on her own was the last thing she needed.

"Got anything else to tell me?" he asked dryly.

"Yes."

He'd expected her to back off. Instead, now, he waited with anticipation. Only the Lord knew what else she could come up with to show she was unsuitable for a hired gun.

"I killed my brother, Mr. Proffitt."

"You said was an accident." But even though he said the right words, a small bit of worry channeled through him.

What if she had been more at fault than she was admitting?

She caught his whiff of unease. "See, I knew you'd begin to think twice. I'm not fit for marriage. I have another person's death on my hands."

Because what she was saying was much like the ugly thoughts he'd filled his mind with in the early hours of the morning, his voice came out harder than he'd intended. "I promise you, honey, it's going to take a heck of a lot more to scandalize me."

Her lips formed a small "Oh."

"Sweetheart, what do you think I've been doing for the last couple of years? Killing people with sharp words?" He forced himself to laugh off his pain. To pretend he didn't feel responsible for far too many souls. "Fact is, if you're anticipating a future of being eternally damned, well, you're in good company."

After that settled in, she turned her back on him. "I don't understand why we're even talking about this," she said over her shoulder. "Those men are waiting. You should go out there and speak to them. There's no telling what they think we're doing."

"I don't matter what they're imagining. They brought this conversation on, not you or me. Shoot, they can wait all day for what I care."

"But —"

"Ain't no buts about it, Rosemarie. All that matters right now is what we want to do."

"And?"

Here it was. Slowly, he pulled her to her feet.

And then he said all the words he hadn't wanted to say.

"I, for one, think we should get married."

She blinked. Opened her mouth. Shut it

again. Just like he'd finally managed to stun her to silence. "Oh, Scout," she said.

She'd called him by his Christian name. That had to mean something, even though he'd heard the sadness in her voice. Truthfully, he'd felt his mind twist and turn a bit, too. He was no savior, and he sure wasn't the sort of man to marry. Ever.

But it kind of seemed like the right thing to do.

She was a decent woman, a good woman. He knew that in his heart. And if giving her his name was going to improve her lot in life, then he was going to do it.

Helping her raised his spirits. He knew it in his soul, just as he knew that offering himself to her was the first decent thing he'd ever tried to do.

Well, since that disaster with Kitty.

"We couldn't. We shouldn't," she protested. But there wasn't the same kind of force or dismay tingeing her tone as before.

It was time to push a little bit more. "If it means anything to you, you should know that I'm not going to marry anyone else. I'd kind of given up on that dream some time ago."

"I understand."

He was somewhat surprised that she wasn't trying to convince him of his worth.

And surprised that he was a little dismayed by that. Keeping his voice even, he murmured, "Like I said, I don't think I've got all that many days left. Sometime, somewhere, somebody is going to seek their revenge. Or try to make a name for themselves."

"Make a name by killing you?"

"In some circles, gunning down a no-good man like me is worth something." He shrugged. "But I've saved a whole lot of money, Rosemarie. Enough for a lifetime. So I figure you ain't got much to lose and whole lot to gain."

"You shouldn't speak like that."

"And just so you know . . . you aren't too skinny, Rosemarie. A lot of men would think you were pretty."

"What do you think?"

Now it was his turn to be uncomfortable. He wasn't ready to reveal what he'd been thinking. It was too close to his heart. "Me? I think you're just fine."

Her pretty rose-colored lips turned into a sweet "Oh." And for the first time in their acquaintance, Scout wondered what it would feel like to kiss her. To hold her close and feel that slim body curve into his.

"So, you ready? 'Cause I think those men are riling up my horse."

"Scout —"

He exhaled and said the words that needed to be said. Because every woman needed to be hear them at least once in her life.

Even if the circumstances had much to be desired. "Will you marry me, Rosemarie? I don't have a whole lot to offer you, but I can promise I've never hurt a woman intentionally in my whole life. And I'll try to do right by you."

A sweet, lilting softness transformed her features, and for a brief amount of time, Scout was certain he spied something more than gratitude in the violet-blue depths of her eyes.

"Yes, Mr. Proffitt," she said at last. "Yes, I will marry you."

Once again, he held out his hand for her to take. For the first time, she took it easily. Like they were becoming a pair instead of merely two lost souls stuck on some of the worst land in the great state of Texas. And when her slender fingers, cool and soft, slipped in between his, Scout was struck how right it felt.

How right the moment felt. So soft and sweet. So heartbreaking.

13

A week had passed since Slim and Big Jim had first told Miles about the rustlers. Since then, a dozen head had been taken. None of the two dozen men on patrol had seen or heard a thing, and Miles felt more helpless than ever.

The only good thing that had happened was that he'd heard from Clayton. Almost immediately, the bank had received a telegraph. In it, Clayton stated that he was on his way.

At first, Miles had berated himself for seeking Clayton's help. But he tamped down that weakness. Men were in danger, ranches' futures were in danger, too. Miles was not going to let anything happen to their home without doing everything he possibly could. And that included asking Clayton Proffitt for help.

He'd checked in with Sheriff Brower, too. The lawman assured him that a plan was in place, but it was so half-formed that he wasn't prepared to share it yet.

Not able to sit and wait, Miles set the men up on twenty-four-hour patrols, hoping against hope to get lucky and find some signs about who had been on their property.

He'd asked Miss Annabeth to hire some kitchen help, too, so at least the men practically living on horseback would have some decent sustenance when they came home each night.

But so far, none of the men had found a thing. It seemed all any of them had discovered was that they all liked a whole lot more sleep than they were getting.

In a sad attempt to boost morale, Miles had talked up the dance. It had worked.

But it also had made him feel obligated to attend. And, because Miss Annabeth was in such a tizzy, he decided to make her happy and ask Tracy to the dance.

In a strange, twisted-up way, Miles figured shooting his stepfather had been easier than raising his hand to Tracy's door. Both felt momentous, but when he'd shot Price Venture, he'd felt no sense of confusion. A whole lifetime of pain and hurt had led him to that event.

Unfortunately, confusion was pretty much all he felt at the moment. He liked Tracy as a sister, not as a prospective bride. He was also well aware that Slim would far rather be the man doing the knocking.

But every time Miles had tried to bring up the idea of Slim being Tracy's escort to the dance, all Miles had got was a firm refusal.

He'd been standing there at the front of the Hope Hotel — which had to be the worst name for a hotel ever — for a good twenty minutes, hoping for an excuse to turn around and leave. It was also taking everything he had not to start pulling on the collar of his shirt. It really was feeling a little snug.

Though it was bitter cold, he felt his shirt become damp under his arms and along the center of his back. Scared sweat was what he had.

Lord have mercy.

What should he do? Walk on in the hotel? Knock?

How did one go about asking a hotel employee to a dance?

One more time he raised his fist, prepared to place knuckle to wood . . . and one more time he dropped his hand as all his practiced words became a jumble of mixed up nouns and verbs in his brain.

Then he heard feminine laughter.

He tensed, sure Tracy was peeking out through a window, giggling at his ineptitude . . . then realized the noise came from behind him.

Two ladies were coming his way. Not anxious to be watched — and surely they would stop and stare — he knocked quickly. The last thing in the world he wanted was to be the focus of their conversation.

Almost immediately, the door swung open and Tracy herself stared at him. "Mr. Grant. Hello."

Had she been standing there, waiting? Or was she really surprised to see him? He tipped his hat. "Tracy," he said, so plumb startled that he'd completely forgotten to speak to her properly.

"Yes?"

He opened his mouth. Closed it. Opened it again. Just like a blasted trout.

"Um . . ." She peeked behind him. "Is there something wrong?"

Oh, but her eyes were green. Up close, they seemed to mirror fresh spring grass in the foothills.

Her expression went from curious to concerned in two seconds flat. "Maybe you should come in and sit down for a spell?"

"No."

"No?"

It was now or never. Clearing his throat, he dived in head first. "Actually, Trace . . . I mean, Miss Wood, I came here to see if you could help me." He took a deep breath and dived in. "Would you attend the dance with me?"

"You are asking me to attend with you? As your date?"

He nodded. "Yes." Inwardly, he cringed. Now, why couldn't he have just asked straight out?

She closed her eyes as her cheeks turned the color of poppies in the summer. "Why are you asking me? Why not someone like Laurel White?"

There was no way he was going to confide that courting Laurel scared the stuffing out of him. "I don't know."

"Oh."

She looked so dismayed by that, he felt like the worst sort of heel. "No, that's not true." Lifting his chin, he said, "I'm asking for the usual reasons, I suppose. I want to accompany you. I would enjoy it. Very much." He kind of wouldn't, not with poor Slim being disappointed. But what else was there for him to say?

"Oh," she said again.

Now he was feeling ill at ease all over again. "So, what do you say? Is your answer

185

yes or no?"

Her mouth opened and shut a few times, just like his mouth had done when he'd asked her.

She looked him over, then seemed to be looking inside of herself, too. After what felt like far too long, but in reality had only been a few seconds, she nodded. "It is a yes, Mr. Grant."

He couldn't help but smile. Then smile a whole lot more. He'd done it! "Thank you. I'll pick you up tomorrow at six." He paused. "That all right with you?"

"I think six sounds just fine. I will, ah, see you then." Then, looking bemused and dazed and all kinds of troubled, she closed the door.

Right in his face.

The two women standing on the street giggled. "Mr. Grant, did you just get a door slammed in your face?"

He took a moment to get his bearings before he turned around. "Not at all, ladies. Miss Wood just agreed to attend the dance with me."

"Well, who would have thought?" They looked at each other and then started marching up the path to Tracy's door. "We better go help," one said over her shoulder.

He stepped to the side before their wide,

186

stiff black taffeta skirts bowled him over. "Go help with what?"

"Oh, Mr. Grant, don't you know anything? Tracy ain't got a thing to wear to the dance."

What did that mean? Did he need to buy her some fabric? Oh, wait, no woman could make a dress in such short time. Maybe she could get something ready-made?

Did a man offer money for that?

While he was puzzling that out, the women looked at him hard, shook their heads, and shared some kind of strange knowing look that they understood, but left him feeling like he was never going to understand the ways and wiles of the feminine mind.

"Mr. Grant," one said. "Get on home, would ya? If you stand here much longer, you're going to cause gossip for the next year. And you're going to make Tracy nervous. We've got things to do."

"You do? Are y'all going to the dance, too?"

"Mr. Grant, you are a handsome man, and the richest in these parts, true. But sometimes, I swear you have less sense than a stuffed-up hound dog."

He took exception to that. "Hold on, now —"

"Mr. Grant, we're going to have to help her get something altered, and it's going to take every spare minute we've got." She shooed him away with a swift hand motion. "Now go so she don't see that you're still standing here looking like you've got nowhere else to go."

"Especially since we were starting to taking bets about whether or not you were ever going to knock on that door," the older of the two women said.

"You saw that, huh?"

"We couldn't help it, Mr. Grant." Kindly, she patted his shoulder. "But don't fret, it was truly the most entertaining sight we'd seen for some time."

"I'm glad I could amuse you," he murmured.

Then he hightailed it out of there. He'd done his part for Miss Annabeth.

He needed no further prodding.

Wearily, Rosemarie took a seat and clenched her fists together in her lap. Scout was telling the men good-bye and watching them leave.

More likely, he was trying to give her a bit of time to get used to the fact that she was a married woman now.

She closed her eyes and thought of the last thirty minutes. With the law and the preacher there everything had been legal and spiritually right. Mr. King and Mr. Kendrick served as witnesses. Both men were of a gossipy nature, so it was likely that word of the nuptials would be common knowledge in a matter of hours.

The six of them had stood in a semicircle of sorts, out in the front yard.

She hadn't been real eager for the men to see the shambles of the house, with its lack of furniture and the bedding spread out across the kitchen floor. Scout had felt the same.

And the barn didn't seem like the right place neither.

So the wind had kissed her cheeks as the men stood watch. The preacher had spoken of matrimony as a special union and a holy covenant not to be taken lightly.

Not a one of them even blinked an eye about how what they were doing was so very different than that. Instead, she kept her hand clasped in Scout's and let her mind drift to a better place. A place where her man loved her and her wedding day was filled with orange blossoms and rose petals and sunshine.

Hope.

And repeated the words after the preacher. Scout had done the same.

And in less than ten minutes, they were a

real couple. A husband and wife. Somehow they were now not sinful, even though they'd said words they didn't mean and made promises they didn't intend to keep.

Rose supposed that no man could ever find fault with what had just occurred. The wedding had been legal and blessed by the Lord, too.

What had been done was done. But even knowing that the inevitable had been accomplished didn't mean acceptance. Or all that more easier to bear.

As the four men who'd entered their life left in a flurry of satisfied glory, only the echo of pounding hooves and the rush of dust flying around was what was left of their shadows. Now only she and Scout stood together. Letting the breeze flap her skirts and pull strands of hair loose from her hastily pinned topknot.

"What are you thinking?" Scout asked.

What *wasn't* she thinking? Too much filled her mind to try to explain. So she settled for something simple and that was almost the truth. "I'm thinking it's a shame you had to get leg-shackled to me."

"I'll have no more of that talk, Rosemarie. We need to move forward with pride. Not look back in shame."

"You sound like a sampler quote."

To her surprise, he laughed. "I suppose I do. Who would have thought? I've never been much for flowery sayings."

Neither had she. She'd always figured they were intended for happier women with time to think about how they wanted to be treated.

He walked forward and crouched in front of her. "So . . . you okay?"

She didn't know. She felt scared and confused. And, to her shame, proud. In spite of all she was, she'd married a fine man. And though their marriage had been coerced and there was a real good chance her groom wouldn't last long . . . it was surely more than she'd dared to dream of. "Why did you do it, Scout?" she asked. "Why did you give in so easily? I never would have thought you were that kind of man."

"The man who would marry?"

"The kind of man who would marry at the bidding of others."

"Let's just say that I might be the kind of man who is willing to put a woman's needs before my own." He paused. "My brother, Clayton —" He stopped, like it was too hard to continue.

She prodded him. "Yes?"

"Well, Clayton is a good man. The best.

He's a man of honor, a man who doesn't make promises lightly." He looked away. "I heard he married recently."

"Oh?"

"He married a woman to save her."

"Like me?"

"No. I married you because it was the right thing to do. Clayton married Vanessa to save her from being abused by her stepfather."

She nodded in understanding. "So he is a man of honor."

"He is, but it was more than that. He married her, promising only to treasure her and keep her healthy . . . even though he loved her beyond everything else. He put her needs above his always. At least, that's what I heard."

The words humbled her. They made her feel curiously light-headed, too. Actions like that were the stuff of daydreams. And the kind of thing she imagined happening to her years ago. "I think I'll go check on the chickens."

"The chickens? That's all you're going to say?"

"Well, no matter what we did today, I still need to make supper."

"I suppose I can understand that."

She was glad he did because she didn't understand much of anything at all.

14

"Russell? You ever going to wake up? Come on, we're waiting on you."

He shook himself up, realizing with a start that he'd fallen asleep moments after the campfire had gotten good and hot. Now the fire was tamped out and his cohorts had already saddled their horses.

"Why didn't y'all wake me up?"

"We tried," Joe Bob said. "You didn't budge."

As he gazed at the empty fire, he fought back a groan. Not only was he cold and cranky and running late, but it looked like he'd missed out on coffee, too.

Stretching his arms, he fought the chill in the air as he climbed to his feet. His body popped and pulled as he encouraged sound-asleep body parts to come to attention.

Joe Bob folded his arms across his chest. "The day's awastin'. How much longer you gonna be?"

"Not long," he bit out. "Give me a sec, would you?"

"Sure," Joe Bob replied, but his look was perturbed. "You can get shut-eye like no other man I've known."

From his horse, Tuff laughed. "It's true. You sleep like the dead, Russell."

"I ain't never seen nothing like it," Andrew added.

Though the other man was showing his impatience, and Russell was feeling irritated that the man couldn't give him a moment longer to collect his thoughts, Russell forced himself to smile. "Being able to sleep in a flash comes in handy. It comes from practice — trying to get rest wherever I can get it."

When the Walton Gang had been riding hard, sleeping in fits and spurts had been the only way to survive. He'd thought those days were over, but they seemed to have begun again.

They'd been riding hard for days now, going east as quickly as they were able. Stopping only to rest the horses. Good horseflesh was sparse these days, and everyone agreed that the needs of the animals should always come first.

It was about the only thing the men agreed on.

There were still varied opinions scattered

around the benefits of seeking out Scout Proffitt.

Russell was one of the men who wasn't sure that seeking out a man like Scout without warning was all that good of an idea. Men who didn't want to be found preferred to keep things that way.

Russell had worked hard during his last nineteen years to stay alive and in one piece. He was in no hurry to tempt fate by coming upon a recognized gunslinger without a whole lot of warning.

After seeing to his needs and making sure his horse had been watered and fed by whoever had been on duty, he swung into the saddle. Starlight, his roan gelding, pranced a bit.

Russell was glad to see the horse anxious to be on its way.

"How far do think we have to go?" Andrew asked. "I want to get this over with."

Russell knew they were close, but he wasn't all that familiar with this part of the state. "I'm not sure. What do you think, Joe Bob?" Joe Bob was their best surveyor and had set a good pace.

"I think we're close. Real close."

Andrew took it from there. "If we're lucky, we'll make it to Broken Promise today or tomorrow. Once there, we'll have to do some fast talking and see if anyone's heard of Scout."

"Everyone's heard of Scout Proffitt," Tuff pointed out.

"Yeah, but not everyone actually knows Scout Proffitt. All we're gonna have to do is let folks know that a friend of his is in town," Joe Bob said with a grin. "Then we'll get directions."

The simple plan brought forth a fresh wave of worry. These men were counting on him to cajole Scout into seeing them and to listening to their plans, too — all based on the slimmest of relationships. And then Russell was supposed to bring Scout to their way of thinking and agree with their plan.

Which, by the way, they'd learned about from a bunch of harlots half a state away.

Russell didn't know if he could do follow through with any of it. By his estimation, Scout had never been the type of person to give much credence to other people's ideas. He was definitely a loner, and hard as nails, too.

But sharing that news was sure to be unwelcome. Probably ignored, too. The men he was with had no interest in Russell disabusing their fantasies about Scout. They had a serious case of hero worship, and it wasn't going to be amended anytime soon.

Clouds formed above them, darkening the skies and making the grueling ride even more unpleasant. They stopped for water, then slowed when a homestead appeared on the horizon. Usually, they would avoid it — most folks didn't take kindly to bands of unwashed men appearing at their doorsteps — but there was a woman out front of the home, waving her hands.

Tuff frowned. "Does that look to y'all like she wants us to approach?"

"It does." Russell swallowed uncomfortably. All of them had been without company for a long time. His cohorts were unpredictable, and he didn't want to cause any trouble. "Maybe we should ignore her?"

Joe Bob rose up in his stirrups and whistled low. "Russell, that ain't gonna happen. She's real pretty. A sweet young thing, for sure." He nudged his horse forward in anticipation.

Russell knew not a one of them could see more than a flowing skirt. "Hold on a sec —"

"I'm not gonna. You see what she's doing, she's calling for us," Joe Bob said over his shoulder. "And don't look at me that way, Russell. I'm not gonna hurt her."

Riding far more slowly by his side, Andrew's eyes widened. "What do you reckon she wants, Russell?"

"Don't know."

"I'm used to women avoiding us like the plague."

"I'm guessing she needs help."

Andrew nodded. "Then I guess I better go see if I can help her. That woman could be like my Betsy."

Russell was so irritated by the two men's lack of caution he didn't even feel like making a joke about Andrew's elusive, picture-perfect Betsy.

Instead, he looked at Tuff, the only one to stay by his side. "If we approach, we're going to be obliged to help."

Right before his eyes, Tuff's eager expression fell to looks of worry. "That might not be good. I don't know much about helping womenfolk."

Russell agreed. As Starlight pranced and fussed under his legs, he watched the woman. Joe Bob and Andrew were closer, but it still looked to him that she was waving him and Tuff to her side as well. "It looks like Joe and Andrew were right. Something's wrong. We can't ignore a woman in trouble."

Their pace was slow as they guided their horses through a batch of mesquite shrubs and across a spell of uneven land, parched and cracked from months of drought. As they got closer, Scout noticed that the woman was indeed a pretty thing. Her eyes were wide-set and dark, her hair looking like flyaway spun gold.

Joe Bob, for all his leadership abilities, seemed to have been struck dumb.

In no time flat, the other men silently moved a bit behind Russell, making him once again their reluctant leader.

He would have argued against the position, but he was grateful for it just then. If the other men were so far willing to follow his lead, then perhaps they would get through this meet and greet without doing any harm.

When they were close enough to see stains on her yellow calico, he brought them all to a halt. "Good afternoon, Miss," he said politely. Tipping his hat for good measure. "Were you calling to us?"

Joe Bob guffawed behind him, and Russell knew he deserved every bit of the chiding. Not only was he as awkward as a preacher in a cathouse, it had been more than obvious that the woman had been signaling for them. Painfully obvious.

Luckily, she didn't seem to notice the other man's amusement.

"Indeed I have been calling for you. I've

been so worried and scared to death, too. You men are surely a sight for sore eyes."

"What's wrong?" Russell looked around, but nothing seemed outwardly in disarray.

"My sister's been ailing something awful, and I don't have a clue what to do next."

"What's wrong with her?" Oh Lord, he silently prayed. Please don't let it be influenza.

"She's in a family way," she said after a moment's embarrassment. "I'm afraid something's wrong with the baby."

As she gestured for them to dismount and follow her, all four of them froze like ice chips.

And Russell had to give the Lord credit. It sure wasn't influenza.

Nothing could create a greater panic in a man than a woman expecting a baby . . . and expecting him to be of use.

"Ah, ma'am —"

"It's Miss."

He cleared his throat. "Miss. I, uh, I'm just not sure we can do much for you."

Her eyes widened as pure panic tinged her voice. "But you have to. I need your help."

Joe Bob spoke up. "Where's her man?"

She faltered, and even in the dim, hazy light, Russell could see that she was struggling to put her thoughts to words. "She doesn't have one. She was violated when a band of men came through. It's just her and me." With each word, her voice had become softer. The last had been no more than a whisper.

Russell wondered what she hadn't said. Perhaps that she, too, had been hurt by the men . . . only she didn't have a pregnancy to remember it by?

"I understand," he said.

Almost by magic, his acceptance of their new responsibility changed the rest of the men's demeanor completely. Sometimes God didn't give men choices to take.

Sometimes He put the problems right there in front of them so they couldn't be avoided.

Surely this was one of those times.

Without looking behind him, Russell dismounted. Clicking to Starlight, he led the horse closer.

"Russell?" Joe Bob called out. "What should we do?"

He wanted their help. He wanted one of them to step up and take his place. To suddenly announce that he'd delivered babies before and had an inkling of what to do.

But by the looks for the place, there was likely no room for all of them inside. They'd probably frighten the poor woman anyhow. Looking at the slim pile of wood outside the door and the sorry looking pump twenty paces away, he shrugged. "Looks like there's work to be done."

The woman who'd hailed them said not a word as she continued her journey to the door. After tying up Starlight, Russell took a deep breath and followed her in.

Then, when he saw what was waiting for him inside, he wished he hadn't.

The woman's sister was in a bad way, a true mess of soiled sheets, sweat, and pain.

"She's been like this for hours," the woman said. "But now I think she's pretty close to her time."

Russell gulped. Looked at his dirty hands. "You got a place I can wash up?"

She pointed to a pitcher of water and a bar of what smelled like lye soap. He rolled up his sleeves and made quick use of it.

The sister moaned again.

Closing his eyes, he said a prayer. Prayed for the Lord to work through him, though he was so very undeserving. Prayed for the Lord to give him strength. And to bless these poor women with a newborn's cries instead of more pain and sorrow.

"What's her name, Miss?"

"Mary."

Well, that figured, didn't it? Perching on the edge of the bed, he grasped Mary's hand. "Mary, I'm Russell. I ain't done this before, but together, we're going to figure it out. Okay?"

Some of the wildness in her eyes calmed. Beside him, the sister exhaled softly.

When another pain came, he coaxed her through it and helped the sister rearrange Mary, too.

And then they waited. Coaxing and pushing and praying and crying. And less than an hour later, Mary was holding a newborn girl.

After washing up with the pitcher and soap again, he rolled down his sleeves and pulled back on his duster. "I'd best go."

The sister nodded. "Can I give you something to eat? We don't got much — but what I have is yours."

"I don't need a thing, ma'am. I'm just glad y'all are all okay." He turned and left then, half-afraid if he didn't, he'd be tempted to stay a little longer.

Seeing new life come into the world had to be truly one of the Lord's greatest blessings.

"Russell, is everything okay?" Andrew asked when he met them at the woodpile that was now a healthy size.

"Yeah. Mary had a baby."

"And . . . is it okay?"

"Yeah," he murmured, half-surprised. "Yeah, she and the baby are just fine."

The other men smiled. Then they mounted their horses and started back on their way.

Only later did Russell realize that he'd never found out what the sister's name had been.

Strange.

15

Rosemarie didn't know if her husband wanted a wedding night. After making him a mess of fried chicken, she made some biscuits to go with them, taking care to roll out the dough.

They'd eaten, sitting across from each other next to the sparse heat of the kitchen stove.

Scout ate heartily in silence, barely doing more than meeting her gaze every few minutes.

Rose, on the other hand, felt like every bite of food she took was ready to be embedded in her throat. She ended up playing with the small amount on her plate, wishing all the while she wasn't wasting it.

Scout watched her. "You're not hungry?"

"Not too much."

"That's too bad because you're a fine cook, Rosemarie. I have to say that's something of a surprise."

It was a thin compliment at best. "Why are you surprised?"

"Don't know. Just figured you probably didn't have a whole lot of experience."

"My pa was poorly for a long while, so my mother had to run the ranch. I, ah, learned to make do." Abruptly, she stopped speaking. To tell him anymore would only make her life sound more pitiful.

Carefully, he wiped his mouth with the dishcloth he'd pulled from the counter. "Well, this was good eating. Thank you."

Slowly, he stood up. She felt his gaze glide over her, head to toe. "So . . . are you all right? Has this wedding of ours shaken you up?"

What to tell him? What to tell him? "Actually, I was thinking about our wedding. About our vows."

"What about it?"

She felt her face flaming so much she was surprised it hadn't caught fire. "Is it true we're married?"

"You were there, same as I. It felt real to me."

Oh, but this was hard. "I mean, don't we have to finish things up?"

His eyes narrowed. "I'm not following. Finish what?"

"The ceremony," she said delicately.

"Don't we need to finish everything?"

He cocked his head to one side. "Like I told you, it's done, Rose." Then, abruptly, he stilled. "Are you talking about the marriage bed?"

Warily, she nodded. "Maybe."

"Maybe?" His perfect brows lowered. "It's either yes or no. Honey, you'd better start talking."

"I thought a couple had to . . ." She searched her mind for the right way to delicately phrase things. "To, ah . . . be together. For . . . things to be right. Legal." And though he was staring at her, though her face was surely flaming, she continued. "I thought doing that was required."

He blinked, looking poleaxed. "Well, now."

She wished he'd do more than question her, that he'd be the one stating the obvious. "Am I not correct?"

He stepped closer, his ice-blue eyes looking so translucent that she was sure he could see into her heart. "Is that what you want to do tonight, Rosemarie?" he drawled. "Make things legal?"

The words warred with their meaning. Yes, she wanted to be legally wed. Now that she'd been forced to go through with the ceremony, she didn't want anything to change the way things were.

But she certainly had no intention of being so forward with him.

Her hesitation looked like it greatly amused him. "Come on, Rosemarie, don't be shy. There's got to be something you want."

She bit her lip as the silence between them lengthened.

"I should have never given this dance more than a passing thought," Miles griped to Miss Annabeth from his new favorite spot — the back corner of the Johnson's barn. "Being here makes my teeth ache."

"That's because you tried Miralee Johnson's peanut brittle. Anyone with sense knows not to get within fifty feet of it. You're lucky you didn't lose a tooth."

Now that she mentioned it, it did seem like more than one person had looked at him with something of a wince when he'd picked up a piece of the treat. "How come nobody warned me that candy was practically lethal?"

She looked him up and down, just like he had no more sense than a bagful of rocks. "There's only one reason no one told you, and that's because you're *Mr. Grant.*"

He had no idea what that meant. "So?"

"So, nothing. You've made that ranch

really prosper. No one's going to tell you 'boo' no more. You should realize that."

He realized it to an extent. But he also realized that most knew all his faults, too. And he had a great many of those.

Looking put upon, his favorite housekeeper jutted a hip out and curved her arms over her chest. "And before you go on again how you're still the same Miles that you were when you were in short pants, I am going to remind you that even if that is there case . . . you're a catch in these here parts."

"Thanks for that."

"I'm just telling it like it is. As I've said before . . . you, Mr. Grant, are a wanted man."

"Wanted, huh?"

"Uh-huh. Wanted both as a husband and potential boss. Those are the facts, and truthfully, you should just get used to it. People think you are a man of worth now, and there ain't a person here who's going to risk ticking you off."

"Thanks," he said sarcastically. "Now I feel real special."

Miss Annabeth snorted. "If you want to feel special, let me know, Boss, and I'll coddle you. I thought you wanted the truth."

"I'll take the truth, you know that."

She leaned to the side and peeked around him. "Now where is your ladylove?"

"If you're speaking of Tracy, she's over there, visiting with those women. And don't you go calling her that, neither."

"She could be . . ."

"I can only think of her like a sister, Miss Annabeth."

"Still —"

"But still, I do like her fine." He glanced Tracy's way again. This time, she caught his gaze — blushed so much that even he could tell her freckles were fading — then turned and chatted with her girlfriends again. "I tell you, I guess she's regretting we came together. I had thought I was doing her a favor, but maybe not. Why, from the time we stepped in here, she's hardly paid me a bit of mind."

"That's the trouble with you, Mr. Grant. You need me to tell you what's what."

"And what are you talking about now?"

"Tracy ain't ignoring you, not even a little bit. Why, I bet she probably hasn't spoken a word that didn't have your name in it since those gals started circling her."

"You think?" This was news to him.

"I think and I know. She got the biggest landowner in the area to take her to the dance. That's a pretty big deal."

He didn't want to ask. He wasn't going to ask. "What do you think I should do now? Can I go over there, or will I just look foolish?"

Miss Annabeth's eyes softened. "Going over there and asking your date for the evening to dance won't make you look foolish at all, Mr. Grant. Go on now. I'm sure you'll do just fine."

After tipping the brim of his Stetson, he turned on his heel before he chickened out and walked right out the door.

As he crossed the barn, Tracy's shy smile turned to giggles and her look to wide-eyed speculation.

Though it wasn't charitable, he reminded himself that she was only a glorified maid. And that he only liked her like a sister. And that Slim really liked her, too.

He should never get so tongue-tied and nervous around a girl who was so obviously not meant for him.

Too bad the reminder didn't do a bit of good. "Miss Wood, care to dance?" he asked.

After looking at two of the women and seeing them nod, she stepped forward. He held out his hand for her to take.

She looked at it like his arm had just become a snake.

Just as he realized he should have offered

her his elbow, not his hand, she'd slipped her hand in his.

Funny, her hand was so much smaller than his. Her personality was so big, he'd half-expected her hand to be as big as his. Which made not a lick of sense.

The band began to play a waltz. Luckily, he knew how to waltz. With a minimum of fuss, he wrapped his other hand around her waist and pulled her close. She was pliant and far more petite than he'd imagined. But there was also a bit of muscle laced under her skin, making her feel more solid than some of the other women he'd held.

Then he remembered that she was not a lady of leisure. She lifted heavy loads of laundry and sheets.

Her body at first felt stiff and woodenlike. With every step he took, she seemed to be a half beat off. The result was that they were walking with slow jerks and beats around the dance floor, not with the easy steps of the beautiful dance.

"Do you think you could relax a bit, Miss Wood?" he asked.

Her eyes widened. "What?"

He didn't know if he was embarrassing her or just ticking her off. But something had to be done. "Let me lead, would you? Relax and match your steps to mine. Waltzing is something I actually do well."

Hurt flashed across her features. "Did I step on your boot? I'm sorry. I'm doing my best."

"So am I, but you're fighting me. Come on, Tracy. Give me a break." After a few more steps and a near-collision with Slim, she got a little closer to him and let him lead. The change was like night and day. He pulled her a little closer, then quickened their pace, even twirling her around a few times.

Little by little, her fierce trepidation gave way to a smile of satisfaction. "You dance real good," she said.

"So do you."

"We know that's not true."

"It is now," he said graciously. It was rare for him to feel so in control. But he did at that moment.

"I never had lessons." She bit her lip, then continued. "Matter of fact, I haven't ever danced the waltz before."

"My sister, Vanessa, had a couple of dancing lessons, back before my mother went into decline. I got roped into being her practice partner a time or two."

"Y'all were real lucky."

"I didn't think so at the time." He smiled, enjoying the spark of interest in her eyes.

And, enjoying the novel feeling of remembering his childhood with something other than regret. "I'm afraid I complained about Vanessa making me dance something awful."

"What happened? Did your daddy set you straight?"

He laughed. "No. As a matter of fact, it was our foreman, Clayton, who got me back on track. He heard me fussing about dancing with her, and he took me to task." What he didn't mention was that he'd spied a look of pain in Clayton's eyes when the foreman had watched Miles dance with her.

He hadn't understood what was wrong then, but now, looking back, he realized that Clayton had loved Vanessa even then. Most likely he'd been feeling jealous.

"Funny thing about them two. They ended up falling in love."

"I heard they married and are living in Colorado Territory."

"That would be true," he said. Not eager to revisit those whole months when so much had happened that didn't bear repeating, he artlessly changed the topic. "You look real pretty, by the by."

She bit her lip. "My dress, it's a made-over one from my cousin. Some ladies helped me with it."

"I think the green color looks real nice."

"It's emerald." She bit her lip, then sighed. "Sorry. I really don't know how to act with you."

He felt the same way. But the dance sure wasn't the spot to let her know. "Whatever it's called, I like it. The color goes well with your brown eyes."

"Goes with brown? I tell you, Mr. Grant, you don't know colors at all."

"Maybe so, but I know enough to know you're supposed to say thank you when I give you a compliment," he blurted. Really, she did bring out the worst in him.

"Thank you."

"Are you glad you came with me?"

"I don't know."

"Ah. Well, that's honest, I suppose." This time he was the one averting his eyes as they danced.

The tension between them rose until a ragtag group of men entered the barn. Immediately, all eyes fastened on the newcomers.

Tracy clung to him a little tighter. "Do you know them, Miles?"

"I don't. Never seen them before." But a sick feeling of dread entered his stomach because he had a very good idea of who the men were: Harlan Jones and his boys.

"Do you think they mean trouble?"

He knew they did. Miles looked at the men a little more closely. Their eyes were old, but their skin looked younger than his own. What had they all seen? He wondered.

Guiding Tracy over to the side of the room, he stopped and unabashedly let his gaze settle on the men.

Slim walked over to them and spoke. After a moment, he gestured for Miles to come closer. Big Jim, too.

"I better go see what he wants, Tracy. I'm sorry about this."

To his pleasure, she smiled instead of looking hurt. "Don't be. I'm glad we're here together."

He bowed slightly. "May I escort you to the other ladies?"

"I can escort myself. You'd best go see what happened before Sheriff Brower gets involved. Or something bad happens."

When Miles reached the circle of men, they made space for him. "These boys just came in town. Offered to help the Circle Z with patrols."

Miles was surprised about what the men were saying. He would've bet money that they'd been the ones rustling. But maybe that was their plan? They'd doing a little rustling and mayhem, rile up a community, then offer to be of assistance? "Thank you, but we don't need your help."

Slim looked flummoxed. "You sure, Mr. Grant?"

Miles eyed the newcomers once more, noticed the sharp blend of evil in their eyes. "Positive. We don't need your kind here. I suggest you get along now."

"I ain't never heard a man like you refuse us," one of the men said, his voice gravelly and hard. "I don't take kindly to it."

"I'm afraid your feelings aren't my concern," Miles said. He stood motionless until they grudgingly turned away.

When all four of them had walked out of the barn's front entrance, a visible sigh of relief went through the whole group.

"I'm sorry, Slim. I trust your judgment, and I know we could use the help, but there was something about them that set me off."

"You're the boss, Boss."

"They looked to me like they had an agenda." Briefly, he told Big Jim and Slim about his idea that they were actually part of Harlan Jones's gang.

Big Jim folded his arms across his chest and nodded. "Mr. Grant, we're going to have to step up our patrols, I'm afraid."

"I know it. And I know y'all are tired, too." Looking to Slim, he said, "I'm going to go

218

visit with Sheriff Brower, but I feel real bad about not being with Tracy. Could you go do me a favor and dance with her?"

Slim's eyes widened. "Boss . . ."

"It's just a dance, Slim."

"All right."

Miles watched Slim ask Tracy to dance, saw her hesitantly accept, then noticed that the two of them seemed a whole lot more at ease than he'd been with Tracy.

With a satisfied smile, he went to go talk to the sheriff.

Hours later, when the dance ended, Miles escorted Tracy back to the Hope Hotel, then talked with Slim and Big Jim. "I'm going out to the south pasture tonight."

"Mr. Grant, I sure wish you'd stay home," Big Jim said.

"I know you do, but I can't do that anymore. Not when all of y'all are losing sleep most every night."

After a pause, Slim nodded reluctantly. "Who do you want to go with?"

"I'll be fine on my own."

Slim shook his head. "Boss, we don't work like that."

"There's no need to watch over me, Slim."

"But Boss —"

"Slim, I know y'all think I'm weak, but I'm not. I can handle a shotgun as well as any man on this ranch. I'll be fine."

"All right," he said softly. "But I don't like it."

Miles rode out within the hour, feeling rather proud of himself. Finally, he was doing his part to save the stock. Doing his part to defend his birthright.

Finally doing what Clayton would have done, no matter what.

But of course, he regretted his decision around three in the morning. When the clouds had swept over the glow of a pale moon, and the band of men he'd refused work to came out of the shadows.

Miles wished he would have listened to Slim, listened to his own directives, and had a partner to work with when the Jones Gang rushed forward.

He tried to fight back when he was knocked off his horse. But then, all he had time to think about was the Lord's prayer when the men's fists met his jaw. And his shoulders.

Then their boots kicked his legs and stomach and chest.

Then, well, he didn't think at all — because he'd been beaten unconscious.

16

Scout recalled the first time he'd shot a man. He'd been living on his own for two years and had met his share of liars and low-lifes. Men had seen him for what he was — a too-green kid with little knowledge and a chip on his shoulder that he'd imagined was pride and substance but in reality was nothing more substantial than a cow chip.

Just a few days earlier, he'd gotten beaten up for looking at a man the wrong way. Soon after, he'd managed to get most of his belongings stolen. He'd been broken and beaten that sorry day in Galveston — sitting against a brick wall of a dark alley, hoping to live a few moments pain-free.

As he'd often done then, he'd sought liquid comfort in cheap whiskey, hoping to pass out into the terrible, wonderful state of blacked-out oblivion.

He'd been halfway there and had been in an especially despondent mood. He'd been thinking about Clayton and Corrine, and their father, and wondering how he'd fallen so far from the tree.

Then he'd been found.

He realized now he should be thankful for the man dressed all in black. He'd been vile and vicious. He'd also seen Scout for what he was — an easy target.

"Boy, you are just what I've been looking for," he'd murmured.

Scout, still in his stupor, had simply stared, wondering what he had that the man could possibly want.

Then the man had dropped his gun belt and reached for him.

Maybe it was a sixth sense, maybe it was because every nightmare he'd ever suffered through had suddenly sprung to life. But whatever the reason, Scout realized what was about to happen.

He'd also known he couldn't allow it. There were some things a man just couldn't recover from, not while he was still living and breathing.

"No," he'd bit out. Even to his ears he'd sounded weak and pitiful.

If anything, his sorry protest had pleased the man. He laughed as he'd slapped him hard. Then he grinned when he'd reached down and yanked at Scout's pants.

Right then, right there, Scout decided to change. He was tired of being lied to and cheated. Tired of being hungry and poor and cold.

He was through being beaten.

And he was not going to be raped in a dark alley in Galveston.

When the man grabbed at him again, all the while spouting all kinds of vile things, Scout pretended to crouch down in fear. And then he'd made his move. It had taken barely a second to pilfer the man's well-oiled Colt from his abandoned holster on the dirty ground.

It took less than that to shoot him in the face.

The sound of the bullet firing reverberated through the alley. The blood and tissue that sullied his skin was warmer and wetter than he'd expected.

What he'd done should've sickened him.

The shock that he'd taken another person's life should have made him feel terrible. He should have felt like the worst kind of sinner.

Instead, he felt a cleansing burst of relief.

He was alive. He was not being raped. No one was hurting him, using him, or cheating him.

Finally, he'd taken control of his life.

Only a few steps beyond the man was his knapsack. Inside the canvas bag was another shirt — black like the one he'd been wearing. Since Scout's shirt was hopelessly stained with blood, he switched shirts.

Then he'd found the man's money. Ten dollars — far more money than he'd ever seen at one time in his life.

He took that, too.

Finally, he picked up his would-be rapist's holster and buckled it around his hips. Carefully replaced the pearl-handled Colt in place. The gun's weight on his hip felt right. Good.

After taking one last look at the dead body laying crumbled on the ground, his body already covered by a fine film of dirt and grime, Scout exited the alley a changed man.

He'd worn black ever since, never forgetting the way another man's blood could stain a lighter shade of cloth.

Scout had never forgotten what it had felt like to be completely helpless in a dark alley in the worst sorts of towns. To be at the world's mercy. He'd never forgotten that sometimes only a silver bullet could change a person's fate.

All of that ran through his mind as he stared at Rosemarie as she approached him in a voluminous white nightgown, her auburn hair flowing around her shoulders and back in a mass of curls.

"What did you decide, Rosemarie?" he asked softly. She'd never dream of it, but he had a very good idea of everything she was feeling.

"I would like our marriage to be legal," she said after studying him. "I don't want anyone to ever say I'm not your wife."

Getting hitched to a man like him was nothing to be proud of. Being married to a hired killer certainly wasn't a step up in the world. The only reason he could think she would want to marry him would be to save her reputation.

"You sure this is what you want?" he murmured, trying to think of a way to talk about marital relations without shocking or scaring her. "We don't have to do a thing. I don't mind letting people think we've done more than we have."

She bit her lip. "You might not understand this, but a thing like this, well . . . I'd like to have some control over it. And I trust you."

He did, indeed, understand her need for control. He understood that completely. Her trust in him nearly brought him to his knees. Trust like that didn't come easily.

"I don't fear you, Scout." Raising her chin,

she said quietly, "I've come to understand that there's no guarantee what the future's going to bring. I'd hate to think I waited for something worse."

He almost told her that they could wait. That there was no hurry. But he knew that look, and he knew that fear. He had never forgotten the way his skin had felt when he'd been at another man's mercy in an alley in Galveston. He'd never forgotten that all-encompassing sense of fear and dread.

Even after all this time.

What's more, she was his wife, and she was a pretty thing. That hadn't escaped his notice. In time, well, they could court and flirt and take steps toward having a real union.

He'd actually kind of liked the idea of taking things slow with her. Plus, this was his home now. Surely they had plenty of time?

But when he gazed into her eyes, he knew she couldn't wait. Coming to him had taken everything she had.

There was only one thing to do. "I understand," he said softly. And with that, he held out his hand. Nodded encouragement when she placed her palm in his own.

It would be no hardship to be her husband in every way possible. With some surprise, he realized he desired her, too. And so he pulled her into his arms and held her close.

At dawn, Rosemarie slid out of bed and padded to the kitchen. After stoking the fire in the kitchen stove, she slipped on her boots and coat and walked out to the barn to gather eggs.

The moment the air brushed against her cheeks, she lifted her chin and paused for a minute, enjoying the fresh air.

Because all she seemed to be able to do was think about Scout. Her husband.

How everything had changed between them.

The night before, she'd been so nervous, she'd been sure her knees were knocking together. There, in the dim light illuminated by the controlled flickering of two candles, she'd stood before him, as vulnerable as a woman could be. She'd asked him to be hers, her white nightgown fluttering against her bare ankles as she'd tried to control her nervousness.

And as she'd waited for him to reply, she'd steeled herself for his refusal. For a disparaging comment. Perhaps a tease?

But instead, Scout had held her close for a moment and brushed his lips against hers.

"Guess you haven't done this before?" he asked when he'd stepped back, the room seeming to grow smaller by the second as the feather bed loomed before them.

She'd shaken her head. "This is all new to me." Knowing it was supposed to be new to her didn't help in the slightest. She'd lived her whole life being caught off guard, and each time, she'd been worse for it.

Gazing at Scout, she realized that he, too, looked a little filled with trepidation. A sudden, awful thought occurred to her. "Have you done it?"

He'd looked startled. "Pardon?"

Embarrassed beyond words, she patted the quilt covering the feather bed. The crazy quilt was made out of leftover scraps from Mr. James's ragbag at the mercantile. "Is this new to you, too?"

His eyes narrowed. Swallowed. Bit his lip. "You mean bedding?"

"Well, yes. Because, you know, it's okay if it is."

"That right?" The smallest of smiles had curved his lips, and something almost like tenderness had entered his eyes. That new emotion softened his gaze like nothing ever had before. "Rosemarie, I, uh appreciate that. That's real kind of you, to be understanding and all. But I'm afraid there's only one of us who's the innocent here."

And with that, he leaned over and blew

out one of the candles. All that remained was a short, stubby taper glowing by the doorway. The flickering light created shadows where none had been before.

And those sudden shadows allowed her to finally relax. A new sense of inevitability had formed between them. No longer was she at a disadvantage, being forced to comply with an idea not her own.

No, there in the dark with Scout, it was everything good and right. Everything better.

Remembering what happened next, Rosemarie shivered. Not even a cold wind kissing her cheeks could remove the warmth that filled her.

In retaliation, she quickened her pace. The temperature was still hovering around freezing, especially in the dark morning air. But that, of course wasn't what made her shiver.

It was the remembering.

"I know what to do," she'd said, ready to lie down on the bed and close her eyes tight.

But Scout had stilled her with one hand. "I'm not quite ready to do the deed, sugar."

She'd been confused. "Is something wrong?"

"Not at all. I uh, just think maybe we should maybe wait a bit before we get on that mattress. How about we take things slow?" Scout had asked. "We could take our time with this. After all, we have all night, Rosemarie."

She hadn't known why he was asking her opinion. She hadn't had one.

But then he'd crossed the room, blown out that last candle, and then approached her in the dark. His touch had felt like a lifeline. She accepted it readily, and within minutes, she'd stepped into his arms. He'd felt solid and so much larger. And so much warmer.

But his embrace paled greatly next to his kiss.

Afraid to stand outside in the yard mooning over him much longer, she shook off the tingles.

Entering the barn, Rosemarie greeted the hens like the day was everything wondrous and wonderful.

"Good morning, ladies," she called out as she unlatched the metal gate. "Y'all look snug in your beds. I won't disturb you much. Just need a few eggs." Slipping a hand under Ethel, she grasped an egg, carefully set it in a metal basket she kept near the door, and then moved forward, sneaking eggs from the hens. Some hardly moved, they were so used to her touch.

After visiting each hen, she walked out

with eight eggs. "Thank you kindly, ladies," she said, giving them a little curtsy. Just because no one was around to see her act silly.

After leaving the hens, she fed the horses, giving each special pats as she dished up oats and hay. Next, she fetched water for them.

The hard work, done before a serving of coffee usually made her grimace. But she hardly cared about the work. She concentrated on her bounty instead. She had more than enough to make Scout breakfast and perhaps even some spoon bread, too. She didn't know for sure that he liked spoon bread, but who didn't?

Imagining Scout accepting the dish with pleasure made her steps falter . . . and drift back to the night before.

Right before they'd fallen asleep, Scout had brushed his lips against her brow. "You okay, honey?" he'd murmured.

"Yeah."

But she must not have sounded very convincing, because he'd pushed a chunk of her hair back from her face. "Sure?"

She knew he cared. He hadn't wanted to hurt her. He'd known their circumstances hadn't been near ideal.

The funny thing was that she knew she

should have felt the same way.

But she hadn't. "I'm sure, Scout." For a moment, she'd been tempted to tell him that she'd spent her whole life waiting to be coddled and held. She'd been waiting to be embraced and kissed and made to feel like she mattered.

And in Scout's arms all of that had happened.

He kissed her brow again. "All right, then," he said, this time sounding a bit more pleased.

Then he'd continued to softly run his hand along her temple. His touch was so featherlike, so gentle, she'd closed her eyes. Just enjoyed the feeling. She'd fallen asleep like that. To her surprise, she'd slept the whole night through and had woken up to a sleeping man by her side and a brighter sense of worth.

Standing at the edge of the barn, with a thousand things needing her attention but only the lethargic feeling in her bones mattering to her, Rosemarie felt herself blush. Not from the things they'd done, but from all the things she hadn't said.

Why hadn't she been able to gather her courage and tell him what she'd been feeling? It would have been right to tell Scout that his touch had been a revelation.

That she'd never expected his tender kisses.

That she'd never expected to feel so cherished. Even if it had been the dark, even if he'd been lying . . . even if it never happened again, she was grateful for the experience. Rosemarie doubted there were all that many women on the earth who could say such a thing about the marriage bed.

Her mother and sister had always said the act was only something to be endured. Still in a daze and not all that eager to return to her chores, Rose leaned against the splintery wall of the barn and watched the trail of snowflakes dance down from the heavens. Each one flitted and floated and spun before ultimately coating the ground for a too-brief second before melting into a fine mist.

The snowflakes' journeys were creating a wonderful mystical feeling in the air. Items in the distant turned blurry and smudged. With each second, the fog hung heavier.

Fancifully, she wondered how long the fog would stay. Maybe Scout would wake up, see the fog out the windows, and roll back over. Perhaps the two of them could stay nestled in the empty house. Eating breakfast and sipping coffee.

They could talk, get to know each other better.

Who knows? Maybe she could learn to look at him without blushing. Or even better, maybe Scout would kiss her again. Kiss her many times.

Imagining how one of those long, slow kisses that curled her toes and made her cheeks heat up something fierce.

Or . . . maybe, just maybe . . . Scout would coax her back beside him. Maybe he'd curve his arms around her, cuddle her close, maybe then he'd mention that married folks did some things more than just once . . .

"Look at her, Russell. Think she's ever going to move?"

"Don't know," drawled the reply. "She's been standing there, smiling for nigh-on five minutes. What do you reckon a gal like that has to smile about?"

Spinning to her right, Rosemarie stared at the pair of men looking her over like she was their new treat.

Pure fear coursed through her as the men surrounded her in a half circle. Effectively trapping her. One of the eggs fell to the ground.

She was caught.

From somewhere inside of her, she found the strength to stand her ground. "Who are you? What are you doing here?"

One of them slowly pulled out a pistol and

leveled at her. "None of that is your concern, ma'am. All you need to do is tell us where Scout Proffitt is."

She gasped. Were these the type of men Scout had warned her about? The men who would dare to kill him in his sleep, all in the hopes of making a name for himself?

These men were one of the reasons he'd given for not wanting to marry.

God gave her strength again to not shrink in front of them. Instead, she stood her ground. "I . . . I don't know who you're talking about."

One of the men stepped forward, out of the misty fog and into her direct line of vision. "Now I know you're lying, ma'am. Because everyone — and I mean everyone — has heard of Scout Proffitt."

He was right. And once more, she was no match for a group of men like this. Trembling, she tried to imagine what she could say to them. Tried to imagine what she could say to buy some time.

"Maybe she'd rather not speak with the likes of you, Russell," a deep raspy voice paired with the sharp click of a gun being cocked intoned through the fog.

"Scout!" The youngish man grimaced as he turned on his heel. "Sorry, didn't see you there."

"I figured that." Scout's voice was icy and distant, sounding to Rosemarie like it came from a long, deep trough.

Still holding the pistol, the boy's hand trembled. "I need to talk to you about something."

"Is that right?" Scout's eyes were dark and ominous looking. "All I've seen you do is point a pistol at my wife."

The man's hand started shaking even more violently. "We weren't going to do nothing, Mr. Proffitt."

"All I'm going to do is shoot if you don't drop that six-shooter and step away from my wife."

The skin around the boy's mouth whitened. "I promise, we didn't mean no harm."

Rosemarie gulped. Only Scout's presence had prevented these men doing the most horrible of crimes.

Scout's gun clicked. "Russell, I'm confused why you're still holding that gun."

Looking beyond Russell, at the other men who were standing wide-eyed, looking for all the world like they'd seen a ghost, Scout added, "I hope you boys know you're only alive because I'm curious about your visit. And I have no interest in burying your bodies this afternoon."

The man she'd married had become a

stranger, right before her eyes. Rosemarie trembled. "Scout?"

Though he didn't look her way, his voice softened. "It's okay, honey. Just go on back to the house. Stay there."

"But —" She hated to leave him alone. Surely, she shouldn't leave him alone to face those killers?

"Do as I say."

She had no choice, and no other options. It wasn't like she could defend him against the men. Without another word, she scurried to the house and sat on the one of the ancient ladder back chairs next to the fire.

Praying that she wouldn't hear the telltale sound of a gun firing. Because that would mean the men had either shot her husband or that her husband was still, indeed, a cold-blooded killer.

17

Once Rosemarie was safely inside, Scout looked at the four men in front of him and realized that he'd never really known fear until they'd dared threaten his wife.

His wife.

Never had he thought he'd ever connect such a pair of words with himself. Never had he imagined that they'd mean so much.

The night before, she'd trusted him enough to share her body and her soul with him. He didn't take trust like that lightly, and he never intended for Rosemarie to have reason to doubt all the promises he'd made to her when the candles were snuffed and the only thing separating their bodies were wisps of frosty air.

Remembering how vulnerable she'd been, and remembering how much he'd enjoyed the feeling of contentment that had washed over him when she'd fallen asleep in his arms, he pointed his Colt at the boy who'd dared to lead his sorry set of friends to his home.

He was going to have shoot him. Maybe kill them all. For a brief moment, he felt bad about that. Maybe he really had made some mistakes.

But then he remembered that Russell was almost as far from being a boy as he was. All of them had grown far past their actual ages while being a part of the Walton Gang.

He cocked his pistol, the unmistakable click sounded harsh and over-loud. "I said to drop your weapons. Can you not hear anymore, boy?"

Something crossed over Russell's features that looked a whole lot like disappointment. "I heard you." Like a dead weight, the gun fell to the ground. "Throw down your guns," he muttered to the men behind him.

When they hesitated, Russell spoke more quickly. "His reputation is true. Scout Proffitt will shoot to kill. And he don't lie, neither. I can promise you that."

Almost in unison, the three other men's guns fell to the ground.

Scout looked at each of their faces, immediately determining who was still on edge and who had no other interest in doing further harm. "Joe Bob? You still packing?"

"Sorry, Mr. Proffitt. Forgot about that

one." Slowly, the blond pulled a gun from his boot and silently added it to the pile.

Only when the men stood in front of him, hands loosely at their sides and looking terribly bare did Scout holster his own weapon. "So, boys . . . how did y'all happen to wander on my property?"

Not looking too pleased about being called a "boy," Joe Bob spoke up. "We didn't happen here, and you know that. We've been looking for you."

"Joe Bob, watch it," Russell murmured.

Joe Bob shifted a shoulder with a jerk. "You ain't my boss, Russell. Stop talking to me like you are." Turning back to Scout, he said, "Getting here weren't easy, but finding information wasn't all that hard neither."

This was news. "That so?"

"Uh-huh. We'd heard that you were out in Oklahoma, and when we were riding through, we got lucky."

"The saloon owner in Shawnee was bragging to everyone who'd ever passed the place that he'd served you," Tuff explained.

Joe Bob nodded. "Anyway, a couple of men in Shawnee remembered you winning that hand in poker. Then I remembered something you said one night about always wanting to own some land of your own. In Texas. Thought coming here made sense."

"We started asking questions, and someone said he'd heard you settled in near Broken Promise," Russell explained.

The way they were talking, Scout was surprised people weren't discussing his eating habits. But if he was less inclined to speak of anything other than his past, it was Rosemarie. "My nuptials were a sudden thing," he said shortly.

"Your wife is a tiny thing, but real pretty," Tuff said. "Never imagined red hair could be so tempting."

Before Scout could correct the man's choice of topics, Russell turned on the lanky cowboy. "Shoot, Tuff, shut up! Are you hoping to die today? Don't ever mention Mrs. Proffitt again."

Tuff paled. "Sorry, Mr. Proffitt. Didn't mean no disrespect."

"Good." Scout fought to keep his voice cool and his expression blank, but inside he was twisting around Tuff's words — and his reaction to them. He was feeling a curious sense of pride that another man noticed Rosemarie's beauty and an all-encompassing jealousy that anyone would dare threaten what was his.

His.

Feeling a bit out of sorts with his warring emotions, Scout holstered his weapon. The action gave him a moment to gather his bearings. He needed it, too.

Every cell in his body had screamed for him to take care of those men who'd dared to sneak up on his wife. With some surprise, he'd realized that he would have shot each of them without an ounce of regret if he'd thought they'd meant to do her harm.

"So, now that I know how you found me, why don't you tell me why y'all are here." he said to Russell. "Unless this is a social call?"

Russell visibly gathered his courage, puffed out his chest a bit, then explained. "We have an offer for you."

They'd come all this way, scared his wife, and interrupted his life — all to ask a favor?

Irritation hit him hard. So much so, that it took a whole lot of effort to keep his voice even and calm. "What kind of offer?"

"A good one," Tuff interjected. "The outfit we talked to are willing to pay good money for Scout Proffitt to be involved."

So, it exactly was as he'd feared. "I don't need to make another dollar from killing."

"The job does pay money, but that's not what any of us want," Russell said after glancing his cohorts' way.

"Yeah? And what else might I be wanting that you all do as well?" This question was from his heart. He honestly couldn't think of a single thing these men wanted that he didn't already have.

"It's . . . it's the chance to start fresh," Russell blurted. "If we do this one last job, Sheriff Brower promised our records would be cleared. That's what this job brings."

Scout crossed his arms over his chest and tried to look bored, but inside, every hope and dream that he'd had all his life was standing up at attention.

Of course, that embarrassed him something awful. The last thing in the world he wanted was to make a fool of himself. He didn't need any help with that.

But he was still fool enough to want to listen, and to listen good, not just bide his time until he could push them off his property. "Why don't we go inside and sit down?"

Russell hesitated. "You sure? Your wife, I mean, Mrs. Proffitt, may not want us near her."

"She'll want to hear this. And she can serve up something to eat." Now that he wasn't worried that they hadn't come to kill him, harm his wife, or bring him into a bounty hunter, he looked his guests over with a tad more sympathy. "Y'all look plumb tuckered," he drawled. "Been a rough couple of days?"

Hearing the change in his tone brought a visible relaxing to the band of four.

"We're worse than that," Russell said with a half smile, once again his dimple popping in his cheek. Making him look more naïve and innocent than Scout could ever remember being. "It's been a real hard couple of weeks."

"Then you really need something to eat." He started to turn from them, but decided to give the other men in Russell's merry band a warning gaze. "My wife has a tender heart. And she's shy. You'd best remember that."

The men knew enough to keep their silence as the three of them stepped to Russell's side.

Turning, Scout walked toward the house. When he entered the kitchen, his heart softened as he spied pure relief in Rosemarie's eyes. Ah, she, too, had been worried that the men had come to him with blood on their minds.

"Rose, I rode with one of these men in the Walton Gang. I know they scared you, but they don't mean you no harm."

"Oh?" Her fist grabbed a section of her skirt and held on tight. But that didn't stop the tightening around her mouth.

Scout ached to comfort her, to hold her in his arms and promise that she was never going to have to worry about being harmed again. To promise that he was always going to be by her side, protecting her.

But of course that wasn't who he was.

Keeping his face impassive, he said, "I need to speak with them, but they need to eat, too. Any way you can fix something up?"

"Of course I can." He didn't know where she found the strength, but she turned to the ragtag group of men and graciously inclined her head. "If you all would like to get cleaned up and perhaps sit in our sitting room, I'll put together some soup."

The four men, now looking so young standing without their weapons and in a woman's company just stared.

But Scout knew the look of longing that passed over one or two of them. He knew because he used to look like that. Until he figured out that wishing for things he couldn't have only wore a man out.

Russell spoke up. "Thank you, ma'am. Much obliged."

After another quick, hesitant look Scout's way, she turned to the stove. Leaving Scout to figure out to play host for the first time in his life.

"Spigot is out by the barn," he said gruffly.

"And the sitting room is on the other side of the kitchen." He felt like a fool giving directions, after all, there was only three rooms in their glorified shack.

But the men didn't act like they thought there was anything untoward about the directions. If anything, they looked even younger as they tromped back outside to follow directions.

Standing at the window, watching the men head back to the barn, he felt the presence of Rosemarie behind him. Though a part of him ached to turn around and gentle the look of worry in her eyes, he didn't dare.

It was his fault a band of killers was at their house.

And though he figured they wanted his help and feared his gun to be a worry to Rosemarie, he still felt bad about the interruption. If the men hadn't arrived, he had a feeling that he and Rose would be circling each other, thinking about the night before.

Wondering about the night to come. And for him, he would have enjoyed the feel of her in his arms again.

So instead, he kept his back to her. "Thank you for this," he said. "I hope it won't be too much trouble?"

"It won't be trouble, Scout. It won't be too much trouble at all."

A better man would offer more assurances. At the very least, he'd turn and brush his lips across her brow.

Instead, he nodded, then walked outside to wait for the men.

18

He ain't nothing like I imagined," Tuff said as he unbuttoned the top four buttons of his shirt.

Standing beside him, Russell scooped up two hands of icy water and splashed it across his face. The contact felt frigid, causing goosebumps to form on his forearms.

Only for sake of conversation — and to hide his own nervousness — did Russell comment. "What did you expect?"

"Somebody who didn't look so damned scary," Joe Bob blurted. "I tell you what, Russell, he looks like he could shoot you and then go have supper."

Remembering a time or two in the gang, when Mr. Walton had pretty much asked all of them to behave like that, Russell shivered.

Tuff noticed. "If you're so stinkin' cold, you should dry off, Russell. You're clean enough."

"Yeah. Sure."

He stepped away then and shook the excess water off his hands.

"You ever think about towels?" Scout murmured from behind his right shoulder.

Russell stiffened, then turned slowly to face him. "Like at home? I have."

"Before I left home, either my sister or my aunt would hand me a towel, fresh off the line when I was fixin' to take a bath." Looking off into the distance, Scout added, "I was so foolish, I used to resent the coddling. Thought accepting a towel meant I was weak. Childlike."

"I try not to think about home much," Russell said. Revealing that was easier than mentioning that his mother had been too worn down by his stepfather to offer him much of anything at all.

Scout's dark gaze darted his way and held on tight. "It still hurts, don't it? Remembering?"

Russell nodded.

"The first night I got here to claim this land, Rosemarie handed me a towel to use after I washed up." Lowering his voice, he added, "There was hardly anything here. She was afraid of me. But she still offered me something to dry off with."

Something needed to be said, though Russell knew he didn't have the words. "If a man hasn't lived on the trail, or ridden with men like Addison Kent or James Walton, he probably takes too much for granted," he finally said.

A new awareness — and maybe respect? — entered Scout's eyes. "I reckon you're right, Russell. The years with those men were difficult, indeed. You know, I've been standing here, looking at you and your friends, thinking that the four of you don't know nothing about much. But maybe you know more than I think."

Before Russell could figure out how to comment on that, Scout turned and walked toward the house.

"Come on, you boys," he ordered over his shoulder. "I want to know what you know. Now."

Joe Bob came rushing forward, the hair brushing his collar spiky and damp. When Scout was out of hearing distance, he whispered, "That man scares me like no other. It's like he's the devil."

Now if that wasn't the pot calling the kettle black, he didn't know what was. "He ain't the devil," Russell said. "Unless that's what we all are." When the other men halted, he looked at them all impatiently. "Are we?"

Tuff looked away, a dark sheen staining

his cheeks. "I don't know anymore."

Russell figured that was the most honest thing Tuff had probably ever said. It was right on the money, too. After all this time, all the hiding and lying and scrambling for safety, something right and honest had left them all.

Now all they were doing was figuring how to get it back.

"You boys coming?" Scout called out from the door. "Because I'm not eager to stand here and wait for you much longer. The temperature's dropped."

"Yeah, sure," Russell replied, picking up his pace.

They all left their muddy boots at the door, then padded silently through the kitchen to the miniscule sitting room where Scout waited.

When he gestured for them to sit, they sat, Russell choosing to forgo the settee that had seen better days long before the War of Northern Aggression.

Instead, he leaned against the back wall and held his tongue until Scout was staring at him.

"Speak," he said.

It was time to tell the whole story without prevaricating. "Well, um, first we heard that there was trouble on the other side of Lubbock. We heard the sheriff there was in need of men who had experience fighting outlaws. Then, on our way to the town we met a man from the area. He was broken and had been beaten up something awful."

Scout raised a brow. "Broken?"

"Collar bone shattered. Face swollen," Russell supplied.

"There was a red band around his neck," Joe Bob supplied. "Someone had tried to string him up, but he got loose."

"And?"

Only a man like Scout Proffitt would look so unmoved at the news. His hands clenched and unclenched like he was bored. "That it?"

"No, Mr. Proffitt. He weren't beat up for no reason. He'd been trying to save his cattle," Tuff explained. "Rustlers."

Scout frowned.

Russell took that as a good sign. Nobody cared for rustlers, and that was putting it lightly. "He was hungry, we shared our fire. And that's when he started telling us about the bunch of no-good cowards in the area, stealing cattle and horses. And he backed up the rumors we'd heard." He saw no need to tell Scout about the talk they'd heard from the harlots.

"Law involved?"

"That comes in later," Joe Bob said. When Scout narrowed his eyes at him, he amended his words. "Or now, if you'd like."

"What happened?" Impatience fluttered through his voice, letting them know their allotted explaining time was just about up.

"These rustlers, they're a tough bunch. The law can't seem get a handle on them. They're hurting women and children. Killed a man, too. Stealing cattle, even killing some in the process," Russell said softly. "It's bad enough that the sheriff is getting desperate and had sought out help."

"I still haven't heard why y'all are here."

"Sheriff Brower talked about how Mr. Miles Grant, the largest landowner in the area, was due to get hit hard. So he came up with a plan."

Scout went rigid. "Wait a minute. Did you say Miles Grant?"

"Yeah." For the first time, a ray of hope shone through all the doubts and worries that had consumed him since they'd hatched this godforsaken plan. Scout looked stunned. "Do you know him?"

"Yeah," he said. "Well, I know of him. We're kin."

Russell could hardly believe it. He'd practically lived by Scout's side for two years. Never once had the man spoken of his family. Shoot, Russell had pretty much assumed that Scout had sprouted up from the ground, like a bad seed. "I had no idea."

"Why would I have told you?"

Russell shrugged. Scout was right. They'd all been in a gang together. They'd slept together, fought together, killed together, scraped out an existence together.

But they hadn't been friends.

"Anyway," Joe Bob said impatiently, "Next thing you know, we were talking to the law and he made an offer. If we get you on board and the five of us track down the rustlers so they can be brought to trial, then our names can get cleared."

Scout laughed bitterly. "And you boys took him at his word?"

Joe Bob scowled. "We didn't make a mistake, Mr. Proffitt."

Scout turned to Russell. "You, of all people, know a sheriff will say just about anything to get what he wants. And that it never means squat."

Russell pulled a neatly squared sheet of paper from his pocket. "I have this for you. Sheriff Brower said it might make a difference to you."

"You read it yet?"

Russell wanted to lie, but he knew no good would come out of it. "Yes."

"And what does it say?"

"Sheriff Brower says there comes a time in every man's life to be more than he thought he could be." He swallowed. "He also says that if you come, he'll do his best to make sure you're not a wanted man any more. Not by the Marshals, not by the Rangers."

When Scout's face paled, Russell cleared his throat. "Mr. Proffitt?"

"Just call me Scout, boy."

Russell took a deep breath. "Scout, are you all right?"

Slowly, tired eyes raised and met his gaze. "Yeah," he practically whispered, his voice was so husky. "I would never have imagined that I could be. But yeah, I think I am."

"Supper is ready," Mrs. Proffitt said from the doorway. "It's not much, just cornbread and bean soup." She bit her lip. "And a dried apple pie."

Standing up, Russell knew he spoke for all of them. "Mrs. Proffitt, it sounds like more than enough. Thank you for your kindness."

Stepping forward, Scout pressed a hand on his shoulder before walking to his wife.

The man's touch had been his thanks, Russell realized.

Scout had been thanking him for paying his wife a kindness.

Russell watched how she gazed at her husband hesitantly, then her features slowly relaxed when he treated her to a smile.

Against his will, he thought of Nora, and of his middle-of-the-night daydreams, when he used to imagine such a scene. When he'd used to think that Nora would one day be his and no one else's.

And he wondered if some of Scout's dreams could come true, then maybe some of his could, too?

Then he remembered the things Nora had called him. And the way she'd backed away from him in fear.

And he realized that some dreams just weren't meant to come true.

19

Turned out Miss Annabeth wasn't as good of a nurse as she was a housekeeper.

"I'm sorry, Mr. Grant, but I just don't think I can nurse you no more," she said, looking a little peaked around the mouth.

"Why's that?" It was a struggle even saying two words. Because of that, Miles wasn't real pleased with the woman's statement. He hated to admit it, but he even needed help with the chamber pot. He had no idea how he was going to be able to manage things on his own. "Have I been that poor of a patient?"

She looked shamefaced. "No, sir, it ain't that. I just, well, I just ain't too good with blood." She swallowed hard. "Or open wounds. Or broken bones. And you've got a whole lots of trouble inside you, Boss."

Miles tilted his one good eye in her direction and held on tight. "Stay anyway," he muttered. Miss Annabeth was a woman who could corral a dozen unruly cowboys and keep them in line. No way was he going to believe one beat-up face was too much for her to bear.

"I'm sorry, sir. I know I'm letting you down, but I ain't got no stomach for this. I'm no good with blood. Makes me faint every time. And you've got a whole lot of blood there, Mr. Grant."

"I thought it was dried by now."

She closed her eyes and swayed a bit. "This is what I'm talking about. It's no good to try and persuade me to get over this phobia of mine." Edging closer to the door, she gave a little wave. "I'm real sorry. I promise, I am. But I really gotta go."

When her hand curved around the door handle, he started getting nervous. "Miss Annabeth, it pains to admit it, but I can't handle myself on my own." If he could flush with embarrassment, he would.

"Oh, I know you need help," she replied. Almost like she never doubted his neediness. "But don't fret, sir." Looking a fair bit brighter, she added, "I didn't leave you hanging. I got you some help."

Feeling alarmed, he raised a hand to halt her. Then struggled to sit up. "Who? Who did you find?"

"Oh, Mr. Grant! You should go lay back

down! You're bleeding again!"

"Miss Annabeth, don't you leave just yet. Who did you get?"

"Uh . . . ugh." She gave him one last apologetic look before darting out the door. "I really am sorry," she squeaked again before she shut the door tight.

Now alone, Miles tilted his head back on the pillow and gave into the pain. Boy howdy, did he hurt something awful. His face felt like shredded barbecue, and his arms and chest felt like a slew of ornery cows had had their own little stampede on them.

But worse than his injuries were his worries. The Jones Gang was indeed alive and well and seemed certain to cause as much trouble as possible in the area. And now that he was out of commission, Miles had no idea who they'd attack next.

He'd feel guilty for the rest of his life if one of his hands got hurt, too.

Old doubts and insecurities came back to him, tenfold. For the first time in two years, he recalled the type of man he'd been when Clayton Proffitt had first taken Vanessa under his care and had taken her from the ranch.

Miles had been a far different person then. Worried about his own hide and no one else's, he'd accompanied his stepfather on a cross-country journey in an attempt to get her back. It had been grueling, both because of the urgent journey, but also because Price had been so evil.

And Miles hadn't made up his mind yet to be better than he was.

For a time he'd followed Price and had tried to earn his approval. But Price's mind hadn't been on Miles — he'd been intent on locating Clayton, bringing Vanessa back home to abuse her, and to sample as many women and liquors as he'd been able to along the way.

Only after discovering the Word and making great changes in his life did he become the person he wanted to be. He'd finally decided that he'd earned the hands respect.

But now he was starting to realize that he'd never really been tested during these last two years. When he'd returned to the ranch after his journey to Colorado, both he and the hands had been eager to push the past behind them. He'd earned their respect fairly, but only by being hardworking and fair every day.

Rustlers were a far different story. He was tired, in pain, and hopelessly out of his league. Compounding it all was the curious sense of inevitability. He knew if he didn't handle everything well, he could very well lose everything he'd just gotten back.

Or maybe earned for the very first time.

Two knocks preceded the door opening. "Mr. Grant, are you decent?" a somewhat raspy feminine voice called out. "Can I come on in?"

"Tracy? That you?" Oh, please don't let it be her.

But his bad luck seemed to be in no hurry to change its course.

"It's me," she said as she stepped inside, holding a pan of water and a cloth draped over one arm. "Miss Annabeth stopped over at the hotel early this morning. When she told me about you, and about how she wasn't all that good of a nurse, I told her I'd be happy to lend a hand."

This was horrible. Almost worse than getting beaten all over again. "Over my dead body."

She stopped, staring at him in shock. He didn't blame her surprise — he hadn't intended to actually say the words out loud.

"I'm sorry, Tracy. It ain't nothing personal." Only that it was, of course, all personal. He didn't even want her seeing him like this, let alone tend to his wounds.

Let alone tend to his other needs.

After another pause, she walked forward,

a new determined look in her eyes. "I'm sorry my being here disappoints you, but you might as well learn to live with it. I'm your only option, you see."

Oh, she was acting like he was choosing a different partner to dance with. "I'm obliged, but I don't need your help."

"You're a mess, Miles," she retorted hotly. Completely taking him aback by using his Christian name. "Fact is, there is no one else to nurse you. The hands are either talking with the sheriff or tending to the stock. Doc Holmes in Camp Hope is stuck at a baby's bedside — she's dying of scarlet fever.

"The other women around here are too flighty to do what needs to be done. And Annabeth . . ."

"Miss Annabeth can't deal with me," Miles finished.

With a shrug, Tracy set the pan on the table by his bed and carefully dipped the cloth across her arm. "She can't help it, I guess. Not everyone is a good nurse."

"I have a hard time believing that the sight of blood makes her so squeamish. I've seen her wring a chicken's neck."

For the first time, a flash of humor appeared in her eyes. "I don't think she cares about chickens like she does you, Miles.

Now hold still."

He did as she bid, holding himself stiffly as he waited for the pain of her fingers against his skin. But to his surprise, her touch wasn't hard and brusque. It was featherlight and fine. So light he hardly noticed it.

Well, noticed the pain. Instead, he found himself trying to catch a whiff of her scent. She smelled like lemons and wildflowers. How did she ever get that scent, he wondered. He hadn't seen a lemon in ages.

"Hold still," she murmured. "This was a bad one." She dabbed at the cut near his mouth, the cloth brushing against his lips. Suddenly, his mouth didn't feel so parched and dry.

Instead, he felt his lips part slightly, as if they were moving on their own account.

Like he was imagining a kiss.

A kiss? He snapped his mouth shut and closed his eyes, too, as his shameful thoughts took center stage. Afraid Tracy would suddenly be able to start reading minds.

She leaned forward. A wayward strand of her hair brushed across his shoulder, fell into the crevice of his neck, and settled in. He felt its touch as clearly as if she'd laid a hand on his bare skin. He winced, not liking the direction his thoughts were going.

She was like a sister to him. A sister.

"Am I hurting you, Mr. Grant?"

"Not at all," he croaked.

She leaned back a bit. "I think I've gotten everything that I can on your face." Reaching out, she started unbuttoning his shirt.

He jumped. "What in the Sam-hill are you doing?"

"Same thing I've been doing since I got here, of course. I'm trying to get you cleaned up. Miss Annabeth told me you got beaten up good. And by the looks of this ragtag shirt, she wasn't kidding."

Like a church-going biddy, he grabbed at the neckline of his shirt and held on tight. "There's no call for you to start undressing me, Tracy."

A line formed between his brows. "But —"

It was time to do what was right, even if it didn't feel that way. Her nearness was making him uncomfortable. And until he figured out if he was uncomfortable because of his lack of romantic feelings toward her . . . or because of them, keeping some space between them was a good idea. "If you go now, I won't tell anybody about how you've been making untoward advances in my direction."

She froze. "You and I both know that isn't

what I've been doing."

"We also know that the way you're acting, all wantonly and all, it ain't seemly. You need to get on out of here before you embarrass yourself."

Scrambling to her feet, Tracy backed away, looking like he'd slapped her. "I can't believe I even came in here, hoping to do a good deed. You are the most ungrateful man I've ever met! I should've known better."

"I should've known better than to have let you in."

Spinning on her heel, she turned and ran out the door.

As soon as the door shut with a slam, Miles leaned back against his pillow with a groan.

Now his heart felt like it was breaking in two. Tracy Wood was a sweet woman, and never did she deserve his treatment of her. When he was healed, he was going to have to think of a way to make things right between them.

With some resignation, he realized what he needed to do. He needed help, and not just in the form of hired guns.

He needed the help and support that only family give him. Forcing himself to his feet, he gritted his teeth as he located his boots and put them on.

Tears pricked his eyes when he shifted his shoulders so he could fit his arms into his coat.

Then he followed Tracy's path out the door and walked toward the bank building. It was time to send another telegraph to Clayton. By now he should be fairly close. He decided to send a telegraph to Timber Ridge, the small town near where Clayton's preacher friend lived.

The last thing in the world he wanted was for Clayton to arrive, unprepared. And shoot — if he was about to lose his land to a band of cutthroat rustlers and his humanity to the sure aim of a hired gun, he wanted family to witness it.

There were some things a man shouldn't do alone.

20

Carefully, Rosemarie washed and dried each dish and bowl as she listened to fragments of the men's conversation float her way from the other room.

We need you . . . they've murdered two men that we know about.

They'll hit more ranches, mark my words.

The sheriff's involved.

As Rosemarie listened to the cadence of the voices rise and fall, and heard the dark promise of the whispered dangers, she gulped. All of it was very disturbing.

She was thankful for the work to keep her hands busy. Otherwise, she'd be tempted to lurk by the door just to hear the conversation a little bit better. Because surely she was misunderstanding the gist of it all?

Rustlers at Miles Grant's ranch. Guns. Night watches. Last chance. Help needed.

Sheriff Brower told us flat-out that he needed you.

No one needs me.

You're wrong, Scout.

"Yes, you're wrong, Scout," she murmured. She needed him.

She looked at the doorway warily for about the hundredth time. Rosemarie wasn't sure, but she was fairly certain the men who'd arrived were getting ready to escort him to hunt down a band of bad men so down on their luck that they had nothing more to lose.

She shivered at the thought of Scout going on a mission like that. Why, anything could happen — he could get himself killed!

Then, just as quickly, Rosemarie berated herself. Who'd she think she married? Scout was kind to her, but that didn't change who he was. No matter how handsome he was, or how well he treated her, or how loved he'd made her feel in the darkened bedroom, Scout Proffitt was really only one thing: a known killer and outlaw. A true sinner.

Not that she was any better. She'd known the worst about him, and she'd still been willing to live with him.

No, she'd done even worse than that. She'd married him, all for the sake of some kind of mistaken need for propriety. She, a woman who'd never been held in anyone's high esteem.

Wiping a bowl, she blanched. No, marrying hadn't been the worst thing she'd done. She'd bedded him, all so there would never be any doubt of the sanctity of their marriage.

As if she'd ever deserved that.

Now she was his wife in every way possible. Their vows forever bound them to a life together.

But . . . none of that really mattered. The fact was she owed him her loyalty. No, it was more than that. She owed him everything.

After all, if she'd been left to her own, there was a very good chance that she'd either be dead or reduced to something far worse than a gunslinger's wife.

Rubbing a bowl until it shone, she knew she should be concentrating on those things.

But the rest of her being warred with her Christian sensibilities. She'd now crossed the line between attempting to be a woman of faith and not caring about who she'd become.

Perhaps that was what survival did to a person? It twisted and turned her inside out, so that her most fragile and delicate parts were laid out to be trampled on and injured. And when things got better, she'd put herself together as quickly and painlessly as possible. But unfortunately, all her parts were clipped and fractured.

Though she was alive and married, she wasn't the kind of woman she could respect anymore. She couldn't be, right? What kind of woman was willing to do so much in order to survive?

The men's voices grew louder. Now she had no difficulty at all in determining what was being said.

We need you, Mr. Proffitt. Surely you need this, too? What choice do you have, anyway? No matter how much finesse or decorating we try to do to ourselves, one thing's always the same. We don't deserve much.

With a bit of shock, Rosemarie realized that man could've been talking to her. She'd never thought she deserved much. That was why she hadn't tried harder to be noticed in her home.

Why she hadn't fought all that much when her mother decided to leave her at the ranch instead of taking her with her.

And why she'd been willing to stay with a man she didn't trust and was almost afraid of.

She hadn't thought she deserved much better.

And that, she decided, was a real crying shame.

The voices got even louder. Rosemarie stilled, listening to the argument about leaving for the Circle Z tonight. And how long it would take to put the rustlers back in their place in the world.

She bit her lip. Scout would be leaving tonight? Suddenly, it didn't matter any longer whether or not she deserved the life she'd been given. Now all that mattered was that there was a very real possibility that she was going to lose Scout before she'd gotten hardly a chance to love him. Love him?

How could that be?

"Rosemarie, you're shaking. Is something wrong?"

Everything was wrong. Turning around, she bit her lip hard to bring some color back into her cheeks. "Scout, I'm sorry! I didn't hear you come in. Was there something you needed?"

His gaze slid over her slowly, as carefully as if it had been his hand caressing her skin. "I don't need a thing, honey," he drawled. "I only came in to let you know that the men are going to bed down in the barn."

So they would be alone in the house. She raised her chin. Met his dark gaze.

She forced herself to think of the men and not the way her heart was suddenly beating a little too fast. "Ah, do you think they'll be okay out there? It's pretty cold out." But Lord help her, she had no desire to have them sleep under the same roof as she and Scout.

He stepped closer, bringing with him warmth and the faint scent of tobacco and leather. "They'll be all right, sugar. Believe me, they've slept in worse places than on the floor of a barn. I have, too."

Though she knew he was trying to make her feel better, it didn't. Now that she knew Scout was so much more than a man to be feared, she wondered what kind of a toll living like that for years had on a man.

"Are you going with them?" She hoped not. She wanted to talk to him about what the men wanted. And, damn her soul, she wanted him to herself. If only for just a little bit longer.

He paused. "Turn around, Rose," he said softly.

When she turned, he stepped closer, wrapping his work-hardened fingers around her upper arms. Now they stood so close to each other that her skirts melded into his stance. Her cotton blouse met his thicker shirt.

And she felt his breath against her skin. "Don't be afraid," he rasped. "Though I know those men, I'm not one of them. I'm not like them. Not anymore."

If he wasn't like those men, who was he like? She didn't know another person who was like the man who held her so tightly against him.

Because he was staring at her so intently. Because he looked like he would give just about anything for her to trust him, she said the words that she knew would mean the most to him. "I'm not afraid. I'm not afraid of you, Scout."

His eyelids lowered. "Good," he murmured. Just as he brushed her lips with his own.

The kiss was chaste. The feelings behind it? Anything but.

He stepped away. "I should know better than to hold you so close in the kitchen," he said with a smile. "Especially since holding you makes me forget about the men in the other room."

When he stepped away and his touch wasn't filling all her senses, she forced herself to speak. "Scout, are you going to accept their offer?"

His dark eyes flashed black. "I guess I should've known you would've heard a lot of that."

"I heard. It was hard not to." Unable to tolerate distance between them again, she reached out and flattened her hand on his chest. "I just want to know what's going on. That's all."

"That's your right. We'll talk about this more when we're alone." Running two fingers along her cheek, he said, "Will you heat up some water? It's been a long day. I want to bathe."

"Of course."

He flashed another smile before briefly going into the parlor. Minutes later, he was escorting the band of four through the kitchen and back out into the chilly darkness. Standing with her back against the cabinets, she watched the men pass in front of her. Each one was taller and more solid looking than the next. And each one wore some semblance of the haunted expression Scout had worn when she'd first seen him.

Russell tipped his hat as he passed. "Ma'am."

She nodded.

"Obliged for the soup and coffee, Mrs. Proffitt," the second man said. She nodded in reply to him as well.

Then did the same thing to the next two men.

When she was alone, she lifted the kettle and began the long process of heating enough water for a man like Scout to bathe in. In the past, she would have begrudged the chore.

Tonight? She was glad of it. After all, there was a very good chance she was going to be alone again.

Scout was back within the hour.

"Your bath is just about ready," she said when the door opened again.

He grinned. "That's the best news I've had all day." Crossing to the back wall of the kitchen, he looked longingly at the large tub she'd placed on the floor in front of the fire. It was almost filled. When he picked up a large pitcher, he headed toward the door. "I'll go pump some more water. Be right back," he said over his shoulder.

And sure enough, he was. Soon they were preparing him a bath as if they'd done the task a hundred times before.

But, of course, they'd never done anything like this.

Only when he started undressing did she become aware of how much they still had to learn about each other.

Her husband, on the other hand, seemed to have no such reservations. In no time at all, he was as bare as a babe and sighing when the heated water warmed his skin.

Quickly, she turned around.

Scout chuckled but didn't remark on her shyness. Instead, she heard him soaping his skin, shifting and splashing with the abandonment of a river otter. Against her will, she relaxed. In some ways, Scout Proffitt was one of the easiest people she'd ever been around. There was little artifice about him when it came to the most basic of comforts. He liked being clean, and he liked to eat.

"Hand me that kettle, would you, sweetheart?"

Keeping her eyes averted, otherwise, she was sure she would end up staring at his bare skin, Rosemarie handed him the kettle of steaming water quickly. "Careful. It's hot."

"I know." With methodical movements, he mixed the hot water in with the cool, then poured it over his soapy shoulders. To her surprise, she found herself laughing with him as water slid off his body and splashed to the sides of the tub and on the floor surrounding him.

Especially since he didn't look the slightest bit ashamed of his mess. On the contrary, he looked almost boyish.

"You certainly are no neater than a child."

"You are right about that, ma'am." After shaking his head sharply, making his hair stand on end, he said, "Hand me a sheet, would you?"

She did as he bid, keeping her eyes averted when he got to his feet and dried off. All too soon, the damp sheet lay on the floor and he was reaching for a pair of denims. When he got dressed, he left his shirt untucked and only partially buttoned. His denims hung loosely at his hips.

His black hair was sticking up every which way, his skin smelled clean and fresh. His eyes were brighter, and his smile was perfect.

In short, he had never looked more handsome.

Disturbed by the train of her thoughts, Rosemarie kept busy, fussing with dishes that didn't need cleaning and counters that didn't need wiping down. Soon, he, too, was attacking chores with a gumption that was unwarranted.

Finally, when the tub had been emptied, the floor wiped as clean as the counters, and there was nothing else left to do, Scout sat down on the lone kitchen chair.

"There's no way to say this except right out. I think I'm going to have to go with those boys, Rosemarie."

"But I heard talk about rustlers and guns."

He nodded. "All that's a part of it."

She didn't want to nag, but she couldn't help the next words. "But you could get hurt."

"I know." He swallowed. "Fact is, there's a good chance I won't return. Rustlers aren't known to be all that reliable of opponents. But the fact is, I don't think I have a choice in the matter. Not really, anyway."

She'd lived most of her life without choices. But this didn't seem the same at all. "Why do you say that?"

"There's been an offer from a sheriff who's desperate for help." He glanced her way, his dark eyes looking almost like a plea for understanding. If he'd been that kind of a man. "If I help him with some men in his area, he's promised to help me. I might not be a wanted man anymore. I might not have to keep living in fear that some Ranger is going to ride in and take me into custody."

"I don't see how a small-town sheriff can have so much pull." Surely the lawman was just telling Scout anything at all in order to get him into his territory. "It might even be a trap."

"I was wondering the same thing, but then Russell told me who the sheriff was who made the offer."

"And that meant something to you?"

"Uh-huh. It's a man by the name of Brower. He's a formidable man, feared by many and respected by most everyone I've ever met."

"Have you met him?"

He chuckled softly. "More or less, and not in the best of circumstances."

"What happened?"

"It was years ago — before I hooked up with the Walton Gang. I was in north Texas, trying to get a night or two of sleep in a little shack of a hotel. One evening when I was in the bar, a pair of men wandered in, looking for trouble." His expression turned pained as the memory returned sharp and clear. "They were men down on their luck. Vagrants, most likely." His gaze turned shuttered. "They had on old pieces of uniforms. One of the men had a nasty-looking scar over the whole side of his face."

Rosemarie shivered. She'd seen men like that a time or two in Broken Promise. Their scent had been sharp and pungent, and their mismatched uniforms made her wonder how they'd come about the clothing. Some wore scars, some wore their hair long and matted. Their eyes had been glazed, but their senses had been sharp. And all of them had always looked as if they had nothing in the world to lose.

Once, when an especially scarred man had nodded her way and had said hello, she'd frozen. She hadn't known whether to face him or run.

It had been one of the few times her father had tried to protect her. "Stay away from those men, Rose," he'd ordered grimly. "Pain and suffering don't mean much to them."

With a sigh, Scout continued. "When they entered the saloon, I saw them coming. I used to sit in the back of the saloons, facing the door. Anyway, the moment I saw them, I knew they meant trouble. And they were trouble. Right away, they started manhandling the whores." He averted his eyes. "I'm sorry, Rosemarie, I mean, the uh, women."

"I understand," she said dryly.

After sharing a small smile with her, he finished the story. "Well, as you can imagine, I let my fool mouth get involved when one of the women got her dress torn. Then, they noticed me and guessed who I was."

"They knew you were Scout Proffitt?"

He nodded, his lips turning into a thin line. "They saw what they wanted to see, Rose. They saw a challenge with a pair of ivory-handled six-shooters. I wasn't eager to prove myself."

"What did you do?"

"One of them pushed the woman to the floor, grabbed at the waist of his denims . . . and I realized then and there they'd meant to goad me, come hell or high water. They were going to do whatever it took, even if it meant harming an innocent woman in the process."

She now knew him well enough to know what he did. There was no way the man she married was going to let a woman be violated in front of him. "You shot them, didn't you?"

"Yeah. But only after trying to talk them off a cliff, as it were. But sometimes a man doesn't want to back down from a fight. Even if it means the only other way out is death."

"And that Sherriff Brower was there?"

He grimaced. "Indeed, Brower saw it all. I'd been prepared to run, but there had been no need. The women were crying, and the bartender was grateful. Turned out those men had been causing a heap of trouble for quite a while."

Clearing his throat, he said, "So, if anyone can help me, it would be Sheriff Brower. The last thing he said to me before I left town was that I had surprised him. That for the first time in his life, he'd realized that he'd been taken in by dime novels and exaggerated rumors."

"If he is so great, why can't he take care of the rustlers? Or the men who showed up here?"

"Sheriff Brower can't take care of them without going through the law. And as for Russell and Tuff and the others?" He shook his head. "Fact is, they're not good enough."

"Good enough?"

He frowned. "You know what I mean. They're green. They might talk tough, but there's a world of difference between following orders, or killing a man in a moment of passion . . . and accepting a job as a mercenary."

"You're not like that, Scout." Though he might call himself evil and beyond redemption, she knew differently. No man as coldhearted as he made himself out to be would have let her stay on with him.

Or would have married her.

"Maybe not now. But believe me, I have been. But if you want me to say it, I will. I can shoot better than most men can ride a horse, Rosemarie. I don't miss. Ever."

"But —"

"And I've really got nothing to lose and whole lot to gain."

When she turned to meet his gaze, she knew his expression mirrored her own. Because his was filled with pain and regret.

22

What did he have to lose? Only a convenient wife.

She, on the other hand, could lose everything.

He had her. He was risking their relationship. And what if he died? Or what if it was simply a trap — and someone had finally come up with a way to lure him out of the darkness? "Are you sure you've got nothing to lose?" she said bitterly.

He hesitated. "Rosemarie, there's something else, too. The ranch that they're doing so much damage to . . . the man they just about killed when he dared to stand up to them?"

"Yes?"

"It's Miles Grant, owner of the Circle Z. He's my brother-in-law." A new vulnerability entered his eyes. "Do you understand now? Rose, I've gotta go. I don't have much family, and for most of my life, I'd tried my best to shield myself from them. But now I have a chance to do something to make a difference to them."

She wanted to tell them that just being alive would make the difference to people who cared about him.

But family was something more, and what he wanted to do was something to be proud of.

Since she knew firsthand what it was like, to live a life wishing for a chance to do some good, to get redemption, she knew there was only one thing to say. "When will you go?"

"Tomorrow before dawn."

Pure fear rolled up her spine. "So soon?" she blurted. When his expression turned pained, she tried to explain herself. "I mean, shouldn't you wait a bit? I mean, I imagine you men need to plan."

"We have a plan."

His voice was so different now. Cold and hard. It matched his expression exactly. Gone was her defender, the man who had promised her that she'd never regret their marriage vows. Instead she was faced with the harsh killer that the rest of the world knew.

She ached to have him back. "Or," she said desperately, "I imagine those men are tired from riding all day to get here. Surely even another day off the back of a horse would be much appreciated."

A muscle in his jaw jumped. "They'll be fine. They want to get this over with, too."

She grappled for any excuse. "But what about the horses? I bet they need to rest? If you push them too hard, one can come up lame —"

"The horses are fine, too, sugar," he interrupted. "We're not going to delay this."

"I understand." She turned away, embarrassed to let him see how desperately she longed for him to stay by her side. But instead of walking away, he touched her left shoulder, his callused, warm hand creating a link between them that hadn't been there before. "Rosemarie, I'd be lying if I said I didn't know that you wanted me to stay. And I'll be honest with you, there's a part of me that wishes Russell and his friends never showed up. But they did."

When he paused, the tension between them grew. She could feel how conflicted he was, and how unused he was to explaining himself to a woman.

Reaching up, she covered his palm with her right hand. As it had been with her, she felt the tension in his body ease. "Thank you for saying that."

Doubt and a new awareness filled his eyes. "Rosemarie, truly, it's better that we go now. If it's a trap, I want to know right away. Besides, the sheriff needs help now, and I want to be that help." He smiled softly. "I have to say I've never been recruited by the other side of the law, and I'm finding myself kind of liking that."

She couldn't help it, she smiled. "I suppose I can understand that."

Looking pleased, he nodded. "See? There's really no reason to wait."

There was to her. She'd just gotten him. She'd just begun to feel like she was needed. She'd just starting living again and thinking about the future instead of only living in regret of the past. "I understand now," she finally replied. Though even to her ears, she sounded wan and defeated.

Compassion and tenderness appeared in his gaze as he shook his head slowly. "No, sugar, I know you still don't understand. But maybe the Lord does. Maybe he's looking down from heaven, directing all of this, leading Russell to your ranch."

"Our ranch," she said loyally. "You bought it, fair and square."

He quirked an eyebrow. "Is a ranch bought in a card game bought fair and square?"

Reflecting about where she'd been before

Scout had arrived, and how much her life had changed for the better, she nodded. "I think it is definitely fair." At least for her, anyway. She'd lived the majority of her life feeling guilty and giving penance for an accident. Scout's arrival had changed everything. Now, instead of trying unsuccessfully to make amends for the past, she was dealing with the present.

And that was a very good change, indeed.

Scout's hand trailed from her shoulder, past her elbow, finally curving around her hand in a secure clasp. She loosened her fingers, letting his link through hers. "Rosemarie, I promise, I'm not running away from you. I need to do this last job in order to get a life."

"To get it back."

"No, honey, to begin one. Until I arrived here, I'd only been subsisting. Barely getting by. Barely surviving."

Barely surviving. She knew exactly what he meant.

"Then, and only then, will I be worthy of you."

"Worthy? Scout, you shouldn't think that way. I'm not anyone who you should feel inferior to."

"Don't ever say that again. Not in my presence."

While she gaped at him in astonishment, he leaned down and kissed her. His lips were tender, firm. Coaxing her closer, igniting the memories of being in his arms the night before. Reminding her of how she'd felt, just for a few minutes. Feeling secure and loved.

Stepping closer, she leaned in to him, enjoying the feel of his cotton shirt under her palm, of the feel of his scratchy cheek against her smooth one.

"Rosemarie," he whispered, "I want one more night with you."

She realized then that he wasn't about to push her. He was waiting for her to make the decision. It was her choice. She could accept his love, accept what he was giving her . . . or she could turn it away and hold all her insecurities and doubts and pain close to her heart.

But she'd already had a lifetime of that.

"I want that, too," she said.

Little by little his lips curved. His gaze warmed. And then, in the dim, glowing light of burning embers of a kitchen stove, he held out his hand and led her to bed.

For just one more night. For possibly, the very last time.

The dawn broke in glorious shades of

amber and rose, rising over the rugged ter-
rain like an invitation from the Lord to
begin a new day.

Seated on his gelding by Scout Proffitt's
side, Russell hoped and prayed that he
made the right decision about recruiting
Scout to help out the folks of Camp Hope.
He'd never had much use for sheriffs — and
even wealthy landowners like Miles Grant
could be as deceitful as the most notorious
outlaw.

He'd learned a lot during the last few
years, and that knowledge had kept him
alive. More than anything, he'd learned that
people lied and cheated all the time, and
there was a very good chance that the sheriff
of Camp Hope had come up with his story
for the sole reason of drawing Scout Proffitt
out of hiding.

Which made him feel not only like a fool,
but also like the worst sort of man. It took a
real idiot to promise something to Scout
Proffitt without being completely sure that
the promise could be delivered.

As he glanced at Scout, who sat so straight
and easy on his horse, not a bit of worry or
stress lining his brow, Russell wished he had
a bit more of Scout's confidence.

Okay, he wished he had a whole lot more
of the other man's confidence.

But all he was blessed with was an anxious tongue, ready to deliver him to an early death — or at least a whole lot of pain.

But even given that, he still felt compelled to say something. If only for his own peace of mind. If he was bringing Scout Proffitt to his death, then he wanted the man to know that he hadn't done it intentionally.

"I sought you out because I'm a desperate man, Mr. Proffitt. I thought you might be, too." The moment the words left his mouth, he winced. If a bullet was headed his way, it was no less than he deserved for pushing the man like he was.

But instead of looking perturbed, the man let out a bark of laughter. "Is that so?" he drawled. "If that's the case, you must have been up to no good for the last year. And call me Scout, Russell. Things haven't changed all that much between us."

"All right then." He took a deep breath. "Scout, I am real serious, here. When we heard all the promises Sheriff Brower had given, I knew I had to at least try. I'd do a lot to live out in the open. But now I'm starting to worry he might've been pulling my leg."

"What made you start doubting? You sounded pretty confident last evening." Gesturing behind them, he said, "Anything changed?"

"No. At least, not with the other men."

"Then with who?"

"It was just a feeling I had." Already beginning to regret this conversation, and very aware of the other men in their group riding behind them, he cleared his throat. "You know, it don't matter. Forget about it."

Scout looked at him hard and long, then nodded. "I can do that."

Scout seemed to be a man of his word. For the next mile or so, the man stayed silent, seeming to enjoy keeping his gaze firmly on the horizon, watching the sun rise and greet the day.

Every so often, he would rest his hand on his horse's neck, calming it. Maybe encouraging it?

The temperature was frigid and cold. Their brisk pace kept a cool breeze chafing their ears, making his eyes and nose run. More than once, Russell had to brush his kerchief against his skin to dab up wayward tears.

Scout, on the other hand, seemed impervious to such things as tears or runny noses. His skin didn't turn pink. his posture didn't stiffen as the cold edged into his bones.

"I've always thought favors were strange

293

things," he said, breaking the peace. "I've never trusted a man who needed help."

Russell swallowed hard. He'd be dead if he'd never asked for help. "Why is that?"

"I didn't understand the concept of it," he replied after a while. "Maybe it's because of my brother. He was the most upstanding man I knew. And he led men into battle. He led men into peace. He didn't ask them for help." Once again, he rubbed his horse's flank. "I ended up working alone. I liked depending on myself. Never did I want to have to worry about other people turning on me."

Russell had heard Scout talk of his brother before. "You speaking of Clayton?"

"I am." A thread of amusement entered his tone. "Listen to this: Clayton married Vanessa Grant, who is Miles Grant's sister. Though I've never met the man, we're family. That's why I said yes to you — because Clayton would have said yes. Even if I have my doubts, I'm doing this because I think my brother would do it."

Russell thought about Scout's words. But what really struck him was the tone of his voice. The man truly didn't believe he was worthy of his brother, didn't think he was near as good.

"You led us," he blurted. "Back with Mr.

Walton."

"Mr. Walton. Even after all this time, we can't help but address that man with respect, can we?"

"I guess not." Russell flashed an awkward smile. "I never thought about James Walton in any other way."

"He didn't want us to. That was part of his charm," he added dryly.

"But when we were with him, a lot of us were grateful for your leadership."

Scout shook his head. "You shouldn't be grateful for anything that I've done. Will was the one who turned things around."

Russell didn't even try to hide his disdain for the U.S. Marshal. "Will lied to all of us."

"For good reason, I think."

"It got you kicked out of the gang."

"Will's actions saved my life," Scout corrected. "And, no, I am not about to start talking to you about that."

The ground below them turned rocky. Both Russell and Scout slowed, turning their attention to the needs of their horses.

But though Scout didn't seem to need to finish the conversation, Russell did. "Scout, I just wanted to say that if this is a trap, that if we're all about to arrive at the Circle Z, just to get gunned down like a flock of foolish birds, well, I just wanted to say I was real sorry." While he still had the chance, that was.

"Apology accepted. Though I suppose I should tell you that I never expected to survive this. So, please don't waste your worries on me. I'm not worth it . . . and I've never expected your concern."

Russell knew he should be tougher. Stronger. Braver. But he couldn't resist saying what had been settled in his heart. "I know we shouldn't expect much . . . but if what those men said is true, will we get to live our lives like everyone else?"

"If it saves our lives and we get to live like everyone else even for one day? Shoot. I think then we'd be the luckiest sons of guns in the whole state of Texas."

Russell doubted that would ever happen. But thinking about it, imagining it? It was a wonderful dream.

23

"You're getting around pretty good for a dead man," Slim commented when Miles limped his way into the barn.

His foreman was leaning against the back wall of the tack room, an oiled cloth in one hand. Before Miles had entered the barn, he'd been bent over a finely tooled saddle that had once been Miles's father's. On the other side of the small room was Big Jim, bent over a pair of bridles.

Both men were working hard, just like they always did. Which, of course, shamed him. He'd inherited the ranch. But instead of being trained since birth to be deserving of the accomplishment, he'd always kept to the background. Both his father and the former foreman, Clayton Proffitt, had never had much confidence in him.

Consequently, he'd never spent a day oiling saddles and bridles. He hadn't mucked out the same stalls hundreds of times or sported a cantaloupe-sized bruise from a scuffle with a heifer.

What's more, everyone knew it.

But his feelings of inferiority weren't these men's burdens. Instead, he kept his chin high and his expression light. Teasing them right back. "I've been getting that a lot today. Thanks for the reminder."

The other men didn't laugh. "The rustlers beat you good, Mr. Grant," Slim murmured. "You look durn near black and blue."

"Not so much that I couldn't be put together again," he said lightly. He hated being reminded that he looked so bruised. Most likely, any other man in the area wouldn't have let himself get beat up half so badly.

The hands most likely knew that, too.

The other men's expressions sobered. "No offense, Mr. Grant, but how come you're out here in the barn?" Big Jim asked. "Don't you think you should be taking it easy?"

"You should be lying down. Taking a rest," Slim added.

He hated that the men thought even walking to the barn was too much for him. "I'm okay. Just a little scratched up."

Big Jim winced. "We saw Miss Annabeth at chow. She told us she couldn't even doctor you, you looked so torn up. Mr. Grant, it's true. You do look a mite worse for wear."

The last thing Miles needed in his life was another person talking about how bad he looked. "I would've thought Miss Annabeth could hold her tongue better."

"You can't fault her for talking. We all were asking her questions," Slim said. "You didn't tell us much."

"There was nothing to say."

Jim glared. "Mr. Grant, your face is so misshapen, it's a wonder you can see or talk."

The temptation to touch his swollen cheek, to wipe at his watering eyes was strong. Matter of fact, his face felt like it could never be put back together again. His bones felt displaced, and his right eye had such a shooting pain behind it that he didn't know when he'd ever be able to see clearly.

But instead of giving in to the pain — and the humiliation — he chuckled. "I've known Miss Annabeth for years. All this time, I thought she was invincible. But a little bit of blood has sure set her off something awful. I guess she's shown me that we all have our weaknesses."

Stepping away from his position against the wall, Big Jim looked ready to take Miles's elbow and lead him away like a little old lady. "Mr. Grant, I know you don't want to hear this, but you should really go back inside. I rode over to the Bar M this morning and hired on six men to help us for a while. We'll get along fine without you."

That's what he was afraid of. "They can spare the men?"

"They haven't been attacked like we have. Old Mr. Jamison told me he was happy to give you a hand."

Though it made no sense, Miles found exception to that phrase. There was no giving him a hand. He'd been sitting around while everyone else was doing their job. And since he'd spent much of his childhood doing that — standing off to the side while others did what had to be done — the idea of doing it now set about as well with him as a swarm of locusts.

Stewing on that, his temper flared. "I'm not going to be sitting in bed while you men are working your hides off defending my property. I know y'all think I can't handle hard work, but I can. And I intend to do my part around here. Finally."

Both men stilled. "Mr. Grant, I never said that you ain't a hard worker. I ain't disloyal," Slim said. To Miles's surprise, Slim's voice sounded contrite. And more than a little bit hurt. "We're trying to help you, Boss. That's all."

And that made Miles feel even more frustrated with himself. He ached to be a better leader, a stronger man. He wanted so badly to be more like Clayton.

While he appreciated their words, he didn't want to sugarcoat his faults. "Come now. You men have been here a long time. We both know my history. There's a whole lot of things I'm not."

He held his breath as Slim and Big Jim shared a knowing glance. His heart — that traitorous organ — began to beat faster as the two men silently drew straws over who was going to have to talk first. But Miles forced himself to stand tall and proud. Well, as well as a man who'd been beaten down like a punching bag could.

"We were here with your dad, and with Clayton, and with Price Venture," Big Jim said at last, uttering the man's name with a healthy amount of disdain.

"Venture was a worthless sack of . . . uh, potatoes," Slim added.

That was true. Price had been a lot of things, and not a one of them good. But one thing he had done that wasn't all that different than his father was treat him like a child. "Then you know what I'm referring to."

Big Jim lifted his hat, scratched his head.

Rolled his shoulders. "I'm sorry, but I don't, Mr. Grant," he finally replied. "I've always thought you did the best you could with what you had."

Miles scanned his face, but instead of a smirk, he saw only honesty. He was so used to feeling insignificant, he wasn't sure how to deal with it.

He settled for moving the conversation along. It wouldn't do any of them any good to sit around and rehash the past, especially when the men weren't eager to be honest about it. "I know I'm not up for a long ride with a Winchester, but I want you men to know that I'm ready to help in any way I can. I want to be there for y'all." What was unsaid was "this time."

Slim stepped away from the saddle, his steps unsure, his expression earnest. "Mr. Grant, here's the thing. We're not only working hard to protect the ranch, we aim to protect you."

"I'm sorry?" Miles had no idea what he meant.

"We like the land, and we like our jobs. But you're the reason we're doing patrols around the clock."

Miles wanted to shake them until they saw things the way he did. He might have grown a lot lately, but inside, in his soul, he was still the same man he'd always been. Weak.

He didn't deserve their loyalty. But, weak as he was, he still accepted it. "I'm obliged, then."

Just as he was backing up, Slim's voice stopped him in his tracks. "It's no accident that the ranch has become a success under your watch. I know that it's your doing that we're getting such good prices for the cattle at market. It's because of you that things have been prospering around here."

Miles thought it had a lot more to do with the right timing than any right words from him. But any more talk about it was going to hold the men up longer. They had plenty to do without trying to lift up his self-worth. "You know what? I do believe I'll go on back to the house."

But Big Jim's next words stopped him in his tracks. "Mr. Grant, do you think Scout Proffitt and those other outlaws will really come?"

Finally he could speak about something that he was completely sure of. "I do," he said. "I've never met Scout, but Clayton told me something once back in Colorado. He said his brother was a man to be feared . . . and to be replicated. I've always thought that was a fine description of a man."

303

"If that's how Scout Proffitt really is . . . then I sure hope he arrives soon," Big Jim muttered. "Yesterday was too late."

Only when Miles was alone in his room did he dare reply. "I hope he gets here fast, too," he whispered to his four empty walls. "If things get as bad as I fear they will . . . he needs to get here soon, and be carrying a whole lot of ammunition."

24

Rosemarie had been home alone at the Bar C more times than she could count. In a strange, convoluted way, it seemed to be her destiny. When she'd lived with her family, her father would be off drinking, and her mother would leave the chores in her capable hands so she could visit Annalise. Those visits would stretch two to three days. Sometimes four.

All the while, Rosemarie would rise early, eat a quick meal, then scurry around like a madwoman, doing the chores of two or three people. When the sun set, she would finally sit down with a cup of hot tea.

And then, in the quiet of the early evening, she would close her eyes and begin her prayers. Ending each day that way gave her strength to begin the next one. And the next.

She knew He heard her, too. It was because of Him that she was able to do so much . . . and not get lonely or bitter. Well, not too much.

So, she'd been alone at the homestead a lot. She was used to hard work.

But she'd never felt lonely.

Instead, she'd often be relieved to be out from under her family's criticism and scorn. She'd looked forward to time spent with her animals, away from her father's drinking and her mother's disappointment.

But since Scout had gone, everything had changed. Now, she was lonesome. Several times a day she caught herself scanning the horizon for signs of approaching riders. Because surely any visitor was going to be better than spending each moment worried about Scout and his terrible, dangerous journey.

She'd been proud of herself when Scout had left in the early hours of the morning. She'd rolled out of bed when he did, even though he'd told her there was no reason to.

While he dressed, she'd stirred up the fire, pumped water, and made a heap of rich, extra-strong coffee. Then she walked outside in the dark, frosty air and delivered tin cups of the brew to the other riders. She made them a quick breakfast of biscuits, leaving plenty left over so they could wrap them in kerchiefs and eat them on the trail.

She didn't shed a tear.

All too soon, the men's packs were loaded on their horses, their dusters were on, and the horses were prancing with barely contained energy. It was time for them to go.

She'd ached to cling to him, or at least to beg him to please be careful. But it didn't seem right. After all, he was going on a mission to kill rustlers, and he'd only married her because he'd been forced.

So she'd wrapped a thick blanket more tightly around herself and tried to smile. "Take care, Scout. I wish you Godspeed."

But there, under the hazy confines of the dim morning light, he'd shaken his head. "No, Rose. That won't do."

She'd stared at him dumbly.

Not two seconds later, he pulled her into his arms. Tightly, so that hardly an inch of light was present. "This is what I need," he murmured around a sigh. "I need to feel you close. Just one more time."

She'd wrapped her arms around him, too. Burying her nose in his neck, capturing his scent, trying her best to memorize everything about him.

In case he didn't return.

Reading her mind, he raised his head, lifted her chin with two fingers, and looked directly at her. "I'll be back, Rosemarie."

"Promise?" It had been a foolish question, but she hadn't been able to stop herself.

"You know I can't promise you that. But I can promise that I'll do my best to stay alive. And if I do, I will come back as soon as I can."

His words had been far more than anyone else had ever given her. She held onto them tightly. "I'll look for you, Scout. I'll look and wait and pray for you."

When he stepped away, his eyes were blank and his expression determined. Then he handed her a wad of cash. "Take this."

Taking his money felt like he'd never need it again. She shook her head. "I can't do that. Scout, you're going to need it."

"I have more." He shook his head slowly. "Listen, a few days ago I rode into Broken Promise and deposited a whole lot of money into our account. In case something ever happened to me. It's for you to spend."

She was shocked. And frightened. Everything he was doing was making her feel like his departure was so permanent. "I don't want all that, Scout."

"Don't argue about this. I want to leave here knowing you won't be going hungry. I want to feel like if I never return, at least I'll have left you better off than before I got here."

But of course, he already had. He'd given her comfort when all she'd known was fear. He'd attended to her when she'd been used to being ignored. And he'd shown her love when she'd feared she was unlovable.

The money had felt cold and solid in her hand. Dangerous and tempting, almost like it was the devil's work.

He was offering more money than the ranch had ever seen in its lifetime. More money than she might ever see again.

So though she knew the money had more likely come from the lives of other men worse than Scout, she took it. Because if she'd learned anything in her life it was that handouts didn't come often, and when they did, they were rarely offered twice. "I'll save it for you," she said, hating what she was doing but giving thanks for it — all at the same time. "I'll save it and give it back to you when you return."

"Don't do that. You spend what you need." His voice deepened, heavy with suppressed emotion. "Rosemarie, there's no telling how long this is going to take me." He pressed his lips together, as if weighing each word he was about to say, then continued. "There's even a chance I might not come back."

She couldn't bear to think like that.

"Scout —"

His gaze softened. "Shh, now. It's true. If you don't want to keep it all here, go into town and ask that banker to add it to our account.

He smiled slightly. "But I really think you should go to the mercantile and buy some things for the house and some fabric for some dresses."

She'd shaken her head. "I don't need anything."

"There's wanting and there's needing. Sometimes they're the same thing. Sometimes one is more important than the other. And I hate to say it, but this house is in such poor shape, all it has is needs."

"Mr. Proffitt, we gotta get going," one of the men called out.

"In a sec," Scout called back, then focused all his attention back on her. Clasping her hand, he said, "Rose, do me a favor and take care of yourself. Take care of yourself until I can do it again. I want to ride in that saddle thinking good thoughts about you — not be worried for your health."

He kissed her then. A long, sweet kiss that curled her toes and heated her body.

Then he quickly turned away, mounted his horse with the ease that only a man who'd spent the majority of his life on

310

horseback could do, and glanced at her again.

She stared at him, too. She was too scared to admit it, but she knew she was falling in love with him. She wished there was some way he could read her mind.

After a sidelong look at the other men, he'd kicked his gelding's flank, pulled the brim of his black Stetson down, and moved on. Into the dark of the night.

"Bye, Scout," she said into the empty yard.

Within moments, their shadows had mixed in with the darkness. And moments after that, they were completely gone.

Almost as if they'd never been there at all.

The Circle Z was a formidable estate, spanning several thousand acres. Scout had the feeling of venturing into another world way before he even saw any signs of life.

But he hadn't needed to see well-groomed thoroughbreds or maintained barns or a large house to notice the difference in the land.

There was something about the prime land, the spring with a little patch of rocks that someone had laid so a person could have a sip of water without getting covered in mud.

The way the fields seemed a bit more lush,

the cattle a little heavier. The air a little richer.

Though all that was probably his imagination for sure.

"This is sure something, ain't it?" Russell asked as they slowed down when the house came in sight.

Scout turned to him in surprise. "I thought y'all had already been here before?"

"No. We met the sheriff in Camp Hope." He smiled self-consciously. "I was kind of surprised Mr. Grant was willing for us to come on his land, if you want to know the truth. I imagined he would have liked to keep the riffraff out of his property."

Scout privately thought the same thing. If he was a man like Miles Grant, untouched by most of the seamier things in life, he'd do his best to keep people like him as far away as possible. "Is Mr. Grant married? Do you know?"

Russell shrugged. "I don't know. But I reckon so. I mean a man like him should be. He'd have a whole lot to offer a bride."

"Yeah," he agreed, though his voice came out a little hoarse, on account of the main house coming into view.

Behind them, Joe Bob or Tuff whistled low.

Scout figured the noise was warranted. The place was far better than anything he'd seen in quite some time. It even surpassed James Walton's mansion back in Colorado, and he hadn't imagined anything would top that.

The house was in a Mexican hacienda style and seemed to stretch on forever. Neatly maintained fencing lined the drive-way to the house. Off in the distance were a series of barns, each one well kept and finely constructed.

It was the complete opposite of his spread. More than 180 degrees. More like night and day. Or black and white. Or alive and dead.

Yep, it was far and away from his home with Rosemarie.

Which was fitting, Scout supposed. If he was about to go to his death, it should be in order to defend a ranch like this, owned by a fine, upstanding man with a good reputa-tion.

Not living in a place like he did, where nothing was new or fixed or safe.

Though he would have like to have changed that for Rosemarie.

Unwilling to show how impressed he was, he kept his back stiff and rode right toward a tall, skinny man who was chewing on a piece of hay and watching them ride in.

Just as if he'd never heard of being afraid of a band of gunfighters.

Scout wanted to pull out one of his guns and hit the ground right in front of him — just to show the guy that it didn't pay in life to become too trusting.

"You know this man, Russell?"

"No, sir." Russell lowered his brim — sign that some habits of riding with the Waltons couldn't be forgotten. "He looks like a regular greeting party though, don't he?"

"Maybe he'll give us tea," Tuff said with a smirk.

Joe Bob rode up beside them. "It's so stinkin' cold out, I'd take a whole pot of tea in a heartbeat and thank him kindly for it, too. I swear I lost the feeling in my cheeks a good four hours ago."

"I hear ya," Scout said lightly, though he made sure to keep his gaze on the lone man. With one hand, he saluted the brim of his hat in the universal sign of a peace offering.

The man nodded right back.

Now they were close enough to see the man's face. And perversely, Scout found comfort in the man's steady gaze. He might not have drawn a gun on them, but he didn't trust them.

That was good. The last thing in the world he wanted was to be killing off enemies of men too dumb to survive on their own.

Raising his hand again, he called out,

"Scout Proffitt approaching."

"Thank the good Lord, too," the man yelled back. Two minutes closer, he said in a quieter tone of voice, "From the moment I caught sight of that black hat, I figured it was you."

"Lots of men have black cowboy hats."

"Yes, but you don't see too many men riding a white horse with a black duster. You've got a way about you that's unmistakable, Mr. Proffitt."

Russell chuckled under his breath.

"Come on into the barn," the sentry said. "I'll take your horses then escort you in to see Mr. Grant."

"Guess there's no turning back now," Russell muttered under his breath before nodding and answering back with a cheery "yes, sir."

Scout said nothing, just rode forward and did what he was told.

But he had a feeling that point of no return had already been passed some time ago.

Possibly even years.

25

Pastor Colson's appearance wasn't just a
surprise — it was a shock of gigantic propor-
tions. Rosemarie had just finished collecting
eggs when the pastor rode in on an especially pretty-looking quarterhorse. The mare
had four stockings and a sassy way of swinging her head. She was showy enough to
garner a second look.

And seemed kind of a poor choice for a
man of the cloth.

When Pastor Colson saw her skeptical
expression, he laughed. "You're not the first
person to look at me like that. I can't help
but ride Winter, though. She was a gift."

Approaching, she ran a gentle hand down
the horse's flank. The mare's fine muscles
quivered with suppressed energy. She was a
beautiful piece of horseflesh. "That is some
gift, Pastor."

"She was from my parents," he explained
as he easily dismounted and wrapped the

reins a few times around the hitching post. "They came out to visit me from Kansas City last week." He frowned slightly. "I just wish I had a better seat."

"You'll get there," Rosemarie said generously. "All it takes to ride well is the knowledge that you and the horse are one. I'm afraid you two still seem to be figuring that one out."

"One, huh?"

She shrugged, feeling like the last person on earth to be giving riding lessons. "I think all you really need to do is just relax a bit. Then, before you know it, you and Winter will be getting along just fine."

She had no experience with gift-giving families, or of ever receiving anything that was so expensive.

With the exception of Scout's money, of course.

Pushing all thoughts of Scout away, she quickly set the eggs in a basket by the front door and turned to the pastor. "Is something wrong with my kin?" It was as close as she dared to ask bluntly, why he'd ridden all the way out to the Bar C.

But unfortunately, he didn't seem to follow her line of thinking. "With your mother or sister? No, I don't believe so. But I was

317

thinking you might not be doing all that well."

She strived for nonchalance. "Why is that?" Had something happened to Scout already? Was she already a widow before she'd had much of a chance to be a wife?

"Word came out that your man already left."

"Yes, he did." Though she ached to tell him that she'd expected it or that what he'd done was fine with her.

But, of course, that was far from the truth.

"Rosemarie, there isn't a need to try so hard for me." Resting his hand on her shoulder, he gave a little squeeze. "Why don't we go inside for a few minutes and you can tell me what's been going on?"

She would've taken him up on his offer if she'd trusted him. But she didn't. "There's no reason to get involved, Pastor. I'm sorry you had to waste so much of your day just to see that I'm fine."

Scanning her face, he slowly shook his head. "I don't think so."

Before she could refute that, he walked into her home. Quickly, she followed, scurrying behind him so fast that her skirts flapped against her ankles.

"Look at this!" he said when the kitchen door clicked shut behind them. "Rosemarie, this looks like a whole new place! What have you been doing?"

"Oh, this and that."

"It's more than that, child. Care to explain what 'this' and 'that' looks like to you?"

Because he truly looked interested, and she was proud of all that she'd accomplished, she gave into temptation. "I've been cleaning, and then I went into town and picked up a few things. My husband said I could," she added in a rush.

"I would think so. Your home has never looked so good. What did he say about the changes?"

"He hasn't seen it yet." But of course, he knew that.

"Would you like a cup of coffee?"

Pastor Colson shook his head as he took a chair. "No. I didn't come here to take up too much of your time." Kicking his feet out, he said, "It's none of my business about what business your husband is on. So I'll concentrate on you. How did you feel about him leaving?"

"I don't know," she sputtered.

"Sure you do. I've never known you to not know your mind."

He had a point. But still, she hadn't given herself time to concentrate on her feelings about Scout leaving. Instead, she'd chosen to worry about him. But what he was missing was her new status. "He's my husband, Pastor Colson."

"Having opinions about yourself doesn't necessarily mean you're being disloyal."

"I disagree." But even though her words were firm, her legs were shaky. She took a chair across from him.

Pastor Colson crossed his arms over his chest. "What Scout did, marrying you, it was a commendable thing," he began. "He saved your reputation. Some might even say he saved your life. But you gave him something in return. You gave him a grounding point. You gave him the chance to have a family and a future. You can't discount that, Rosemarie."

She'd never imagined that anyone would look at her as doing something good for Scout.

"I appreciate you saying that."

"It's the truth."

Surprised, she looked at him. Trying to read more than what he was saying in his gaze. But all she saw was an honesty that she'd rarely had the privilege of seeing. "Some folks think I've never deserved much. Because of my brother, you know."

"When I first got here, a couple of people told me about that. But here's the thing,

Rosemarie. What happened was no one's fault, and especially not yours. You were a child, dear. His death was an accident."

"He still died. Sometimes accidents don't matter much."

"I disagree. Accidents happen all the time. Sometimes a person might get hurt riding. Or farming. Or meet the wrong end of a horse."

"You can't compare what I did to that."

"You're right. It's your mother's fault. Or your father's. Or maybe even your sister's."

"What?" She shook her head. "They weren't there. It was my fault."

"Annalise is older than you. Your parents' responsibility was to look after their children. They shouldn't have left him in your care. You were a child yourself."

Tears pricked her eyes. All her life, she'd had the responsibility weighing on her shoulders heavily, so heavily that sometimes that burden had felt almost crippling.

No, it had been crippling. So crippling, she'd hardly ever looked up from the weight of it all.

"I never thought about things that that way."

"Then perhaps it's time you did. God has a plan and a perfect time for everything. I have a feeling things are all happening exactly as they are supposed to."

It did seem like a whole lot was happening all of the sudden. A whole lifetime's worth of new people, new situations, and new relationships.

After all those years of feeling like her whole world was sitting still. Waiting for something to happen.

And after all those weeks of sitting by her father's bedside, waiting for it to be his time to die.

"I appreciate you coming out here, Pastor."

"I wanted to pay you a visit. Is there anything I can do for you?"

It crossed her mind to say no. But then she remembered what most likely counted the most.

"Could you pray for me? And, if it doesn't upset you too much . . . could you pray for my husband, too?"

"Of course, Rosemarie. That's what I'm here for," he said with a smile.

Miles Grant looked like he'd been dragged two miles behind a runaway horse.

But still he stood, his stature proud, his green eyes level and steady. "Miles Grant," he said, holding out his hand. "Thank you for getting here so fast."

While Scout stood to one side, he shook Russell's, Joe Bob's, Tuff's, and Andrew's hands, then gestured them to the pair of large leather couches and two chairs grouped in the center of a massive living room.

Scout was glad that the hand that had greeted them had shown them to the washrooms after helping them get their horses into stalls, then watered and fed. He would've hated to dirty up the fine furniture.

By the way Russell was staring at the couch, he was likely thinking the same thing.

"Couch is leather so a little bit of dust won't harm a thing. Please sit. Miss Annabeth is on her way in with refreshments."

Refreshments? Scout opened his mouth, ready to remind the wealthy landowner that they were visiting for a job, not for a social reason, when a strapping woman pushing a cart loaded with more food than he'd seen in a hotel dining room entered.

Immediately, Russell stood up. "Ma'am," he drawled politely.

She stopped and stared at him, then grinned even wider. "Now, ain't you a darling? Sit down, son. I'm bringing this in here for y'all, not so you will get up and start causing trouble."

While he and the other newcomers tried to sort that out, Miles chuckled. "Gentlemen, please meet Miss Annabeth. She's bossier than a mule and cooks like a dream."

Miss Annabeth lumbered forward, pulled out a stack of china plates from nowhere, and then started loading up the dishes with sandwiches, potato salad, pickles, and fried chicken. "Don't pay Mr. Grant no mind. We're all just doing our part here. Now, eat up. Y'all have been riding for days, yes?"

She continued without waiting for a reply. "Mr. Grant, Tracy came calling. What do you want me to say to her?"

"Tracy?"

"Yes, sir. I told her you had company. But she was pretty determined to see you."

Scout munched his roast beef sandwich while Mr. Grant's ears turned red. Altogether, it was fairly entertaining. "If you need to delay our meeting . . ."

"Of course not." He swallowed. "Miss Annabeth, see if she'll wait an hour, would you please?"

"I will." She winked. "And I have a feeling she won't mind waiting," she added as she sauntered off.

When she closed the door, Russell whistled low. "No disrespect, Mr. Grant, but that is some kind of woman."

"That she is. She keeps me on my toes. I'd be lost without her." He cleared his throat. "Now let's get to business. Sherriff Brower is coming out here at dusk. What do you boys have in mind to tell him?"

With a bit of regret, Scout set his plate back on the table. "That we're aiming to honor his deal. If he meant it."

From his spot on the couch, Russell spoke. "Mr. Grant, is Sheriff Brower the kind of man to honor promises?"

"Yes."

That was the kind of answer Scout liked best. He didn't want a lot of flowery dissertations or poetic arguments about right and wrong.

All he wanted was a clear direction so he could go back to his home. With Rosemarie.

"What else do you want to discuss?"

"Your pay."

Scout had already discussed this with the others. "We're not doing this for the money. We're coming to your aid for our reputations."

"I know more about a suffering reputation than you might imagine, Mr. Proffitt. But I also have to tell you that I've learned that it would be foolish to ever turn away money."

Scout felt the other men's tension and

knew for their benefit that he couldn't brush off further discussion about payment. "What kind of money are you talking about?"

"If you men are able to either apprehend or kill the rustlers, I'm willing to pay each of you a hundred dollars."

Tuff's plate clattered on the table as he hastily set it down.

One by one, the other men did the same.

"That's a whole lot of money, Mr. Grant," Russell said. "That's a whole lot of money even if the five of us divided up one of the payments between us."

"Money's still being made, gentlemen. There's a lot of profit in the cattle business, as more and more folks are hoping to run their cattle to the stockyards and come out with a handy profit." He looked at each of them. "If you're willing to stand up to the Harlan Jones Gang, then you'll be sending out a message to most everyone that we don't put up with thievery. Not only will you be helping out our lives right now, but you'll be helping us in the long run."

"You've thought this through."

"That's my gift, such that it is," Mr. Grant said mildly. "I'm a failure at saving myself from getting beat up by renegades. But finding a profit from nothing? I can do that."

Scout stood up. "You've got yourself a

deal, sir. Now why don't you let us leave you so you can visit with your girl?"

"Tracy?"

Scout nodded. "She is your girl, right?"

There went that blush again. "She nursed me when I was bleeding."

"That's the kind of woman to not keep waiting. If you don't mind my saying so."

"Scout's recently married," Russell supplied. Like that explained his comment.

Scout could have hit the guy, but for the first time, something new showed up in the rancher's eyes.

"My felicitations, Mr. Proffitt. I can see you know what you're talking about." With obvious effort and pain, he got to his feet. "I'll go meet her then. You all, please. Stay here and eat." He winked. "Miss Annabeth will bring you something to drink shortly."

The food was too good to ignore.

As Miles awkwardly crossed the room, opened the door, then shut it behind him, Russell leaned back and smiled. "Y'all may think I'm idiotic, but I like that guy."

"Like him? I'd marry him if I could," Joe Bob said with a low laugh. "That money he's talking about? If it really happens? I could go back home and live like a king."

"I could too," Russell said softly. And with such a look of yearning, Scout wondered who he was wishing for.

As for Scout, already he was imagining what he could do with his portion of the money. He could build a better house. Buy some cattle.

Spoil Rosemarie a little.

The possibilities were endless, as long as he didn't die first.

26

There were few ways a man could regain his dignity while reclined on a settee. His visit to the hands had worn him out, and the meeting with Scout Proffitt and the other men had rattled him something awful.

He'd known being in the company of a known killer would be difficult, but he hadn't been prepared for the look of commitment and pain in the men's eyes. It had become obvious that they didn't take this job lightly.

And it had also hit him hard with the realization that they were doing it on his behalf.

He was still sitting and stewing on that when Miss Annabeth led Tracy in before making a quick exit. No doubt she had business to attend to with the men in the living room.

"I didn't expect to see you here, Tracy."

She'd only stepped a few feet into the room. "Why not? I told you that I wanted to tend to you."

"There's no need. As you can see, I'm better now."

Her chuckle was soft and low, and the sound rolled along his spine. "If you're better, it's not by much," she commented. "Mr. Grant, you still look like someone got ahold of you with the sharp end of a stick."

"Just a couple of bare knuckles."

Without invitation, she perched on the edge of the ladder back chair next to him. Her scent wafted closer, reminding him of spring flowers and roses in June.

"Are you wearing toilet water?"

She looked down at her knees. "Maybe."

"I didn't know you owned any."

"You don't know everything about me, Mr. Grant."

"I know enough."

Her eyes flashed. "Only what you've wanted to see."

He knew he should ask her to leave. But sparring with her was so entertaining he didn't want to stop. He needed her to take his mind off things.

"What is there about you that I'm not seeing?"

For the first time in recent memory, she

looked a little taken aback. "Why don't you tell me what you think you see and I'll tell you if there's more to it."

This was a strange game, and that was the truth.

What he saw was a mass of blond hair and a pointed chin that showed just how determined a woman she was. He saw a slim figure that was the opposite of a lady's like Laurel. Laurel was fragile and willowy.

Tracy? She was far more solid. Sturdy.

"Mr. Grant? Is there nothing you see?"

"I see a capable woman," he said finally. "I see a woman who can patch up a bloodied man and doesn't mind taking the time to pay him a visit. Even though it probably wasn't all that proper neither."

He braced himself. Ready for her to fillet him with a vicious rejoinder. Tell him that he was the last person in the world to go about telling her what to do.

But instead, her eyes filled up with tears.

He was horrified. "Tracy, what did I say?"

She shook her head, her bottom lip trembling. "Nothing."

He didn't understand women, and he didn't understand what that was supposed to mean, either.

"Nothing, like I didn't say the right words? Or 'nothing,' like I didn't hurt your feelings, you just all the sudden decided to start tearing up in my conservatory?"

She got to her feet. "I don't know what I see in you," she said.

"I didn't ask you to see anything! I didn't even ask you to come over." With a groan and a wince, he got to his feet and stomped closer to her. "Now, Tracy, why are you crying?"

Her perfect lips turned into a little circle, and she stomped her foot. "Oh! Mr. Grant, you will be the death of me."

He couldn't help it — he gripped her upper arms to hold her close. "What? What am I doing wrong?"

"Everything!"

Right when she pulled away from him, he gripped her tighter. Somehow that clutch became an embrace.

And for some reason — probably because his mouth was right next to hers — he kissed her.

Right there in his music conservatory room.

Maybe it lasted two seconds. But it lasted long enough.

She stepped away with a gasp. "See what I mean?" she moaned, then turned with a swirl of skirts and left the room.

Leaving him more confused than ever.

Or . . . maybe not? She'd had her golden hair pulled up around her face. Had on perfume. And her dress? It wasn't all loose and worn.

It was well fitted and pretty.

She'd looked pretty. And she'd cried when he'd called her capable. And she'd let him kiss her, though he hadn't really ever kissed anyone much, and he wasn't sure how to go about doing it.

But she hadn't slapped him. No, she hadn't slapped him at all.

In the privacy of the room, his frown slowly slid into a smile. Maybe he wasn't so bad at love and romance after all.

They began that night. Russell rode with Slim and Scout and headed out toward the back fields. Though Russell couldn't say he looked at the gunfighter as his equal, he definitely didn't gape at him with an overwhelming sense of awe like he used to.

That was good — man didn't need to be worrying about his hero when he should be worrying about getting shot. Dark clouds were thick overhead, effectively blocking out all stars. There was little to see beyond what was a few feet in front of them.

But with each passing yard, the prickling became stronger in the back of his neck.

And his sense of foreboding increased. He'd felt the same kind of thing when the Marshals entered James Walton's hotel room and carried him away. And when he'd known he was going to have to finally shoot his father and save Nora. He didn't doubt the feeling even a little bit. It was all going to be over with before daybreak. He was as sure of it as he was that he'd most likely never see sweet Nora ever again.

"Heard your recently married, Mr. Proffitt," Slim said. "That true?"

Russell kept his mouth shut, but inwardly he was impressed by Slim's gumption. He hadn't had the nerve to say a single thing about Mrs. Proffitt. Even though he and Tuff and Joe Bob had talked long into the night after first seeing her.

Mrs. Proffitt was a little thing. Pretty and slim, too. But there was more to her than than pleasing looks. There seemed to be a wariness and vulnerability about her that made a man want to protect her against the world.

"That is true. And call me Scout, Slim. There isn't any reason to stand on formalities."

"All right, Scout. How's married life treating ya?"

"It's been a surprise, if you want me to be

honest. Never thought I'd be married."

"Yours a love match?"

Russell ached to slap the foreman's cheek, just to wake up some sense in him! "That ain't no business of ours, Mister."

"Oh, I mean no disrespect," Slim countered. "Just making conversation."

There in the darkness, Scout chuckled. "Russell, I appreciate your sticking up for me, but there's no need for that. I don't mind talking about Rosemarie."

"Pretty name," Slim said. Just like the fool that he was.

"I think so, too. And to answer your question, no, it wasn't a love match."

"Ah."

'Course, now Russell had a slew of questions. Why wasn't it a love match? How did they meet? What led a man like Scout Proffitt to marry her? And before he knew it, he'd spoken. "If you didn't love her, why'd y'all get married?"

To his right, Slim laughed. "I knew you were interested, boy!"

"I married her because it was the right thing to do," Scout said, his voice all serious.

And the way he said it, his voice gravelly and sure and sounding like it hid a whole lot of information that nobody knew about . . .

It made Russell rethink his life, all over again. What would his life be like if he hadn't given up on Nora? If one day, he turned right around and rode back to her ranch, just to see if she ever thought of him?

And if she did, now wouldn't that be something?

After riding in silence for a few more minutes, Slim cleared his throat. "This is the spot. We've got good coverage here, and if the rustlers are coming for the herd, they'd be coming over here."

Russell could faintly make out the shadows of the cattle. He heard the gentle grunts and moos of them, sleeping and content in the mild night. "What do we do now?" he asked.

"Now we wait," Slim said as he dismounted. Scout and Russell dismounted, too.

There was a faint outcropping of rocks partially hidden by a pair of sad little mesquite trees. The three of them settled in there, their rifles out and cocked.

It was time to sit and wait.

Russell had spent more time doing this than he could remember. He'd sat and waited when he'd been hungry and scared and alone.

And when he'd been the newest, greenest member of the Walton Gang. Then, he'd been thankful that he hadn't been alone. Even if some of the men in the gang had scared him half to death . . . at least they wouldn't shoot him in the back and leave him on the road for the birds to pick at.

So sitting watch wasn't anything new. But sitting in the company of men was something new.

"What do you think, Russell?" Scout drawled so quietly that his voice seemed to fade into the air as soon as the words were released. "Think tonight's our night?"

"Maybe." He rubbed the back of his neck, where it felt like all his nerve endings were lit on fire. "Feels like it."

"Yeah?" Scout Proffitt flashed a grin, his white teeth illuminated in the darkness for a brief moment before making Russell wonder if that smile had been just a memory. "I knew being with you was going to do me some good, boy."

Russell didn't dare smile or comment on that. But the acceptance felt good.

Yep, sitting in the company of men who looked at him as an equal was very new.

He was just wondering how to one day get up the nerve to ask Scout about some of his gunfights — the ones that had been documented in the dime novels — when the faintest crack of a branch clicked behind them.

He exhaled. The rustlers were here.

As one, the three of them picked up their rifles and got ready to fire.

This, of course, was very familiar.

27

After Scout had been gone another week, Rosemarie went back into town, clad in her new navy blue dress. As she parked the buggy, then secured the horse to a hitching post in front of the mercantile, she felt more than one person pass her, then take another look.

It made her a little nervous. She smoothed her hair, wishing all the while she had a smart-looking hat to perch on her head. Just as quickly, she pushed the vain thought away. There were too many things to worry about besides hats and bonnets.

Giving herself a firm little shake, Rosemarie strode into the mercantile. With a little bit of effort, she might be able to pick up her goods and be back in the wagon in less than hour.

"Mrs. Proffitt, hello!" Mr. James called out from the back of the store. "So good to see you again."

She started for a moment, then realized he was speaking to her. The change in the man's manner was uncanny. All her life, she'd been ignored, both at home and in Broken Promise. Now that she was married to a notorious gunslinger with money, she'd gained respect.

She nodded politely. "Mr. James. Good morning."

Leaving the folks whom he was helping at the counter alone, he approached her with an eager gleam in his eye. "Did you make that dress from the fabric you bought last week?"

Brushing out a wrinkle in the skirt, she nodded. "Yes, sir."

"It's real pretty. You do have a way with a needle, ma'am."

"Thank you." Noticing that the family were her Polish neighbors, she cleared her throat a little self-consciously. "I need some things, but perhaps you'd like to finish up with the Kowalchecks?"

He glanced at the family's way, his gaze skimming over both Mr. and Mrs. Kowalcheck and their three children lined up beside them at the counter. "They can wait."

"Certainly not. I'll just go look at the fabric."

"Going to do some more sewing?" he

asked. Just like that was something new and interesting.

She nodded before turning away. She was uncomfortable with the fawning and felt guilty for claiming Mr. James's attention. Especially since she wasn't sure if he was excited about the new money in her account or the fact that she was wedded to an infamous gunslinger.

When the shop owner drifted back to her neighbors, she walked over to the bolts of fabric. Yellows and blues and dark greens and calicos stood prettily in front of her, practically begging for her to run fingers along them. Or to fashion the smooth, fine fabric into another pretty dress.

Or curtains for the kitchen, perhaps?

Rosemarie couldn't help but smile at the thought of their tiny, well-worn kitchen being doctored up by a swag of bright yellow calico.

Just imagining the sight made her feel uplifted. Boy, she was sure Scout would have something to say about that! No doubt he'd tease her about trying to dress up a sow's ear.

When an elderly man entered the shop and claimed Mr. James's attention, Mrs. Kowalcheck approached. "Good morning, Mrs. Proffitt," she said politely.

Feeling her cheeks heat, Rosemarie returned the greeting. "Good morning. How are you today?"

Mrs. Kowalcheck fanned her face. "Enjoying a morning away from the farm. I'm a little warm, though, so I'll go sit outside while my husband finishes his work."

Warm? It was near freezing outside. And though the store was cozy, it was in no way overheated. "Are you ill?"

With a stealthy glance at her husband, Mrs. Kowalcheck shook her head. "I'm in the family way again," she whispered. Her cheeks blushed prettily, and her eyes shone with pure happiness.

Rosemarie smiled. "Congratulations." Taking the lady's arm, she guided her outside and sat with her on the metal chairs.

"Now that we have some privacy, why don't you tell me how you're really doing? How are you, Rose?" Mrs. Kowalcheck asked when they were alone. "You've had so many challenges lately. I've been praying for you."

"I appreciate that. I'm all right." She ached to talk about all her troubles — from her worries about Scout surviving his trip, to the strange grief she felt for her father — a man she'd never liked all that much and who'd always seemed more than happy to show his disdain for her.

Then, of course, there were all the mixed-up feelings she was experiencing on account of her new status in the community. Being a rich outlaw's wife was a precarious thing to be, for sure.

But more than anything, her heart was filled with the new feelings of love and desire she was feeling for her very handsome husband.

Reaching out, Mrs. Kowalcheck wrapped both of her gloved hands around Rosemarie's own. "When your parents still lived at your ranch, it was difficult to reach out to you. But now that you are in charge, I hope you won't mind if I come over sometimes? I would love to be your friend."

"I would like that, too, Mrs. Kowalcheck." She'd had no idea it was her family and not herself who'd been the reason the woman had stayed a stranger.

"Please call me Marta."

"Marta, thank you," she said as the door opened. Looking up, she saw that Mr. Kowalcheck's big body filled the doorway. His expression was concerned and distressed.

"You okay, Marta?"

"I am fine, John. Mrs. Proffitt and I were just catching up."

"Perhaps you could talk another time,

too?" he asked. Three pairs of eyes peeked around his legs, making Rosemarie laugh.

Marta chuckled, too, as she held out her arms for the children to join her. "I am ready now." With a kind smile Rose's way, Mrs. Kowalcheck said, "I'll pay you a visit soon, Rosemarie. And try not to worry about your husband. I bet he'll come home soon."

"Thank you for your thoughts and prayers."

After watching Mr. Kowalcheck help his wife and children into their wagon, Rosemarie went inside and quickly gave her shopping list to Mr. James. In no time at all, he was loading her wagon with more flour, grain for the chickens, a pair of lanterns, and several yards of that yellow calico. Sunny yellow curtains could only help her kitchen.

And looking at them in the morning, when the sun shone through the glass would lift her spirits indeed.

As he took his leave, Mr. James leaned close. "I hope you don't mind my saying so, but everyone here's been real happy about your change in status."

As a matter of fact, she did mind him saying so. It didn't make sense to her, not really. She was the same person inside. Only now she'd had Scout's name backing her up.

But, of course, she couldn't mention what she was thinking. Instead, she smiled absently and hopped in her wagon.

The whole way back she thought a lot about the changes that had happened. Thought, too, about God's plan for her.

But then almost froze in fright when she arrived at the ranch.

She wasn't alone.

Her skin turned cold as she saw the figure looming in the shadows. After a long moment, he tipped his hat.

Her horse pawed the dirt as she worried about what to do. They were alone together. She was at his mercy.

Resigned to her fate, Rosemarie put the brake on the wagon and waited.

"Afternoon, ma'am. I do hope I haven't frightened you too much. I'm sorry to be waiting for you here, but there was really nowhere else." He spoke slowly, keeping his words even and easy. "I don't mean to offend."

She stayed silent, too scared to speak.

The tension between them altered a bit, becoming less menacing. Looking at her closely, he gently asked, "Are you Rosemarie, by chance?"

Her heart started beating faster. How did she know her name? "I am Mrs. Proffitt," she finally replied. "Now, who are you?"

He stood stock-still, just like she was a skittish filly, and he was attempting to wean her from her mother. "Ma'am, I am Clayton Proffitt."

She blinked, not certain she heard him correctly. "Clayton Proffitt? Are you . . ."

"Scout's brother? Indeed, I am." He looked beyond her, his dark, chocolaty eyes giving nothing away. "Is Scout here?"

After a moment's hesitation, she shook her head. There was no way reason to lie. For all she knew, Clayton had already toured the house and barn and had seen for himself that Scout wasn't anywhere in sight. "My husband went east. On a job."

"I know. He's out at Camp Hope. Or thereabouts." He grimaced. "At least, that's what my brother-in-law said."

"Your brother-in-law?"

"Miles Grant." He raised a brow. "Did Scout mention him?" he asked, gently again. Quietlike, as if he was truly afraid of scaring her.

Maybe it was his manner. Maybe it was his calm, soothing voice. But she was breathing easier now. "Yes," she murmured. "He's your wife's brother."

"Yep." His gaze warmed. "I used to work for their father."

There was something about those eyes, so like Scout's, that made the last bit of her hesitancy dissipate. Finally climbing out of the wagon, she said, "Mr. Proffitt, please forgive my manners. Things have been a little hectic lately, and I'm afraid I never know quite who to trust."

Walking toward her, he picked up the five-pound bag of flour with one arm and the ten-pound bag of grain in the other. "Why don't I help you get unloaded and see to your horse while we talk?"

"I'd like that, thank you."

He smiled gently, then followed her around as she showed him to the kitchen for the flour sack, and then into the barn, to the cubby where the grain was stored.

All the while, he walked by her side, easy and relaxed. Like no man she'd ever known, not even Scout. Scout always seemed to have a bundle of suppressed energy hidden inside — his gaze always wary. More often than not, she'd gaze his way and notice his muscles were bunched, ready to spring at any moment.

Clayton, on the other hand, looked as if he'd never been in an out-of-control situation in his life.

He helped her carry the bolts of fabric into the small living room, then together they walked outside again.

"We just need to unhitch the horse . . ."

"Of course, ma'am," he said easily, doing the work himself with such an air of ease that Rosemarie would have felt even more awkward if she'd offered to do the task instead.

After the horse was curried and Clayton was given a brief tour around the barn, they walked outside again. Clayton stood still, gazing at the house. The lone fence post, standing like a stalwart sentry for all to see. Rose figure it looked more lonely than ever — now that there was little hope of it even becoming part of a great whole.

To Rosemarie, the post was a fitting symbol of everything that her father had wished for — and all that she'd long ago given up imagining could be different.

The wind had picked up a bit. Instead of gently brushing her skirts, it now flew through the fields in static bursts, flattening the fabric of her dress against her body in spurts and jolts. She was just about to suggest they go inside when he gestured to the spot where a lone cross loomed in the field.

"What's up there?"

She didn't need to turn to see where he

pointed. "That's where we buried my pa."

"Mind if we go visit the grave?"

She hadn't been there since they'd lowered the coffin in the ground. Since she'd stood next to her mother and sister and the pastor and had been sure that her life had been about to change.

'Course she never could have imagined the changes that had come.

When she'd walked down that hill, she'd promised herself to never return. At least not until the harsh memories of living with a man like her father had faded into something more comforting.

But for some reason, visiting it now with Clayton seemed like a good idea. "I don't mind at all, Mr. Proffitt."

"It's Clayton, Rosemarie," he said with the briefest of smiles. "It's perfectly acceptable to call each other by our Christian names. We're related, you know."

Yes, they were. Somehow, God had taken a woman like herself and put a whole series of events in her life, changing not only her circumstances but her whole outlook on life.

Now she had this man in her life. The man who Scout had said was so good that he could never hope to measure up to him. She just had to hope and pray that Scout would come back to her. She would dearly love to get to know the man she was now bound to for life.

Without another word, they started walking. The longish grasses, long turned yellow and brown in the cold, brushed against her boots. Every once in a while, a piece scratched her calf, threatening to tear her stockings. She lifted her feet a little more until her steps resembled a march. The stiff breeze continued to fan her cheeks.

As the incline sharpened, she glanced Clayton's way. "How did you know where to find Scout?"

"Miles's letter mentioned that he'd heard Scout was out by Broken Promise. A quick stop in town revealed where he was living."

She could only imagine what the townspeople had told Clayton. "It's a small town."

"Indeed." He spared her another glance before he smiled slightly. "After they gave me directions to the Bar C, a few people mentioned that the two of you had recently gotten married."

Rosemarie wondered which of the men had passed on the information. Not that it mattered much. Remembering how scared she'd been, and how embarrassed she'd been that she'd had nowhere else to go and that a man like Scout had been pretty much cornered, she grasped for something to say.

"I suppose you're disappointed that he married me?"

"Not at all. I've long since given up trying to second guess Scout. Or trying to push my way into his life." He frowned slightly. "We're a little too far apart for that."

"Y'all aren't close, are you?"

He turned to her and looked her square in the eye. "I haven't seen Scout since he was fourteen."

With effort, she controlled her gasp. She wouldn't have imagined that Scout had kept in touch. After all, it had been in his best interest to keep his doings private. But this man beside her was a different story. Clayton Proffitt seemed like everything dutiful and responsible. She would've thought he would have moved heaven and earth to keep tabs on his brother.

Glancing her way, he sighed. "Our relationship isn't quite like you imagined, is it?"

"I don't know what I imagined," she replied. And that was the truth. Almost.

"Ah, here we are," he said when they came to the gravesite, switching topics abruptly. Or maybe it had all been a part of the same thing? After all, losing track of a brother was an awful lot like losing a pa you never really had the chance to know.

Standing in front of the mound of dirt, in

front of the crudely designed cross that still meant so much, she looked for something to say. Something that wouldn't betray her feelings, wouldn't give Clayton a hint about all she lost. "We buried my father here less than a month ago."

"Recently."

Yes, it had been recently, though in a lot of ways it felt like a lifetime ago. "Scout appeared the day he died." She'd used the word *appeared* on purpose. It felt like he'd come out of nowhere.

And perhaps he had?

There was really no good explanation for how his poker game with her father in the middle of Oklahoma would result in her marrying him.

Especially not that she would fall in love with him.

Sneaking a sideways glance his way, she said, "When I get to heaven, I'm going to ask God what that was all about."

"I hope He tells you." Clayton grinned. "As for me, I don't expect too many answers. He's given me enough."

She didn't know what to say to that. As another burst of wind passed by, she curved her arms around her chest. Trying to get warm.

"Clayton, I don't know my husband as

well as I wished I did. But I do know that I'm not ready to say good-bye to him. I certainly don't want to visit his grave anytime soon."

A muscle in his jaw jumped. "Rosemarie, I don't know Scout all that well either, truth to be told. But even if I don't know him, I love him with everything that I am. I'll do all I can to prevent you from making this walk to see him."

And with that, he turned around. She scurried to follow, then realized that he'd stopped and had his arm out for her to hold. To steady her on her journey back down the hill. She grasped his strong arm and held on tight.

And she thought grasping hold of Clayton Proffitt was somehow fitting. As sure as all the men Scout had told her had served under him in the war, she'd already taken to depending on him, too. And she didn't even feel guilty about it. It just seemed like it was meant to be.

Clayton Proffitt was that kind of man.

28

Back when he was fourteen, Scout Proffitt used to dream of war. Before he'd left his aunt's house and his sister's side, he'd taken to going into town and listening to the injured men talk about their glory days.

There, in the darkened corners of smoky saloons, he'd sip sarsaparilla and try to imagine what it had been like. Try to imagine having done something worth talking about. Tried to imagine being a hero.

Some of the men had lost their sight. Some a limb. Maybe two. A few had been broken down, others still wore portions of their uniforms as a matter of pride. As if to show everyone that they'd given up much to fight for a cause.

Some drank too much. Many of the men were simply bitter. Others had come home, expecting open arms, only to find that their homes had been burned and looted.

Or their sweethearts had moved on.

In relation to them, Scout had felt insignificant. Coddled. He hadn't understood his father's insistence that he be kept protected from battle. He'd resented his brother's drive to fulfill that promise.

His sister's love had felt confining, and even her husband's terrible stories about the harsh realities on the battlefield, filled with the stench of blood and sulfur and gunpowder and despair, hadn't diminished Scout's goal of wanting to be more than himself.

Instead, it only compounded his need to be stronger than he was. Less innocent. The strong survived. And those who didn't even try?

Well, they were worse than the cowards.

Which was, of course, why he'd ended up going out on his own. The way he'd seen it — in his fourteen-year-old brain — was that if a man wasn't given opportunities to fight and earn honor he had to create those opportunities himself.

"And this is what you've become," he muttered to himself, sitting crouched behind a rock in between a man who was better suited to riding horses and mending fences than defending them and another man who was really little more than a kid.

"Sorry?" Russell whispered. "I didn't hear you."

"Nothing. Just talking to myself," Scout murmured as he leaned farther into the darkness and watched a team of four men approach on horseback.

Scout felt the muscles in his legs tighten as he prepared to spring to his feet and announce himself. Sheriff Brower had insisted that they at least attempt to stop the men without gunshot.

"Sometimes, announcing your intentions does a world of good," he'd reminded them.

Back then, that bit of advice seemed a bit useless.

Scout had figured if it had been that easy to apprehend the rustlers they wouldn't have needed Russell and his friends . . . and certainly not him.

After all, his reputation hadn't been made on caring conversation or bringing men to justice.

The rustlers approaching were obviously unafraid and beyond worried about being caught. Ribald humor played between them as they rode forward, caustic laughter rising up to the sky like a signal flare.

The cattle, startled by the unexpected noise and the rushing horses, began to moo and bawl fiercely.

The man in front of them all whooped a bit, frightening the poor cows even further.

Beside him, Slim tensed.

It was time. "Ready?" Scout asked.

"Ready as I'll ever be," Slim muttered.

"I've been ready. Let's do it," Russell added.

Scout couldn't resist adding a word of warning. "Russell, I know you're good with a gun, but if you shoot, aim to kill," he whispered.

And with that, he stood up and made himself known. "You're under arrest!" he called out. "Stand down if you want to live!" Completely feeling the irony of his words.

A horse whinnied in fright. Cattle shifted and bawled some more.

And as he expected, one of the men turned his way and fired.

Scout had been ready for that.

Grasping both guns in his hands, Scout did what was now second nature to him.

Slim and Russell did the same. Guns blazing, they fired their rifles at the men on horseback. A horse screamed, whether from the noise or because it was hit, Scout didn't know.

More shots flew their way. Bullets were exchanged, the staccato pangs echoing through the prairie. Beside him, Slim flinched, grunting in pain.

Scout was barely aware of it all. Instead, he aimed for hearts and heads and fired. Taking care to not leave a single man standing. If one got away, he would be a failure.

That's what he told himself.

He didn't sweat, he didn't flinch. He didn't think about dying or about killing. Instead, he turned his mind off and pretended he was fourteen again.

Wishing he could somehow make a difference. Wishing someone else would be proud of him. Imagining he could somehow be a hero.

Wishing and hoping that one day he would be the man in the tattered uniform recounting old stories of valor and terror. That he'd be sitting in a saloon telling stories instead of sitting with his back to the wall, waiting to be gunned down.

Wishing that he would have something great to be proud of.

So he aimed and fired. In the darkness. Undercover. Doing it all for a gentleman. And his brother's wife.

And, so selfishly, for himself. So he could one day have a better life.

The whole thing had taken less than three minutes. Four men now lay on the ground, silent and still. Their horses breathing heavily. Obviously agitated and frightened.

The cows, dumb animals that they were, milled around, bawled and mooed, their tones mournful and pained. Finally when the air cleared, they grew quiet.

The men beside him slowly lowered their weapons.

His voice still thick with worry and tension, Slim muttered, "Think we got 'em all, Mr. Proffitt?"

"Hope so," Scout said. "Russell, you got a light?"

With a shaking hand, Russell lit a match and put it to the end of a cheroot, then stood up to locate a branch to use as a torch. Scout watched the boy in surprise. He didn't know why he'd been surprised that the boy had a cigar but he was.

Slim was far more shaken, which stood to reason. Russell had ridden with the Waltons. He was used to killing in the dark.

The cowhand most definitely was not.

Crouching beside him, Scout tried to see the ranch hand's face. "You get hit?"

"Yeah."

"Where? Do you know?"

"It ain't bad. I think they only got my shoulder." He grimaced. "Stings like the devil though."

Scout leaned closer, looking for the telltale signs of blood. He spied a red patch on the man's shoulder, but otherwise, he didn't look to be injured anywhere else. "Hold on, okay?"

"I'll be all right."

Scout left Slim's side. Still holding a Colt in his left hand, he walked toward Russell. "What have we got?"

Russell had been trained very well. In his left, he held a burning branch, in his right, a pistol. His eyes were wary, obviously ready for any of the men to roll over and take them by surprise.

It had happened, of course. Gun battles between men of no honor wasn't a pretty thing.

Scout walked toward the first body they saw and gently nudged him with his foot. When he saw no flinch, he rolled him over to see his face. "Recognize him, Russell?"

"Nah. But I don't know rustlers."

They did the same thing with the other men, examining the last as they heard the rumble of approaching riders.

There was no place to hide. The sun was now peaking over the horizon, turning the pitch-black darkness into various shades of gray.

Russell stomped out his torch and gripped

his other gun.

At two hundred paces out, one of the riders raised a hand. "Brower!" he called out.

Russell relaxed, but Scout remained vigilant. Only when the next rider appeared, none other than Miles Grant himself, did he holster his weapons.

A chill bit his skin as he waited for the men to approach. Was Brower going to go back on his word now and arrest him?

Was Miles going to lie and say he'd never wanted the men to lie in wait and commit murder on his property?

Scout had seen enough lying and cheating in his life to not take anything for granted. Not even from a man who was almost family.

"They dead?" Brower called out.

Scout nodded.

In silence, the men dismounted, tied up their horses, and approached the fallen men.

The sun had risen a bit, casting the first rays of sunlight across the land. In its rays, the braying cattle's black coats shone like crude oil.

And four men, their eyes open in death, stared back at them, their gazes unseeing.

"Look familiar, Mr. Grant?" Brower asked.

Miles Grant stepped across the uneven

ground, glanced Slim's way for a full few seconds, then strode over to the bodies laying prone on the ground.

Scout half-expected the man to blanch. Maybe look a little faint. He wouldn't have faulted the rancher for doing it, neither. It wasn't easy to look a dead man in the eye. A man looked different when his soul was gone.

Miles swallowed hard, then raised his chin and nodded. "These are the men. These are the men who paid me a visit, anyway."

"Then that's good enough for me," Brower said with a satisfied expression. "All right, men, let's bring these men on into Camp Hope. And get you to the doctor, Slim."

"Won't argue with that, Sheriff," Slim said. "Darn bullet burns like the devil."

Faint laughter filled the air as they lifted bodies and carefully placed them on the back of the horses.

But Scout noticed the laughter wasn't merry — only forced. Russell looked haunted, and Miles Grant looked disturbed.

No, the only person who looked satisfied was the Sheriff. But was it because justice had been served . . . or that he'd finally had a concrete reason to string up the notorious Scout Proffitt to the closest tree?

29

Russell knew when he died, he was going to have to answer for the pain he'd caused other men. He was going to have to answer for killing his father.

But more than that, he was going to have to pay penance for standing guard while others had murdered during his time with the Walton Gang. At first, his membership in the gang had been a blessing for him. He'd been so thankful to not be scared and alone. A man couldn't discount the days that pain and hunger and living in isolation could do to his soul.

Little by little, he'd realized the things he'd given up for security. When he'd stood by and watched Kent beat a witness or abuse a woman, Russell had known he'd lost most of his heart.

He'd given up decency and compassion. Those qualities had had to be firmly punched down or he wouldn't have been able to survive. The day he'd left the gang, it had been cloudy and dark. A storm had been brewing, and Mr. James Walton had been taken away in handcuffs.

Addison Kent, and everything he'd stood for, had become just a memory — Scout had killed him on Mr. Walton's orders before he'd taken off.

That's when he'd realized that his reason for being in the gang — for security and comfort — had been merely smokescreens. There had been no security living with men intent to do harm.

But now, as they rode toward Mr. Grant's mansion in the dawn's morning light, Russell realized for the first time that he felt proud of himself.

"You okay?" Scout asked as he rode next to him. "You seem a little quiet."

"I'm okay. Just wondering if Brower is going to keep his end of the bargain."

"He seems inclined." What Scout didn't say was that no man could really be trusted. They were all prisoners to greed and their own agendas.

"I hope so."

"What are you going to do when you're a free man?"

Russell pretended to think about his answer for a time. But it was all an act. He knew exactly what he wanted to do. "Go home."

"Yeah? Where's home?"

"Arkansas." Russell glanced in Scout's direction. Hoping to see some kind of response in his gaze. But of course, his black Stetson shaded most of his features.

"Arkansas is a nice place."

"Is it?" Russell looked at the land surrounding them at the moment. With its red clay and squatty mesquite and thin creeks and rocky buttes, it looked like a dozen other places he'd been to. No better or worse than any of them.

"Nice enough."

"That's true." Any home was nice — as long as there were people there who cared about you. He wasn't sure he had that, though.

"So, who's still home? Your mother?"

"Maybe. She kicked me out years ago, so she might not want me back."

"You going back for a girl?"

There it was. Though everything inside of him ached to lie and keep his secret to himself, he decided to give into weakness. "Her name's Nora."

"Pretty name."

That, he didn't have to think about. "It is. The prettiest."

"Have you been writing her?"

Russell shook his head. "No. She may not want me back either. I . . . I killed someone in order to protect her." Amazed that the truth could still hurt after all this time, he struggled over the next words. "I stabbed my stepfather for . . . for trying to rape her."

"So you loved her."

"I did." He still did. He'd met a lot of women, some good, some not so much. But none of them affected him like she had. None of the women made him yearn for a future like Nora did. "If I don't go see her, I don't think I'll ever know if I did the right thing."

"Russell, she might have moved on."

"I know. And I wouldn't blame her. But I gotta know." He looked at Scout, sitting so erect and sure in the saddle. "I need to make sure she's all right."

"I can understand that." He coughed. "Family and home and a man's past are important. It's what makes him who he is."

There was something in Scout's voice — a note of yearning — that made Russell ask more than he should probably have dared. "Have you ever gone back home? Have you ever gone back to see your family?"

"Me? No."

"Maybe you should take some of your

366

own advice?"

"My life is different, Russell. First off, I've found Rosemarie, and she's more than I deserve. I can't imagine the Lord giving me more people in my life. Then, there's a big difference between me and you."

"I've killed too. And I've been part of the Walton Gang."

"You were just a pup. You might have thought you played a big part in our missions, but we all did our part to try to keep you sheltered." He paused. "Will and me, anyway."

"I still sinned."

"I appreciate your sins, but I have to tell you that you'd have to do more than you'd ever care to to get to my level. I made that choice in order to stay alive." He paused. "But that doesn't mean my family has to still want anything to do with me."

"Maybe —"

"I promise you. They won't want me." His voice hardened as they got closer to the barn and the men in front of them began to dismount. "Well, let's see what the sheriff has to say." With a wry, bitter smile, he added, "If he strings me to a tree, cut me down and bury me decent, would you?"

Mouth dry, Russell nodded. He knew in his heart that Scout wasn't kidding. He really thought there was a very good chance that he was about to die.

"Clayton, will you be heading to Mr. Grant's home soon?"

"That had been the plan, but now I'm thinking it might be best if I stay here until Scout gets back. If it's not too much of an inconvenience, ma'am."

With each hour in his company, Rosemarie understood just what a decent man Clayton Proffitt really was. With some shock, she realized that if she refused his offer, he would leave.

But that he was most likely looking out for her, his brother's wife.

"I'll be fine on my own. I've been alone much of my life."

"No longer. Now you have family who will take care of you."

That was the difference, wasn't it? She had a sister and a mother, but they had only focused on her faults. And because of that, she'd never stood a chance in their regard. No one could overcome a lifetime of perceived faults.

"If you'd like to stay here, I'd be grateful for your company."

"I'm relieved to hear it."

"Why is that?"

"I don't want to offend you, but there's quite a few things that need doing."

She giggled. "There's a great many things that need doing. What did you have in mind?"

"I thought I might build you and Scout a fence. At least get started on it."

Tears pricked her eyes. The fence symbolized everything that was so wrong with the farm. And symbolized the many, many things that had been lacking in her life. "I think a fence would be much appreciated, Clayton."

"Good." A satisfied gleam appeared in his eyes. "Because I went out early and spoke with your neighbor, Mr. Kowalcheck. He's going to round up some men this evening and start helping me make post holes."

Post holes? In November! "Is there anything you can't do?"

"Plenty, Mrs. Proffitt. I just don't dwell on them."

Now that was good advice.

30

Miles had never been one for ceremony, but even he had to admit that the men standing in front of him could use a small celebration.

Fact was, the men grouped around him looked pleased as punch. Even Slim, who'd needed doctoring, but since the bullet had been dislodged easily and his arm patched up without a problem, he was only looking mildly achy.

The other men, on the other hand, looked far different. Each of them looked lost and afraid and wary. Even though they'd just captured and stopped some of the worst criminals in the state, they still had a haunted look about them.

After conferring with Sheriff Brower and hearing that they had, indeed, gotten their men, Miles decided to give them their due. "Gentleman, I am in your debt. Your hard work and bravery have not only saved the ranches in the area from losing all their profits for the year, but also have saved lives. Congratulations for a job well done."

But instead of cheers or laughter or slaps on the back, the men stood motionless, their eyes trained on Sheriff Brower. This man, it turned out, had what they most needed. A key to their future.

Miles nudged him to speak.

He cleared his throat and began. "I am ready to fulfill my end of the bargain. It will now be my honor to expunge your records and now forever declare you free men."

"Unless you create your own trouble in the future," Miles warned with a small smile.

Little by little, Scout and Russell and the others' expressions slowly thawed. Doubt and wariness were replaced by smiles and a look of hope in their eyes.

Finally, Joe Bob, the blond with the smattering of freckles across his nose, grinned. "See? I told ya it would all work out."

With that quip, the other men relaxed and moved from formation. Scout Proffitt went right over to the sheriff and shook his hand.

Russell and two others came up to him and grinned.

"This is a mighty big day in my life, Mr. Grant," Russell said.

"It's a big one for me, too," he replied. A little louder, he said, "My housekeeper is bossy and talks too much. But she makes a good breakfast, and at the moment it's cooling inside. Come on in and eat."

If he'd thought he'd have to argue and cajole to get the men to eat, he'd been very wrong. Hardly a minute passed before they filed into the grand dining room and began heaping their plates full.

Miles kept to the background. He'd learned that the men he paid appreciated a bit of a distance between himself and them. Sitting across from them while eating a plate of eggs and sausage only made them uncomfortable.

Instead, he went into his office, pulled out a couple envelopes, opened his safe, then started writing notes and slipping cash in envelopes.

Though money didn't make everything better in a man's life, Miles knew that it did come in handy. Living on mere praise might sound okay from a pulpit, but nothing made a man feel appreciated like the ability to provide for his wife and children.

He was just about done when Scout appeared at the doorway. "Miles, I'm about to take off. Just wanted to thank you."

Gesturing to his beat-up face, he shrugged

off the praise. "You saved my ranch and my life, at no small expense to you. They could've killed you, Scout. I'm grateful."

Scout nodded, appeared to be ready to leave . . . then glanced at him again. "Mind if I ask you something?"

"Ask me whatever you want."

"Clayton . . . did he ever mention me?"

Miles paused, knowing deep in his heart that his next words were going to mean the world to this much-feared man in front of him.

"He mentioned you all the time," he said. "I've spent a lot of time with him over the last year. And hardly a day went by when either he or Corrine didn't mention you."

Pulling off his black hat, Scout ran a hand through his hair. "So . . . you don't think they hate me?"

"No," he blurted, shocked that Scout could think of that. "They don't hate you at all."

"I don't deserve their love."

Getting to his feet, Miles walked to stand in front of him. Scout Proffitt was taller, more handsome, and in a lot of ways, far more respected than Miles could ever hope to be. The man had had books written about him, and more women than Miles could ever imagine practically falling at his feet.

He was a hero to some. And whether others feared him or wished he was dead, there seemed to be a universal truth that all acknowledged. He was the best shot that anyone had ever seen.

But with a sudden sense of knowledge, Miles understood that he had one thing the famous gunfighter didn't have.

Hardly believing he was doing it, he enfolded the man's hand in between his own. "You deserve it," he murmured. "That's what Grace is all about. None of us is perfect enough to deserve God's love, but we get it anyway. And that's how Clayton and Corrine feel about you. They love you no matter what. Not because of who you are, or of who you should've been. They love you because you're their brother."

Scout's jaw clenched, and he blinked and looked away quickly. "You really believe it, don't you?"

"I know it because I was given the same generous love from my sister, and I promise you, I deserved her love and forgiveness even less than you do." He squeezed Scout's hand again. "I wrote Clayton and Vanessa and told them about what's been going on. I imagine Clayton's on his way out here right now. You ought to wait for him. You're welcome to stay here as long as you want."

"You'd really have me? As your guest?"

"Of course."

For a moment, Miles thought Scout was going to consider it. But then he released Miles's hand and stepped back. "I appreciate it, but I think I'd best get on home. I have a wife now . . ."

"And she needs to know that you're coming home."

"Yeah."

"If you're leaving, hold on a minute. Let me give you an envelope."

"If it's money, I don't want it."

"I promise, the money won't be missed, and you deserve it."

"Give my share to those boys." He smiled softly. "They're young and needy. They'll put that money to good use."

Miles had to smile. Scout's description of the boys was exactly right. Those boys really were needy. And not near as old and jaded as they supposed they were.

Now there was just one more thing to take care of. "When Clayton comes back here, may I tell him where you are?"

Scout breathed deep. Exhaled. Then in an action so quick Miles almost missed it, he nodded.

Then he turned around and went out the front door. Minutes later, Miles saw a man in a familiar black duster riding away on a silver horse.

He closed his eyes and offered him a prayer for safe travels.

Then he stood up, envelopes in hand, to go see the men at the table.

Rosemarie had watched Clayton saw wood and pound boards for two days straight. He'd slept in the barn and had risen well before dawn, often milking the cow and fetching her eggs before she had the coffee ready each morning.

Yesterday, she'd been embarrassed. "Clayton, this is no way for me to treat a guest. Please let me wait on you some."

"I'm not a guest, I'm family. And I'd expect nothing less from Scout for my Vanessa."

Vanessa. There it was again. Clayton spoke his wife's name in such a way that told volumes about how much he cared for her. Rosemarie had no doubt that he would expect Scout — or every man he met — to tend to her needs.

She had to be a special woman.

Now, as she stood beside him while he nailed the fence posts together, she ached to learn more about the woman who had so claimed her brother-in-law's heart.

"What's she like?" she asked, hoping she sounded merely curious and not slightly jealous of a woman to have such a man's high regard.

He paused, holding the hammer loose for a long moment. "Vanessa's just about the prettiest thing you ever saw. And though she looks a little on the delicate side, it's deceiving. She's stronger than she looks."

"Do y'all have children?"

He held up a finger. "One. A boy. I named him after my father."

"I'm sure y'all will have a fine family one day."

"God willing. Though I have to tell you that we have a fine family right now. I'm already happier than I imagined I ever could be."

The way he talked about his life . . . the way his eyes softened when he spoke of his wife, Rosemarie knew Clayton was only telling a small portion of how much he cared for his wife. "She's a lucky woman to have you," she murmured. "Have y'all been married long?"

"Two years."

"The way you talk about her . . . the way you two seem so close, I would've imagined y'all been married longer."

"I've known her much longer. I was foreman of her ranch for years. Her father hired me, then I stayed on after he passed away."

"And then one day you two fell in love?"

"No, it wasn't like that." Looking out toward the west, his voice hardened. "One evening . . . something happened. She was in need. I risked everything to take her away."

That sounded incredibly romantic. "And then you fell in love?"

"Ever since I can remember, I loved her." His lips curved into the smallest of smiles. "And then I married her."

"And then?"

"And then we both became brave enough to fall in love."

Rosemarie was startled by the words. "Brave enough to fall in love." That seemed to say it all.

Falling in love did take courage. With some surprise, she realized that she hadn't been fearing Scout as much as her feelings for him. She hadn't been afraid for her life or her safety.

Instead, she'd been afraid for her heart.

"What about you and Scout? Is yours a love match?"

"You know that he and I recently met. And you most likely know that he was asked to marry me in order to save my reputation."

"The folks in town did tell me that."

She was surprised at the way he didn't sidestep around her awful truth. But she also appreciated the honesty. Like falling in love, being honest wasn't an easy thing to do.

"Rosemarie, did you wish that you hadn't married him?"

"I didn't want to marry him, but not for the reasons you might expect."

He stared at her hard, then nodded. "I understand."

"No, I don't think you do." She took a deep breath and continued to tell the truth. To tell him more than she'd hardly been able to tell herself. "I have to tell you that I wasn't afraid of him. I wasn't worried about being married to him."

"He's been a wanted man. A notorious man."

"That is true. But there's also far more to him than I think most people have ever cared to see." Thinking about Scout, and the way he'd stood up to the banker and sheriff, she tried to put into words everything she was thinking. "He's tough, but he's honest, too. He's also a very decent sort of man."

"Decent?"

She realized then that Clayton wasn't just asking about Scout for her sake . . . he was asking for his sake, too. He wanted to know more about his brother.

The brother he'd never really known.

"I don't think Scout has enjoyed his life much," she said hesitantly. "But I think he's come to terms with his faults and his sins. I know he believes in God and has asked forgiveness."

Time seemed to stand still as a new light of hope flickered in his eyes.

Finally, he spoke. "Our father was a God-fearing man. Our mother, she was a sweet soul. Both had an enormous, positive impact on our lives. When Scout was born, so much bad was happening. His birth brought about our mother's death . . . which brought our father's faith into precarious places. I'm afraid Scout grew up aware of that."

He picked up another board, ran his hand along the wood's grain. "Corrine and me have a relationship with the Lord. But I never felt like I did a very good job of teaching Scout about Jesus. By the time he got old enough to understand, our father was off to war. And then I went to battle, too."

"I might be wrong, but I think we all have to make peace with our faith at one time or another. Faith and believing in a higher power? It's a personal thing. Something that can't be forced or taught." She thought some more. "Or spoon-fed to a person like a baby. But if a person's will is in the right place, the Lord will lend his hand."

"So you're saying that Scout might have found it on his own?"

Though Clayton seemed indomitable, Rosemarie knew she had to tread carefully. "I have a feeling that you and your sister and father gave him the seeds, but Scout took the time to water and nurture that faith. It's true he did, indeed, experience a drought. Possibly he was in danger of losing everything good that he had. But in his own time, he did grow his faith into something strong."

"You really believe that?"

"I wouldn't have said it if I didn't."

He blinked quickly. "I don't know if you can ever understand how much hearing that means to me."

She understood family. And she understood faith. And now, thanks to Scout, she understood love. "I hope you won't take this the wrong way, but I already do know."

To her relief, he didn't ask her to explain. Didn't ask her to say more than she was ready to. Instead, he picked up another piece of wood. Ran his hand along the grain.

"Scout's going to be so happy about this fence," she said. It was a rather silly thing to say, but it couldn't be helped.

"I hope so."

"I hope Scout comes back soon." Actually, she hoped he came back. She'd hate to lose someone who she'd just found.

"I do, too," he said softly.

31

Russell now had more money in his pocket than he'd ever had in his whole life. The amount that Mr. Grant had given each of them had been staggering.

This whole time, he hadn't dared to imagine a payment for helping Mr. Grant and Sheriff Brower. The idea of being a free man, of finally having a future? That had been more than enough for him.

But now he had enough money to start a new life. He liked the weight of the wad of bills in his pocket. Liked the idea of having possibilities in his life.

Looking at the other men in the bunkhouse — the men he'd spent the last nine months with. Some even longer. He felt a sad sort of melancholy fall over him. All this time, they'd stuck together out of fear and out of necessity.

Now they each could do what they wanted.

And it was a bit humbling to realize that given the choice, none of them wanted to be with the others.

The only person who had a set place he intended to ride to was Andrew. From the moment he'd stuffed the envelope in his pocket, he'd had a dreamy gaze on his face.

"You still going to see Betsy, Drew?" Russell asked.

If anything, that dreamy look deepened. "Uh-huh. I'm gonna leave first thing in the morning, I don't care if I hit snow the whole time."

Tuff chuckled. "You will when you're half-freezing to death."

"I don't care. I can't hardly wait to see Betsy's face when I show up. I haven't seen her in practically forever."

Russell kind of expected the other men to tease Andrew, but it seemed like they were feeling . . . a little bit envious. And a little bit pleased that at least one of them was going to ride off to have a happy life.

"You know, I don't even know where Betsy lives," Tuff said. "Where does she hail from?"

"Kentucky. Louisville."

Louisville was a long distance from Texas. It was also worlds away from how they'd been living. "It's going to take a while to get to her," Joe Bob said.

"Hope not. But I'll get there," Andrew said with his usual confidence.

Tuff cleared his throat. "No offense, but do you think her family will let you court her?"

"They've known about me for years. I know they're not happy with what I've been doing, but I can win them over. I'm sure of it. Plus, I've got Betsy on my side."

"You think so?" Russell asked. He didn't mean to sound so skeptical, but life had surely taught him that a woman's word could be a mercurial thing.

"I know so," Andrew said. "By the time we finish talking with them — and they see how happy I make Betsy — they won't raise any objections." He paused for a breath, then his voice hardened. "At the end of the day, it don't matter none what they think, anyway. Betsy's mine. I have her heart, and she has mine."

The words, so honest and heartfelt and private, made Russell uncomfortable. He could only imagine such a relationship.

Could only imagine a woman waiting for a man like that.

But, then again, Andrew's circumstances were far different than his own. In the grand scheme of things, his friend didn't have all that much to overcome. Andrew hadn't lived with the Walton Gang. But still . . . "I hope seeing her is everything you want it to be."

"I hear what you're saying. Or rather, what you're not saying. But I promise you this, it's all right." Andrew smiled. "Her family is a bit different than most. See, her father fought in the war, but he also helped get slaves to the North. He believed in the South, but not slavery. Betsy's much the same way. Loyal but a freethinker, too. She'll have me, even though I'm not perfect."

"You're nowhere near perfect," Tuff said with a grin. "If Betsy thinks you are, she's gonna be in for a big shock!"

Russell knew he didn't need to see Tuff's face to know that underneath that grin was a good chunk of envy. Andrew had a goal, and a way to achieve it, too.

Russell didn't blame him. He was jealous of Andrew's future, too. It must be something to know where you were headed, instead of being afraid to go there at all.

Lighting up a cheroot, Andrew took a puff. "What are you going to do, Russell?"

The tart-sweet scent of tobacco turned his stomach. It reminded him of James Walton's cigars and the many terrible things he'd done in order to stay a part of the gang.

And of the feeling that his future was out of his control.

"Me?" he asked. "I don't know." Fact was, he was afraid to say too much about his dreams. Then they'd all know how much he had to lose . . . or maybe how much he'd never had.

"You should go see that girl you've been mooning about." He tapped the end of the cheroot, sprinkling ashes to the ground. "What was her name? Nancy?"

"Nora," he said automatically. Before he remembered that he'd been trying to keep Nora's identity — and his love for her — private. "I'm surprised you remembered her name. She wasn't all that special to me."

Sharing a look with the other boys, Andrew said snidely, "Russell, did you really think you'd kept her a secret? All of us have known you've been stuck on a girl."

"Since when?"

"Since forever."

"I should've kept her a secret. Things between Nora and me aren't like how they are with Betsy and Andrew. Shoot, I don't even know if she'll have me again." Feeling like he had nothing to lose, he added, "The last time I saw her, she said she didn't want to see me again." Actually, that was putting it mildly. He was fairly certain she didn't want to see him again.

"Girls always say that," Tuff blurted. "But it ain't always the truth."

"It's not always the truth, but it ain't always a bad idea either," he said. Remembering. "What I did was unforgivable." He hadn't thought so at the time, but now he knew better.

Tuff stilled. "What did you do? Did you hurt her, Russell?"

Even the thought of hurting Nora made him sick to his stomach. "Of course not."

"Then I bet what you did might be forgivable." Tuff waggled his brows. "Take it from me. Most things are."

"Betsy's forgiven me for lots of things," Andrew added.

"She's not going to forgive me for what I did." Figuring he had nothing to lose . . . after all, he'd probably never see these men again, he confessed it all. "I . . . I killed a man. He was hurting her."

Joe Bob cocked his head to one side. "And she got mad at you for that?"

There was no going back now. He inhaled. "The man I killed? He was my stepfather. My stepfather, he was a vicious man. He used to beat my mother." He took a breath. "And me," he added, feeling like he'd just

388

made the biggest choice of his life.

For the first time, he'd chosen honesty instead of another lie. These were the first men he'd ever admitted his past to, and doing so made him feel bare and at risk.

But telling the complete truth, holding himself out there, letting them see his weaknesses also had a freeing effect. He now felt like he could breathe easier, without the weight of more mistakes bearing down on him.

As he took another deep breath, no one spoke.

The other men were silent. Russell closed his eyes briefly and pretended his heart wasn't breaking. Revealing that he'd let himself get beaten had been a mistake.

Sharing that he'd killed his stepfather had been a mistake, too. He was a fool. Though he might never see them again, he'd wanted to leave with their respect.

Or at least their compassion.

Now they probably thought he was nothing better than a weakling and a common murderer. He hung his head as a tear traipsed down his cheek. He'd been a fool to trust these men, just as he'd been a fool to imagine Nora would even dream about ever accepting him back into her life.

Then to his surprise, he felt strong arms

curve around his shoulders. Holding him close. Offering him support. "It's okay, Russell," Andrew murmured. "I would've killed him, too."

Maybe it was Andrew's words. Or the hug . . . no one had hugged him in a decade.

Or maybe it was because he wasn't going to know them any longer and he was suddenly sad about that. Whatever the reason, Russell closed his eyes and leaned closer. Letting the tears fall.

Another hand patted his back — Joe Bob's.

"Go ahead and cry, Russell. We won't tell nobody."

"I won't tell a soul," Andrew murmured. "Promise."

So Russell did cry, but whether it was from his past or the uncertainty of his future, he didn't know.

All he did know was at that moment, it didn't really matter at all.

32

Rosemarie had been up at dawn, throwing up. Tears pricked her eyes as the queasiness strengthened.

She wasn't going to be able to leave the company of her chamber pot anytime soon.

She groaned as she heard the door open.

"Rosemarie, are you all right?"

"I'm fine, Clayton," she called out. Hoping, hoping he didn't decide to peek into her bedroom.

He did. His eyebrows rose when he saw her sitting here, hugging the chamber pot. "You don't look all right," he said mildly. "It looks to me like you aren't feeling so well."

"I'll be okay soon. I guess I must have eaten something that didn't agree with me."

To her shame, he walked closer. Leaned on the door jamb. "We've been eating the same things. Unless you've been sneaking food?"

"I haven't been sneaking food," she said with a laugh. "I don't know what's wrong." Loosening her grip on the chamber pot, she made a shooing motion with her hand. "Please don't worry. I'll be good as gold soon." Just as soon as she didn't feel clammy and the smell of eggs didn't make her feel worse.

He smiled slightly. "This probably isn't seemly for me to mention it. But, any chance you could be in the family way?"

Family way? It took a moment to realize what he was talking about. But then it hit her hard. "Do you mean . . . a baby?"

"Well, yes." He nodded. "My wife just had our son," he said. "You're acting a lot like she did the first few months she was carrying our boy."

If she had a mirror in front of her, she knew she'd see her cheeks were bright red. "I . . . I suppose it could be a possibility," she finally said.

He grinned broadly. "If it is, that's good news indeed." Gentling his voice, he said, "Why don't you lie down for a little while? I can take care of things."

Lying down on a pillow sounded so nice. But she had a guest in the house. Scout's brother! "Please don't trouble yourself," she said quickly. "I'm sure I'll be up and fine in no time at all. There's no way I could look at Scout and let him know that I left you to fend for yourself."

"And there's no way I could look at my brother and let him know that I let you wait on me while you were feeling under the weather."

She chuckled. "I guess you could say we're in a bit of a quandary. Neither of us wants to let the other get put to work."

"Or you could listen to me. I promise, Mrs. Proffitt, a man will forgive his wife easier than his brother. Let me tend to you for a bit."

She supposed he had a point. Besides, she didn't feel like she was up to much at the moment, and there might even be a baby to think about. "Thank you," she said weakly.

"Anytime. Sleep, now," he coaxed, then closed her door.

Moments later, she heard him washing dishes in the sink, then turning on the stove and clanging a few pots and pans around. Obviously, he was no stranger to the kitchen.

He seemed to be just as able to fend for himself as Scout was. As she heard more pans clang, Rosemarie wondered what he was making. For a brief moment, she thought about lending him a hand. Maybe her nausea would subside if she moved around a bit?

But that musing soon faded as she curved her hands around her stomach. Could Clayton be right? Could she really have a baby on the way? Was her "flu" really a bout of morning sickness?

Thinking back, Rose remembered that Annalise's stomach had been upset for nine straight months when she'd been carrying. Her mother had commented on it almost daily.

And when her mother hadn't been fretting, Annalise had.

But there had been times when Annalise had sported kind of a dreamy expression.

Goodness. A baby! Someone to have and hold all her own. Someone to love — and who would love her back, always.

Wouldn't it be something if she would always have a part of Scout with her? The idea of telling him when he got back that she was carrying his child made her smile.

She just hoped that he would indeed get back to the Bar C. She couldn't bear to imagine what her life would be like if he didn't.

She couldn't bear to imagine having to spend the rest of her days wishing she'd said more to Scout. That she'd dared to trust him enough to share her feelings.

And wishing that she'd made more promises to keep.

Though they wouldn't have guessed it, it actually *had* occurred to Scout to say goodbye to Russell and the boys. At the very least, he knew he owed them his thanks. It was because of them that he was riding a relatively free man.

It was because of them that he'd finally met the elusive Miles Grant and learned more about his brother and sister.

But what would he say?

Even a good turn of events couldn't turn around a lifetime of living and working independently. He was still a man afraid to venture too far from his comfort zone. Scout had never been one for hugs or handshakes or good-byes anyway.

Shoot. He hadn't really ever been one for hellos, either.

But even if he had been that sort of person, he doubted he would have spared the time to chat. Hours were wasting.

He was too eager to see Rosemarie.

He couldn't count the number of times he'd replayed their good-byes. When he'd hugged her so close he could have sworn he'd felt her heart beat.

And thought for sure that she'd heard his.

When he'd held her so close, then silence had hung between them. And for a very brief moment she'd looked into his eyes and all the barriers fell down between them.

And that had only been their hug good-bye! He could hardly bring himself to recall the feel of her in their marriage bed. He now knew the difference between her slenderness and the bony figure he'd imagined her having.

And, like the selfish man he was, he'd enjoyed the feminine feel of her. But what had held his memory tight were those pretty blue eyes of hers. The way they gazed at him with something an awful lot like trust.

And, in his weaker moments, he'd let himself believe that there had been love there, too. And that, of course, was what his heart had craved so much.

He'd spent time under the sheets with a number of women, that was a fact. But he'd never held close a woman that he'd fallen in love with. Until Rosemarie.

Now he couldn't wait to return to her and settle into a life with no surprises. He was eager to work hard at the back end of a plow, once he figured out how to do that, of course. He couldn't wait to sweat and worry over crops, not whether the man at the other end of the saloon was going to take a shot in order to make a name for himself.

One day, perhaps they'd both be ready to start a family, and they could have a daughter or a son. And it would be just the three of them against the world.

That was fine with him. Being part of a family of three was two more people than he was used to worrying about.

All he had to do was get to her and hope she'd forgive him for putting his body at risk in order to have a life together.

When he heard the gallop of the rider behind him, he pushed away all the dreams with a sinking heart.

Looking over his shoulder, he spied Sherriff Brower.

He'd been a fool to imagine that life was fair or that he deserved anything. Preferring to wait for the man to explain himself and either shoot or take him into custody. He pulled on Rio's reins and watched the esteemed lawman approach.

"Look at you, Scout Proffitt, waiting on me. I'm honored."

"I thought we might as well get it over with," he drawled. "How are you going to do it, Sheriff?"

The sheriff blinked. "I don't follow."

"Come on. We both know there's only one

reason you would be here, riding after me."

The sheriff reined in his horse. "And that is?"

He was really going to make Scout say it? "You're going to kill me. Right?"

"That would be wrong, cowboy."

The sheriff's drawl was so world-weary and full of dry humor that Scout didn't even pretend to hold back his surprise. "I don't follow." Was this a new kind of trick?

"May I?" The sheriff motioned to the space beside Scout. Not taking a single thing for granted.

Flummoxed, Scout nodded.

When Sheriff Brower sidled up beside him, he raised the brim of his Stetson slightly, so that his eyes were plainly visible. As was his quizzical smile. "You just don't get it, do you, Proffitt? You don't believe you're really a free man."

There was no way to tell the truth and save his pride. Since his death was imminent — and since there weren't a whole lot of witnesses, only one — Scout told the truth. "I find that almost impossible to believe." And that was putting it mildly.

"I'm a man of my word, Mr. Proffitt. I've already telegraphed the news of your assistance with Harlan Jones. You are now officially pardoned." With a look of satisfaction, he continued. "I conveyed my thanks to both the U.S. Marshals and the Texas Rangers, too, for removing you off any and all wanted posters and lists. Before long, every sheriff far and wide will hear that you are now as innocent as any other man."

Scout scoffed. "And you think they'll believe all that and will actually listen and take me off their 'most wanted' lists?"

"I do, son. I promise, there're still plenty of bad outlaws, criminals, and murderers out there for them to hunt down. Losing you won't bother them none. If anything, they'll be relieved."

Scout didn't think that was likely. But he hoped it was true. No, he hoped and prayed it was true. "You sound so certain, I might just believe you."

"Absolutely, you should believe it. I only rode out here to tell you the news to your face."

"Why go to the trouble?" He still didn't understand.

"This is going to sound like a heap of lies. Or maybe it just won't make a lick of sense. But the truth is I respect you, Scout."

"I'm not worth it."

"I beg to differ. I've strung up my fair share of criminals, I promise. You're not like most."

"But I am like some."

"Heck, yeah," Brower replied. "You're not perfect. Of course you ain't! But I haven't reached the ripe old age of fifty and not realized that no man is. It seems to me that a man must have some flaws in order to survive. Otherwise, he's just too good to live."

Scout grinned. "I reckon you might be on to something there."

"So you heading home to your wife?"

"I am." Suddenly curious, he looked at Brower. "What about you? Are you married?"

He shook his head. "Can't say I've ever had that honor."

"Never found the right woman?"

"Oh, I found her. But, ah . . . she went and found a different man and then even had the good sense to stay married to him for twenty years. My luck, huh?"

"I'm not going to touch that one."

Brower grinned. "See, I knew you were smart." Holding his hand out, he said, "Good-bye, Scout Proffitt. I hope you won't take this the wrong way, but I'm going to have a grand time telling folks that I've actually met you."

Scout gripped the sheriff's hand as he returned the retort. "Well, I hope you won't take this the wrong way, but I most likely won't be telling a soul that we had this conversation."

"Fair enough." Giving a little salute, he said, "Good-bye, son."

And then he turned his horse around and left at a good trot.

As Scout continued back to Broken Promise and the Bar C, he thought about Russell and his boys. About Miles and about Sheriff Brower.

But most of all, he thought about Rosemarie and about how he was anxious to try out married life with her.

Thirty hours later, he spied the run-down shack with the surprisingly pretty red door. He spied the barn with the repaired wall that he'd fixed himself.

And then, he noticed the fence.

It was double-planked and pretty as a picture. And, of course, brand new.

He slowed his horse, wondering who would have done such a thing. Had Rosemarie gone crazy and decided to pay some fool to spend every waking minute working on a fence?

Or was she in danger? Had someone kicked her out and took over things and now she had nowhere to go?

"Rosemarie?" he called out. "Rose? Rose, you here?" For a second, he flushed. His voice had been as eager as any child's on Christmas morning.

But, of course, that was how he felt — anxious and excited and stunned that he'd actually made it home.

Head cocked, he waited. Listening for her steps.

Nothing.

"Rosemarie?" He started to feel sick. What was he going to do if she'd come to harm?

The red door flew open. And out came his wife. Her hair down, a neat blue dress fitting her form. She looked older and more polished and even prettier than he'd even remembered.

But the smile on her face, the look of pleasure and relief and happiness in her eyes — all of it was just for him and made him catch his breath. It was beautiful.

Close to being miraculous, really.

"Scout, you're back!"

When she started running to him, he reined in Rio and quickly swung his leg over the horn on his saddle. Leaving the reins dangling, he brushed past the horse and walked to her.

What could he say? How could he tell

Rosemarie just how much she meant to him?

But then there was no time to talk because she flung herself into his arms. Automatically, he curved his arms around her and held on tight. Her hair smelled like lavender and fresh spring water. In his arms, she felt so right. As little as ever, but more firm, too. Like she'd finally begun to take care of herself.

"You're here! With me. You came back," she gasped. "I was so worried." Biting her lip, she examined him from head to toe. "Are you hurt?"

He'd been worried, too. "You shouldn't have fretted so much, you could've made yourself sick, honey." It was so much easier to be strong now that he knew his life was in her arms.

"I couldn't help it." A few tears traipsed down her cheeks. Pressing his lips to her brow, he chuckled softly. "Rosemarie, it's okay, honey. It's over."

"It's over."

"You sure?"

"I am. Honey, I promise, I'm fine."

Stepping back, he looked into her eyes. "Now. Care to tell me about this fence?"

She bit her lip, looking all the sudden like a woman with a secret. "There's a story there. I'm not quite sure where to start."

A smidge of uneasiness entered the band of warmth that had been surrounding him. "How about you start at the beginning, sugar?"

"Well, you should know that we have a visitor."

"What?" A thousand questions burst into his mind. Who could it have been? And why did she look so wary? Had something happened to her that she was afraid to tell him?

Did she like whoever showed up better than him? Did Rose want him to leave?

She dropped her arms and hesitantly looked behind him.

His spine tingled. And he wondered how he could have been so foolish. He hadn't even looked around to see if another man was there. He deserved to be shot.

Ah, perhaps another outlaw had found him, finally? An outlaw had found him and had decided to wait here for Scout to get back . . . all so he could make a name for himself?

Before he knew it, he held one of his Colts in his right hand. And with a strong feeling of trepidation, he turned around.

And there, standing over six feet tall, solid and sure, was the best man he'd ever known.

The one man he'd always feared seeing.

And what had he done? Scout had pulled a gun on him.

His mouth went dry.

Feeling ashamed and disturbed, he slowly slipped his gun back into his holster. Then finally forced himself to meet his brother's gaze.

The look in Clayton's eyes was filled with pain and doubt. It seemed like he was trying to both see everything in Scout's heart and weigh his actions all at the same time.

Scout remained motionless. He deserved whatever anger his brother was no doubt feeling. He'd become everything Clayton was not. Once more, he'd become that way through no one else's fault but his own. Clayton and Corrine and his father had all tried to shield him from the harsh ways of the world.

He, on the other hand, had merely embraced it all.

As Scout's pulse quickened and his cheeks grew warm, Clayton continued to stare.

And then at last he spoke. "Hello, Scout," he said. "I have to tell you that there were times that I thought this day would never come."

Like the fool he was, Scout just nodded. Because truly?

There was nothing left to say.

33

"Guess things are back to normal, Mr. Grant," Miss Annabeth said as she bustled by his office, her arms full of sheets. "Before you know it, those stinking rustlers will have been a thing of the past. Just a memory."

Rubbing his cheek that was still slightly swollen, he nodded. "I suspect you're right. One day this will all fade." Maybe it would — eventually.

But of course one thing he didn't feel like sharing with her was the complete sense of loss he felt now that all the excitement was over.

He felt curiously deflated instead of triumphant now that Scout and Russell and the rest of the men were gone.

For some reason, the place now felt even more isolated than ever.

But perhaps that was his life?

Unceremoniously, Annabeth plopped the pile of laundry on the hall floor and wandered in uninvited. "Do you know what I think you should do now?" she demanded impatiently, her arms folded over her chest.

"Does it matter if I want to hear what you think or not? 'Cause I've got a feeling that I'm going to get an earful whether I want to hear it or not."

"You should go see Tracy Wood."

Just to goad her, he tried to look irritated. "And do what?"

She made a shooing motion with her hands. "And do what men do, of course. Go courting. Sir."

"Miss Annabeth, I appreciate your interest in my love life, but I think I'll take care of it by myself."

"I know you're gonna do what you want to do. But I have to tell ya, I think you're slower than molasses."

To his embarrassment, he was. Shoot, most men would be planning their weddings by now. He could hardly figure out if he "liked" Tracy or not! "I do things in my own time."

"If you don't take a wife, I'm going to be an old lady, rattling around this big old house, carrying your laundry to the washroom."

The picture she presented wasn't a pretty one. Neither was the idea that she probably had a good point. It was extremely likely that he wasn't going to be squiring a wife any time soon around the halls of the home.

"Thank you for voicing your opinion, Miss Annabeth."

"I'm not trying to be cheeky. Just honest."

"I'm not upset."

He kept his composure until she left, then collapsed against his chair when he was alone.

He'd never tell her, but he completely agreed with his bossy housekeeper. It was time he took a wife. Past time.

But he'd been frozen in time . . . first concentrating on all that he needed to do on the ranch in order to prove himself to the men that he was worthy of them.

Of course, he had other villains in his head to battle, too. Memories of his parents' marriage warred with images of Price abusing his mother. And of her letting the abuse happen, because being with a man like that was better than being alone.

Oh, he didn't think he was about to hurt a poor perspective bride. Far from that. He would never hurt a woman, certainly he'd never do the things that Price had done. But there was a time or two when he worried about taking a wife not for love, but because of loneliness.

That seemed like an awfully terrible reason for love.

So far he'd never met a woman who had taken his regard like Vanessa had for Clayton. No one could be in the same room with the two of them and not be struck at how in love they were. So much so, that more than one person had commented that they could probably leave the room and neither Vanessa or Clayton would notice.

Miles was happy for them. They deserved every bit of happiness.

But he wasn't sure if he was destined for a relationship like that. Laurel White wasn't his destiny.

And Tracy? He just wasn't sure. He'd appreciated her ministrations. And talking with her always seemed to ignite a few sparks between them. But he didn't know if that was because she irritated him so much or that was part of their destiny.

And while he knew some couples had that fiery chemistry, he just wasn't sure that was what he wanted at the end of every day. He'd always hoped for a more comforting kind of love. A love that felt like a soft blanket. Cozy and secure. Warm and soft.

He inhaled, imagining such a life, then abruptly coughed. Love like a soft blanket? Lord have mercy!

His thoughts were beyond embarrassing.

Lighting the lantern on the corner of his desk, he opened up his check register and began to sort through the mess of bills that had accumulated during the past week.

What he needed to do, he knew, was concentrate on the bills and forget about making things happen. The Lord would provide. He always did.

Picking up a pen, he read the latest bill from the blacksmith and got to work.

An hour must have passed when Annabeth trotted in.

"Mr. Grant —"

No way was he going to go through this again. "I'm busy, Miss Annabeth."

"No, sir." She coughed. "You have a visitor. I mean, someone needs to see you."

He got to his feet. "Who is it?"

And then to his surprise, a lovely woman with lovely brown hair pinned in a lopsided chignon and skin so fine it looked like it had been dipped in cream appeared in the doorway.

"Me," she said. Looking mildly embarrassed. After a quick look behind her, and Annabeth's gentle nod, she continued. "I'm sorry to bother you, sir. But my . . . ah, wagon broke down."

Unable to help himself, he gazed at her,

letting his eyes traipse over her hair, her face, her figure. She had to be the most beautiful woman he'd ever seen — though she wasn't even the prettiest. There was just something about her dark blue eyes that struck him senseless.

Quickly, he walked around his desk and strode to her side.

He fought to speak. "Miss, are you all right? I hope you aren't injured?"

"I'm perfectly fine." She smiled self-consciously. "Well, apart from sore feet. Me and my son walked here. It must have been three or four miles."

It was a wonder she hadn't gotten attacked by coyotes. Or had gotten lost in the dark and cold. He came around his desk. "You and your son? What about your husband? Is he with the wagon?"

She bit her lip. Then, making a decision, she shook her head. "I don't have a husband. It's just me and my son, sir. We decided to come to Texas to start a new life."

He noticed she didn't say she was a widow. Perhaps she thought it was understood? Perhaps there never had been one.

To Miles, it didn't matter. All that mattered to him was that he wanted her to stay a little longer. Smiling slightly, he held out a hand. "Please forgive my sorry manners.

I'm Miles Grant."

"I'm Katherine Sherrill."

Her hand was delicate and clad in a kid glove that had seen better days at least a year ago. "Miss Sherrill, it's a pleasure. Now, where is your son?"

She smiled slightly, bringing a dimple to life in her cheek and drawing his eye once again to her lovely face. "Brock is in the barn. He wanted to see the horses, and your hands told me they'd watch over him while he did so." She chuckled. "He's four. Everything is an adventure to him."

He knew the boy would be in good hands if Slim and Big Jim were looking out for him. No doubt, they'd probably already set him on the back of a horse and were teaching him a thing or two about riding.

"I can't wait to meet him," he said.

"I don't want to cause you any trouble. If someone wouldn't mind walking back with me to the wagon and helping me with the repairs . . ."

"There's no need for you to worry about that, ma'am. I'll ask a couple of the hands to ride out in that direction and handle things."

"I don't want to be any trouble," she said again.

"It's no trouble." Glancing at the doorway,

where Annabeth was lurking unabashedly, he said, "Please don't take this the wrong way, but your timing couldn't have been better. You came on exactly the right day."

Looking beyond the woman, he met Annabeth's understanding gaze. "Wouldn't you say, Miss Annabeth?" he asked softly.

Tears pricked her eyes as she met his gaze.

It had happened. He'd found his match and they both knew it. "I would say that exactly, Mr. Grant." Stepping away, she called over her shoulder, "After you see that boy, you tell him to come see me. I'll have some cookies ready for him."

Katherine blinked. "Cookies?"

Miles held out his elbow, "May I escort you to the barn, Miss Sherill. I'd love to meet Brock."

Looking at him in a daze, she slowly placed her hand on his elbow. "Please don't take this the wrong way, but I do have a feeling he's going to be very glad our wagon broke."

Miles simply smiled. But inside he was grinning broadly. He knew that feeling well. He, too, was very glad their wagon broke.

34

It had taken a while, but finally Scout had found his voice. "Clayton?" Scout said, still looking at his brother like he was an apparition. "What are you doing here?"

"Miles telegraphed me about the rustlers on the ranch. I decided to offer what assistance I could. But then I heard you were living here and that you'd recently gotten married. I thought I might stay here with Rosemarie. I knew you'd rather have me stay with her so she's not alone than be by your side."

Scout glanced Rosemarie's way and felt himself flush. His words were true. He'd lived all his life on his own. He certainly didn't need his older brother there for his success.

And if he'd known that Rosemarie had been watched over, it would have given him a greater sense of peace.

What was surprising, though, was how

Clayton had sensed that was the right decision. Even though they'd both lived their lives virtually apart.

How was it that an older brother whom he hadn't seen in more than a dozen years could still make him wish he was more like him? Stronger, taller, better? "This marriage of ours, it was kind of a sudden thing."

"It was a blessing, to be sure," he murmured. "You've got yourself a real fine lady here. It's been a pleasure to get to know her."

Rosemarie smiled. "I feel the same way. You've been a real help, Clayton. And, you are an excellent fence builder."

Looking at the fence, now surrounding the barn and house, he nodded. "It's a very fine fence," Scout allowed, realizing all of the sudden that the fence was so much more than a mere enclosure. "It suits the place."

"It makes the Bar C seem like it's something special, after all," Rosemarie added.

"I wanted to do something for you," Clayton said. His voice was husky, his words stilted. "I wanted you to know I still care."

And he had. After all these years, his older brother was looking out for him, again.

Scout tried to think of a way to reply to that, but the words seemed to be stuck in his throat. The emotion was too deep. What

Clayton was saying were the things that he used to hope and wish for but had never imagined that would ever come to pass. He'd either thought he would be dead or have done so many unforgiveable things that Clayton wouldn't want to claim him as kin.

Clayton pursed his lips, seemed to make a mental decision, then mumbled something under his breath. "I can't do this," he said as he strode forward.

Scout's stomach flipped. Had he somehow ruined everything between them before it had even begun again?

"You can't do what?" Scout blurted. Then all words failed him when Clayton enveloped him in a hug. His brother was his same height. Just as strong. The feel of him brought back faded memories of their father.

Brought back memories of being loved.

Slowly, inch by inch, Scout's hands circled his brother's back.

And immediately felt like he'd come home, all over again.

When Clayton's arms tightened, Scout's did too. Suddenly, it didn't feel like he was alone any more. Suddenly, it didn't feel like he'd cut every tie. He exhaled — a long, shaky sigh.

Raising his head slightly, he looked for

Rosemarie. She was standing to the side, tears running down her cheeks. Letting him know that everything that he was feeling was right with her.

Briefly, he closed his eyes and said a prayer.

Finally, he had seen his brother again. Years of hopes and dreams and made-up scenarios fluttered in his head, making him realize that they were nothing like he imagined.

Being with his hero brother was like everything and nothing he'd ever dreamed.

When Clayton pulled away, his eyes were damp. "I'm sorry," he bit out. "I didn't mean to make you feel uncomfortable." After clearing his throat, he added, "It's just for a while there, I was afraid I'd never see you again. Not alive, anyway."

He'd felt the same thing, except that he would have bet money on it. More than one morning, he'd awoken sure that the day was his last day on the earth.

He was at a loss for words. What do you tell a brother who had lived his life doing everything right that he was still grateful for him, even though he'd done everything wrong?

As if she sensed his tension, Rosemarie stepped toward the two men. "Scout, I know you've got to be starving. Why don't you let me feed you?"

He couldn't help but touch her. Reaching out, he ran a finger along the soft, fragile skin on her hand. "Only if you'll eat, too."

His touch caused her hand to tremble, making him realize that she wasn't immune to his touch. "We, I mean, Clayton and me, ate a few hours ago."

"I see." He tried not to feel jealous, but he was. He and Rosemarie had done so little together, he didn't trust their relationship yet.

"Come on," Clayton said, clasping his shoulder with a heavy hand as they walked into the tiny room, warm and toasty thanks to a warm fire in the wood-burning stove. "Sit down and talk to me. I've got all kinds of news about Vanessa and Corrine and her brood of kids. And you need to tell me what happened at the Circle Z."

Scout was ready to do that. But before he filled him in on the gunfight, he ached for honesty between them. "I'll tell you everything you want to know. But, I just need to know one thing. Do you hate me?"

A second passed. Then another. Then finally Clayton spoke, saying the words that Scout had long given up ever hearing. "I could never hate you. Never. I love you,

Scout. Of course I do," he drawled, emotion thick in his words. "You're my brother."

He wanted to believe the words, but life was short and he didn't want there to be anything fake in this moment. "But I wasn't good like you. I've been as far from your example as possible."

Clayton looked at him closely. "Do you hate me, Scout?"

He couldn't believe Clayton was asking him such a thing. "Never." The words were hard to say. Unfamiliar and rusty. "I love you, too. You're everything I've ever admired. You're my brother."

"Then that's all that matters. I don't care who you are or what you did. Or even what you didn't do. All that matters to me is that I've finally found you. I want to know you, Scout. I want to know you, and I want you to be a part of my life now. There's no going back."

Scout treasured the words, for both what they said and what they didn't. I want to know you. He didn't ask him to change. Not to improve. He wasn't there to save him.

"I want to know you, too."

Clayton nodded. Just like the decision had been made and all was right with the world again. "Then that's all we need to know, right?"

Rosemarie patted his shoulder as she walked to the stove and started dishing up stew.

"What happened with the rustlers?" Clayton asked. "Is Miles all right?"

Scout sat down across from him and started out slowly. "Miles is okay, but they'd beaten him something awful before we got there."

"Is he going to be all right?"

"Oh, yeah. He's banged and bruised and is sporting a good-sized cut or two. But he's going to be fine."

"Thank God for that."

"But those men were lethal, Clayton. They've been running wild across the county. Killed two other ranchers."

With halting words, he told the story of gunning them down. Every few minutes, he looked at Clayton again, half-sure he had finally said something to completely ruin their fragile new bond.

But Clayton only remained silent and sipped the coffee Rosemarie poured for him.

When she put a plate of steak and eggs in front of him, it was Scout's turn to sit quietly while Clayton talked of Corrine's three children and her life with her husband, Merritt.

"And Vanessa?" Scout asked. "Miles said

she's very happy."

"We're very happy indeed. We have a son. And I'm ranching with Merritt. Life is quiet now. It's good."

They talked more. One subject floating into the next. After a bit, Rosemarie sat down next to them, sipping hot tea and smiling softly.

The hours passed.

When Rosemarie's yawns began to occur with more frequency, Scout stood up and faced his brother. "We should probably let her sleep. You're not going in the morning, are you?"

Clayton winked at Rosemarie. "I promised your wife I'd stay a day or two after you arrived. Long enough to finish that fence, at the very least, and long enough to make plans."

Looking around, Scout wondered where his brother had been sleeping. "Have you been bedding down here on the floor?"

"No, out in the barn."

"I can't let you stay out there." Though it was a pitiful offer, he said, "I'll get a pallet for you here in the kitchen. It's not much, but at least you'll be warm."

Clayton's lips curved up slightly. "Thank you, but no. I don't mind the barn. I've slept next to horses more times than I could count."

"But —"

"Don't worry about me, Scout," he said gently. "I'll see you both in the morning."

After he left, Scout turned to Rosemarie. "I can't hardly believe this. I never thought I'd make it back, let alone see my brother again."

"I know."

Like his tongue was loose, he just kept talking. "After a lifetime of not expecting much, now so much has happened."

"I know," she said again. Standing up, she said, "Would you like to bathe, Scout? I can heat up your water."

"I'll wash up outside. I'm not going to keep you up any longer. I know you're exhausted."

She hesitated. "I am tired, but I have something to tell you."

He sat down. Then, unable to help himself, he pulled her onto his lap. "Do you want to tell me now or in the morning?" Unable to resist, he kissed her bare neck.

She made a little noise, letting him know he was pleasing her. He kissed her again. "We can talk about anything right now."

"I should probably wait . . ."

Worry overtook him. Was something

wrong? He'd been so eager to talk to Clayton, he'd hardly spared her more than a few private words once the two of them started talking.

"Sugar, are you upset? I have so much to tell you about what happened with the sheriff and with Miles. And about how much I missed you."

"Did you? Did you miss me?"

"More than you'll ever know." He kissed her softly on the lips. Ready to deepen the kiss when she yawned again.

So instead of kissing her, he picked her up easily in his arms and carried her to bed. A quick shake of the sheets, and she was in bed. Secure with a pair of quilts nestled over her.

"How about we talk tomorrow, Rose?"

He got no answer. In the safety of his arms, she slept.

35

Clayton stayed for two more days. Rose-marie loved watching the two men together. So much that she decided to share her news with Scout after Clayton left.

Selfishly, she wanted to celebrate the news when she was alone with Scout.

That was, she hoped he would be excited about the news.

Clayton left early that morning, the sun barely peeking over the horizon. He was off to the Circle Z to see Miles before heading back to Colorado.

Though he never said a word, she knew he was thinking the same thing she was — that her news to tell would be better done in private.

"I hate to see you go so soon," Scout said.

"It's probably time. Miles is no doubt wondering where I am."

"All right then."

"Scout, I'm going to keep you to your

promise. You're going to bring Rosemarie out to Colorado within the year, right?"

"I told you I would. I want to see Corrine and her kids and meet Vanessa." With a quick look in Rosemarie's direction, he quirked an eyebrow. "Who knows? We might even get out there sooner than later. I have a feeling traveling with Rosemarie would make a nice adventure."

Rose said nothing, knowing that a lot was going to change when she had a baby in her arms.

After another round of good-byes, including a soft kiss on her brow from Clayton, she was standing alone with Scout.

Right next to the fence post where she'd been standing when he rode into her life.

Perhaps this was the most fitting place to share her news.

When Clayton's silhouette was long gone, Scout turned to her and pulled her into his arms. "I'm sad to see him go, but I'm thankful to be alone with you."

"Me, too."

A look of concern appeared in his eyes. "You're trembling. Are you cold?"

"Not so much."

"Let's go inside, sugar."

"No . . . I want to tell you something first."

"You look serious."

"That's because this is important."

"Well, when it's that important, I think it's best just to say what's on your mind."

"All right." She took a deep breath. "I don't know if I'll be able to go to Colorado in the spring."

"No?" He looked crushed, but held his chin up. "Are you worried about meeting all those people? I'm worried, too, but I'll stay by your side." Running two fingers along her cheek, he said, "You know, maybe we could take this visiting thing a little more slowly. We could go see Miles Grant first. He is my brother-in-law, you know."

"I'd like that. But —"

"Shh. If you're not ready, we'll wait. But I don't want to leave you ever again, Rosemarie. I've been alone all my life. I don't want to live that way again."

Here was her chance. "I don't think you will be that way anytime soon."

"Good." He brushed his lips against hers once. Twice. "I'm glad to hear that. You know, maybe I should take that bath now? And then we could warm each other up . . ."

"I'm with child."

He stilled. "I'm sorry . . . what did you say?"

She laughed. "Scout, we're going to be parents."

"But, it was only that once . . ."

"Twice," she corrected with a blush.

"So fast . . ."

"I guess God decided that you needed a family real fast, Mr. Proffitt. You got a wife, a brother, a brother-in-law, and a whole string of relatives four states away . . . all waiting for you."

He kissed her, gently caressing her back, then tenderly brushing his fingers along the planes of her flat stomach. "Are you sure?"

She nodded. "I've been so tired. And so queasy. Clayton said Vanessa was the same way."

He slowly smiled. "Clayton knew?"

"Uh-huh. That's one of the reasons he left so quickly. Because he knew I was waiting to tell you."

Then, all at once, Scout smiled darkly, bent slightly at the waist, and scooped her up in his arms.

Rosemarie squealed with delight. "Scout! What are you doing?"

"Carrying you inside." He drawled as he practically marched into their cozy home.

Only when the door closed behind him did he slowly set her back on her feet.

"Don't you remember what I said when I carried you over the threshold on our wedding day?"

She remembered. She remembered everything that had ever happened with them.
"That it was a tradition you wanted to
repeat?"

"Uh-huh. Because I don't want to forget
this moment." His voice cracked. "Rosemarie, every day I thank God for meeting
your father at that run-down poker table in
Oklahoma. You've given me more than I
ever wished for. You've given me your love
and your life and your smile. Now you've
given me a child and a family.

A future.

Rosemarie, you've given me more than
I've ever deserved."

She believed in him. And she believed in
their future. But she didn't agree with his
words. "No, Scout, I've given you everything
that's been waiting for you right there all
along. All you had to do was choose to accept it."

"How did you get so smart?"

"Because I feel the same way. Because I
feel the very same way."

And that's when Scout Proffitt, former
notorious outlaw, reached out to Rosemarie
Cousins Proffitt and held onto her tight.

In his arms, she felt wanted and loved and
secure.

But most of all?
She knew he would never let her go.

DISCUSSION QUESTIONS

1. The Scripture verse from Ecclesiastes 8:7 ("Since no man knows the future, who can tell him what is to come?") seemed to fit the central characters in *A Texan's Choice* well. How might it relate to your life?
2. Scout Proffitt is one of my most favorite characters, and probably the one with the worst history. In your opinion, did he deserve to be a hero? If he resonated with you, why did he?
3. How are Scout and Rosemarie alike? How did their past hurts help make them perfect partners for each other?
4. What did you think of Russell and his band of friends? I thought their interactions were a nice counterpoint to Scout's and Rosemarie's romance. What do you think is going to happen to them when they set out on their own?
5. I looked forward to making Miles Grant

a hero in this book. For those of you who've read *A Texan's Promise,* how has he changed?

6. One common theme in the novel is self-doubt. Many of the characters doubted themselves and their worth. It is only when they see themselves through the eyes of people they love that they are able to accept themselves. Have you ever been in a situation where you needed other people's perspectives to truly "see" yourself?

7. Why do you think Russell, Miles, and Scout all needed to stand up to the rustlers?

8. The reunion between Clayton and Scout was a favorite scene for me. How did each of the men need the other?

9. What do you think will happen to Rosemarie and her family?

10. Rosemarie realized that she had to lose almost everything in order to find herself and her future. How could that be true today?

The employees of Thorndike Press hope you have enjoyed this Large Print book. All our Thorndike, Wheeler, and Kennebec Large Print titles are designed for easy reading, and all our books are made to last. Other Thorndike Press Large Print books are available at your library, through selected bookstores, or directly from us.

For information about titles, please call:
  (800) 223-1244

or visit our Web site at:
  http://gale.cengage.com/thorndike

To share your comments, please write:
Publisher
Thorndike Press
10 Water St., Suite 310
Waterville, ME 04901